AF406220

# CODE NAME:
# ARIES

USA TODAY BESTSELLING AUTHOR

## JANIE CROUCH

CODE NAME: ARIES • SPECIAL EDITION

*To my mother.*
*I miss you.*

# CHAPTER ONE

"STRIKE FIRST. STRIKE HARD. NO MERCY."

"Did you really just quote *Cobra Kai* to Baxter as life advice?" Sarge asked.

Landon crossed his arms over his chest and leaned back in the conference room chair with a good-natured grin. "Not so much life advice as *dating* advice, but yeah. I'm surprised you got the reference, Sarge. Did they even have movies when you were growing up?"

Sarge tilted his head to the side and narrowed his eyes at Landon. "You know what they did have when I was growing up? Ways for me to kick your scrawny ass, and that's still true."

Ian DeRose leaned back in his own chair at the head of the table. He could have put an end to the bickering between his two right-hand men, Landon Black and Harrison McEwan—a.k.a. Sarge—but didn't. It was harmless enough.

Besides, he'd recognized the actions for what they were: Landon had been deliberately trying to get a rise out of Sarge. Nothing unusual there. But this time he had done it for a reason. It kept Sarge focused in the room.

Besides, quoting the spin-off of an eighties karate movie as dating advice for Isaac Baxter, Zodiac's new employee who looked like a movie star himself, was ridiculous.

They'd just finished their monthly conference call with the other Zodiac Tactical offices around the world. There were branches on nearly every continent—Paris, Singapore, Rio de Janeiro, New York, and the home office there in Denver.

Each office specialized in an area of what they were experts in as security contractors—risk consulting, intelligence gathering, private and corporate bodyguarding, hostage rescue.

If the law couldn't or wouldn't handle it, their team would. So Ian had some of the best tactical minds in the world working for him. *Cobra Kai* references notwithstanding.

"I think I'll try taking her out to dinner," Isaac muttered. He was new but so far was fitting in well. Landon and Sarge continued bickering like an old married couple, hardly paying Isaac any mind even though he was the one they were supposedly giving advice to.

It was currently zero six hundred, not when they were normally in the office, but it was impossible to find a time for their monthly meeting that was within regular business hours for all the different locations. They varied the time of their interoffice call each month, but someone always had to get up in the middle of the night. And this month had been their turn.

Ian might be the owner and head of Zodiac Tactical, but he tried to make it a practice to never require his people to do things he wasn't willing to do himself.

The meeting had been relatively uneventful.

He stood up. "Let's get some breakfast and head home."

Isaac immediately nodded. "Yes, please. Thank God. I was afraid Landon was about to tell me to *wax on, wax off* once I got this girl to say yes to a date, and I was afraid to find out what that meant."

"Oh," Landon replied with a grin. "I can gladly demonstrate the *wax on, wax off* if Sarge here would volunteer to bend over—"

"Fuck off." Sarge flipped him the bird.

Landon stood and patted the older man on the shoulder. "Now Sarge, it won't hurt a bit if I do it righ—"

"Breakfast," Ian interrupted. "If it will shut you guys up, I'm buying."

Landon kept taunting Sarge with details of the so-called waxing on and off as they walked out of the conference room, but he stopped midsentence as he received a text on his phone.

His eyes narrowed. "We've got an incoming email from Linear Tactical, boss. Intel on Mosaic."

All of them immediately fell into combat readiness, even though there was no battle to fight. Mosaic, or more specifically this new version of Mosaic, was a pretty word for a very ugly group of people.

"Anything concerning Bronwyn Rourke?" Sarge asked.

That was the reason Landon had been using all his annoyance skills to get Sarge focused on him. To distract Sarge from Bronwyn.

Landon shook his head. "Sorry, man. Nothing mentioned about her. Only says Linear has some sort of hard drive, and they hope to crack it soon. It contains intel on Mosaic, but they don't know what."

Ian squeezed Sarge's shoulder. "We're going to get her back."

Sarge nodded. "Yeah, I know."

Ian hadn't been aware Sarge knew Bronwyn Rourke, one of Zodiac's most unique agents who was based out of the Paris office, but he'd nearly lost his shit when they'd gotten word she was missing. She was supposed to have been on a special and highly dangerous solo mission in Marrakesh.

When she hadn't reported in, they'd sent multiple contacts to ground looking for her. Nothing. She'd disappeared.

Eventually, they'd assumed the worst. However, the worst wasn't what they'd thought. She wasn't dead, but it was arguable that what she was going through now was worse. She was at Mosaic's mercy. And they'd made sure Ian knew it.

He kept a tight lid on his own personal weaknesses, which

simmered close to the surface when it came to Mosaic. Landon saw it and raised an eyebrow at him. He was the only one who knew the truth.

But fuck that. Ian wasn't about to let any emotion get the best of him.

"Can we trust the intel?" Sarge demanded.

Ian had to hand it to Landon. He didn't say anything when Sarge snatched Landon's phone out of his hand to read the email himself.

Landon may have been egging Sarge on before, but that had been for a purpose. He cared about the other man. For whatever reason, Sarge was taking Bronwyn's disappearance harder than anyone else.

"Can we trust intel from Linear? Hell, yes." Ian responded.

Sarge handed Landon back his phone and scrubbed a hand down his face. "Sorry."

"Help a new guy out. What is Linear Tactical?" Isaac asked. "Is that a sister company or something?"

"No. They work with civilians out in Wyoming, teaching survival and self-defense courses. They don't do what we do"—face danger on the front lines almost daily—"but they're good men. I respect the hell out of them. Almost all of them are former Special Forces."

Ian had been a Navy SEAL, not an Army Green Beret like the LT guys, but he'd fight shoulder to shoulder with any of the Linear men. They may no longer be active duty, but they definitely hadn't given up their warrior instincts.

Landon turned to him. "Kendrick Foster, LT's computer guru, wants to meet face-to-face. Says there's too many potential breaches in electronic transference of data to take the chance."

"Then let's get the jet ready. Looks like we're going to Wyoming."

He'd never spent much time in Oak Creek itself, just knew the town was small enough that his assistant called it a logistical nightmare—few hotels, no car rentals. Only a couple of restaurants, none of which took reservations. She had to line every-thing up via phone.

"You want me to come?" Sarge asked.

Isaac took a step closer. "I'm available too. Whatever you need."

Everyone in their office knew that taking down Mosaic, or this *new version* of Mosaic, was the most important thing. The old version had been bad enough: information and weapons sales, providing the tools any organization needed for its own little terrorist attack. But this new version of Mosaic, if they could believe the videos they'd received that included footage of one of their own, had branched out into human trafficking.

"Landon and I will go. You guys stay here in case we have any actionable intel. I want you to be able to move at a moment's notice."

Sarge nodded. "Then I'm going to head home. I don't feel much like anything to eat."

Isaac nodded too. "We'll be ready if you need us." Both men took off down the hallway. Sarge slammed the end of his fist against the wall as he went, frustration strumming through him.

Landon and Ian turned the other direction toward the elevator.

"Kendrick wants forty-eight hours to crack the drive. Says it's delicate, and he doesn't want to take a chance on losing any data."

Ian rubbed his eyes. "I'm not waiting that long. We need answers."

He'd met Kendrick a couple times, and he seemed competent, but if he couldn't get the job done, Ian would find someone who could.

"Roger that. I'll have our tech team standing by. Nothing gets the nerds salivating more than a computer puzzle to solve."

"We need to shut Mosaic down. It's hard to operate with a guillotine hanging over my head."

Landon stopped walking. "This is not your battle to fight

alone this time, Ian. We need to bring everybody in on this. Let them know . . . the details."

*The details.* Such a benign way of putting what had happened.

Ian shook his head. "No, not unless we have to. I know what my weaknesses are. I've got everything under control."

After all, his code name was Aries, right? And like the sign, he was confident, bold, a man of action.

Giving in to his weaknesses was a luxury he didn't allow himself.

Landon was the only one at Zodiac who knew exactly how strong his ties to Mosaic were and the price he had paid to cut those ties the first time. And now it looked like he was right back where he'd started.

"Grant is dead." Landon started walking again. "You don't have to keep fighting him."

Ian pulled out the key card that opened the elevator to his penthouse apartment. Living in the same building as his office had proved invaluable over the years.

Landon stepped in along with him, both of them silent. He knew better than to talk to him while they were in an elevator. He focused on breathing and keeping his heart rate steady for the few seconds it took to get up to the penthouse.

And even though he managed to do it, Ian still stepped out of the metal box the second the doors opened. Landon followed at a more normal pace.

"I may not have to fight Grant, but someone has resurrected my brother's ghost and given their villainous organization the same name as his. Then they brought the fight to my doorstep when they kidnapped one of my employees."

"But it's not Grant. Grant is dead."

Because Ian had killed him.

But in his defense, Grant had killed him first.

All he knew was that he'd stopped Mosaic the first time, and he would stop this new version of them too.

He just hoped it didn't cost him his life.
Again.

"HONEY, are you sure? I don't like the thought of leaving you here for an evening shift alone. And this is supposed to be your day off to work on your little art project."

*Little art project.*

Wavy Bollinger forced a smile at the woman she'd been working with at the Frontier Diner for ten years and had known her entire life. Leeann didn't mean any harm. "Little" was her preferred adjective for almost everything.

Still, it made her teeth grind to hear her passion referred to as such.

She kept the smile plastered on her face. "No problem. I can always use more tips." It wasn't like her art was going to make her money any time soon.

"Are you sure?" Leeann's voice dropped to a near whisper. "Those *collage* people sound dangerous."

It took her a second. "You mean *Mosaic*?"

She nodded with way too much enthusiasm. She'd overheard the Linear guys talking about Mosaic but didn't know the details about the organization. Wavy had bugged her brother Finn until he'd told her more. Evidently, Mosaic was truly bad news...a main course of terrorism with a side of weapon sales and human trafficking to round out the meal.

Leeann would have a coronary if she knew. She'd watch over Wavy like a mother hen and turn a suspicious eye towards people they'd known for years.

The good thing about a town the size of Oak Creek was that people looked out for one another. That's why she loved living there.

The bad thing about a town the size of Oak Creek was, good Lord have mercy, people were always up in your business. That's why the town drove her crazy. It was time for her to get out. She'd been feeling that way more and more. But a lifetime's worth of ties to one place wasn't easy to unravel.

Wavy sent Leeann on her way. She'd been looking forward to spending the evening painting, but her art would wait. After all, it had been waiting a decade for her to actually do something productive with it.

The shift went like most any given weeknight at the diner. Leeann had gotten them through the dinner rush, so now it was just a few stragglers for the couple hours until they closed. Some teenagers sitting at separate booths but flirting back and forth. A young family who'd decided to splurge and go out for pie.

And then a man walked in fifteen minutes before closing. Everything about him had her on high alert.

She couldn't see the color of his eyes but recognized the fierceness in his gaze. Strong chin and carved jaw. Broad shoulders, trim waist. A warrior's awareness.

Everything about this man screamed danger.

And sex.

But mostly danger.

"Can I get you something?" He had chosen the very back booth and had his back to the wall so he could see the whole restaurant.

He only glanced at her, but she had no doubt he was aware of everything happening in the diner. Brown eyes, she could see them now, with little specks of gold.

"Just coffee. Thanks."

Wavy nodded and walked to get it. He was probably stopping for coffee before a long road trip or something. No need to turn into Leeann and assume the worst just because he sat in the back booth and was aware of what was going on around him.

To make up for being suspicious, she made a fresh pot before taking a steaming mug over to him. Those brown eyes might be intense, but they were also…tired. Like he'd spent way too long carrying a burden not meant for one person to bear.

She offered him a smile as she set down the coffee. "You need creamer?"

"No, black is fine."

Of course it was. How could someone who had a jaw that chiseled drink anything but black coffee? *Dark and dangerous.*

Wavy wanted to paint him. She didn't normally like to create anything having to do with people, but she'd love to paint this man.

Naked.

*No!* No, not naked. Regular.

Or…*half* naked. Which half?

"Um, are you okay?" He was looking at her with one dark eyebrow raised.

She swallowed hard, trying to offer him another smile that didn't come off as pervy-perv.

"Yeah. Sorry, I'm fine. I—"

His phone lit up on the table, a text message coming in. She couldn't read the whole thing, but one word very definitely caught her attention.

*Mosaic.*

Oh *shit.* All thoughts of painting him flew from her mind as he slid the phone so she couldn't see the message anymore.

She backed up one step, then another. "I'll— I'll be over here if you need anything else."

"Thanks."

Dark and Dangerous's phone chirped behind her as she walked to the kitchen. She couldn't hear most of his conversation but one word caught her attention once again.

*Kendrick.*

Shit, shit, shit.

Wavy took out her phone and texted her brother Finn.

*Stranger just came in diner. He got a text with word Mosaic, and is talking to someone about Kendrick.*

Finn's response was immediate.

*Get out.*

No. She wasn't going to leave like some ninny. She peeked out the kitchen window to see the guy still sitting in the booth. If Linear could get information from him, maybe it would help put those Mosaic criminal people behind bars. Human traffickers were the scum of the earth, and she wanted to do her part to take them down.

But damn it, why did the first guy she'd been attracted to in…*way too long* have to be a bad guy?

Wavy looked over at Nolan, but the cook had his headphones on. She didn't want to involve him in all this if she didn't have to. In a physical altercation, Dark and Dangerous would win. Nolan would be no match. Neither would Matthew, the teenage dishwasher.

She'd have to keep the guy here herself until help arrived. She shot off another text to Finn.

*I'll keep him here, you send someone as backup.*

Again, his response was immediate. *No. Get out.*

Damn it, she was going to do her part. *You better hurry.*

She slipped her phone back into her apron pocket, ignoring it when it started buzzing a few seconds later, Finn calling rather than texting.

The guy looked like he was fishing for his wallet, so she loaded a tray full of slices of the diner's different pies and walked it over to him.

Wavy forced herself to smile. "Hi. I know you said you only wanted coffee, but we're about to close, and I've still got all these pies. I'd hate for them to go to waste. We'll just have to throw them out." Her brothers would have a heart attack if she ever once threw away extra pie from the Frontier. "Can I offer you a free slice?"

The guy was going to turn her down. She could already see it.

So she did what anybody would do—she tripped and dumped the tray in his lap.

"Oh my God! I'm so clumsy. I'm so sorry." Wavy set down her tray and immediately started wiping at huge chunks of pie flowing all down his front. Chocolate smeared into apple, and lemon meringue covered it all.

It kept him in the booth. So she kept wiping.

But oh God, had she just brushed his crotch? Now her mortification wasn't acting.

He grabbed her hands, more gently than she would've expected given the current circumstances. "I've got it." He set her away from him. "You have a bathroom?"

Wavy pointed to the hall near the back corner. He stood and began walking in that direction. Finn better hurry up. Short of undressing the guy, she was out of ways to keep him here.

Dark and Dangerous's phone rang again right as he got to the hallway.

"Where the hell are you? I'm going to put a fucking cap in your ass myself. This town is already on my last nerve."

She was pretty sure her eyes were bugging out of her head. Maybe she should've gotten out when Finn told her to.

She pretended to wipe down the table so she could watch him go into the bathroom. She needed to call in more backup while he was in there. But instead of going into the bathroom, he went through the door that led to the side alley outside.

Damn it. That was where some of the customers went when they needed a smoke. It didn't really lead anywhere, but you could get out if you wound around the side and went through the back.

If she didn't stop him, he was going to get away.

Knowing she was all sorts of stupid, especially since he'd threatened to put a cap in someone's ass, Wavy ran for the side employee door. She would cut him off and crack him on the head with her tray. He wouldn't be expecting anyone coming at him from the opposite direction.

She hoped.

She rushed toward the back door through the kitchen. Nolan saw her, but she didn't have time to explain.

Out back, the guy was still on the phone, talking about taking whatever opportunity presented itself. He ended the call and muttered something about *fucking pie*.

He was getting closer. She backed herself against the darkened wall, waiting for him to come around the corner. When he did, Wavy brought her tray down on the side of his head as hard as she could.

He let out a roar. "Mother fuc—"

She moved backward, then brought the tray back up to hit him again, was swinging back down when someone caught it from the side.

"Sorry, lady, I can't let you beat up my boss, even if he did threaten to put a cap in my ass. Seriously, who *says* that?"

She waited for a blow or to be shoved to the ground, but it didn't happen.

Should she scream? Hope that Nolan and Matthew could hear her inside.

Dark and Dangerous turned to her. "What the hell is wrong with you, lady?"

"I don't like human traffickers. That's what's wrong with me."

"What are you talking about?" The guy was covered in pie and rubbing the side of his head, glaring at her. Now she really expected some sort of violence.

*She could take a hit. She grew up with two brothers who rough-housed all the time.*

"I'm gonna have to ask you to step away from my sister."

*Baby.* Thank God.

Wavy's younger brother walked farther into the back alley, the moonlight gleaming off the gun he was pointing at the two men. Dark and Dangerous and the other guy backed up, holding their hands up near their heads.

"Your sister has assaulted me with both pie and her tray in the past three minutes."

"Yeah, she's a sassy one," Baby said. "And although she and I are going to have words about her wasting pie like that, I'm still going to need you to move farther away from her."

Baby stepped into the light, and both men took another step back.

"Look, I think there is some mistake here," said the man who'd stopped her from getting my second thwack in. "We don't mean any harm."

Dark and Dangerous glared at her and muttered, "Speak for yourself."

"Wavy doesn't generally attack her customers without due cause," Baby said. "Bad for tips."

Wavy turned to Baby. "This guy was talking about Mosaic and Kendrick. That was enough for me to let Finn know there was trouble."

"And Finn told you to attack him?" Baby cocked his head. "Using *pie*?"

She shrugged. "More or less."

"Can I join the party back here?" Zac Mackay, one of the Linear Tactical guys, came through the same entrance she had used. "Finn called. Asked me to stop by since I was already in town."

He was slightly breathless. Zac might be acting cool, but he'd rushed to get there.

"Wavy might have caught a couple members of Mosaic," Baby said.

"Oh for fuck's sake," Dark and Dangerous said. "I'm not—" She held up the tray like she was going to hit him again. He rolled his eyes and turned to Zac. "You going to tell them or let me be assaulted by Killer Waitress again?"

Zac chuckled, and she grimaced. Zac laughing in this situation wasn't good.

"Wavy and Baby Bollinger, can I introduce Ian DeRose? He owns Zodiac Tactical. We work with them occasionally. He is also the world's foremost expert on Mosaic and how to stop them."

Ian DeRose. *Shit*. She'd heard the guys talk about him and Zodiac before.

Baby lowered his weapon, laughing. "Sorry, man. I got a panicked call that Wavy here had a possible tango, and that I needed to get my ass over to help, stat."

"Thanks for checking your info before shooting," Ian said. He stared at her. Message clear: She *hadn't* checked.

Boo-hoo. She hadn't had a real weapon either.

"This is Landon Black, my right hand," Ian said. "We got a message from Kendrick that he might have an update. He's not at his place."

Zac nodded. "Yeah, I can help you with that. He's at a safe house."

"I'm getting back home to my fiancée. I'll let Finn know to stand down." Baby reached in to hug her and whispered in her ear, "Way to take down the enemy, sis."

"Piss off." But she kissed his cheek.

He laughed as he walked away.

"I'm going to grab a slice of pie." Zac glanced at Ian's shirt and pants. "If there's any left."

"I'll take some of that action," Landon said. "I've already heard about the pie here."

That left Wavy and Ian *Dark and Dangerous* DeRose out there alone.

"I guess I owe you an apology." Why was that so hard to say? With anyone else, she would've already apologized while laughing at how she'd been such a moron, then make a joke about free pie for life.

But somehow, she was too aware of Ian DeRose to laugh like she did with everyone else. Instead, she had this unnerving need to run away from him.

Or step closer.

"You were trying to detain a member of Mosaic, so that justifies a lot." He looked at her with brown eyes that were way too intense. Like he never let his guard down.

Her fingers itched to run through the dark hair behind his ear. A touch to soothe. To connect.

She had no idea why. He didn't seem like he would accept that sort of touch from anyone, much less a stranger.

"Still, bad guy or not, I'm sorry I hit you."

He took a step closer, and she couldn't help but take a step back. His smile turned the slightest bit predatory as he moved toward her again.

Wavy's back was to the wall. Literally and figuratively.

He got closer.

He reached down, and she thought he was going to touch her, but he grabbed the tray in her hand instead.

"Next time, come at your enemy's temple with the edge of the tray where it's hardest." He tapped the edge with his knuckles. "You're a lot more likely to do damage that way, Wavy Bollinger."

And then he was gone.

# CHAPTER
# THREE

THE NEXT DAY, Landon and Ian were on their way into Reddington City, the largest city in western Wyoming. Hell, it was pretty much the *only* city in western Wyoming.

They'd already been there once, him covered in pie, to meet with Kendrick at the safehouse where he was still trying to crack the drive. Ian wasn't surprised to find the drive was more difficult to access than anyone had figured.

Mosaic had never made anything easy for anyone.

He'd wanted to take the drive and give it to his people to work on, but the head of his tech team had assured him that if Kendrick and his girlfriend Neo couldn't crack it, the Zodiac nerds wouldn't be able to either. "Elite white hat hackers" was the term his team leader had used to describe them, awe clear in her tone. She joked about getting their autographs.

At least he thought she was joking.

So Kendrick and Neo were continuing their computer voodoo. Landon and Ian were on their way to check out a building they'd suspected was a front for Mosaic activities and had an entire secret underground level.

His tech team had been up all night getting as many details about the Hemingway building as possible. The layers of electronic and personnel security for the facility were way too high for a building that housed a couple of lawyers' offices, an accounting firm, and a travel agency.

Last he checked, none of those had need for guards with Uzis and electronic key-coding that rivaled military bases. It meant Mosaic was protecting something. He wanted to know what that was.

Landon and Ian had decided not to wait. They were going in themselves. Landon would be posing as a wealthy businessman interested in renting an entire floor of offices while Ian gained access to the hidden level to see what he could find.

They should be going over the details of the mission to make them as solid as possible, but Landon was more interested in giving him shit about the past eighteen hours they'd spent in Oak Creek.

Specifically, the minutes involving Wavy Bollinger.

"All I'm saying is that you didn't stop her from hitting you with the tray."

Ian raised his gaze heavenward with a long-suffering sigh. "You weren't there. How do you know she didn't get the drop on me?"

Landon scoffed. "She's an untrained civilian who weighs a buck twenty sopping wet, half of that in her smile. I've seen you take down guys twice as big as her trained in hand-to-hand combat and subterfuge."

He kept on driving. "Maybe she got lucky."

Or maybe he'd known that stopping the tray would have meant hurting her in some way. Or at the very least, knocking the wind from her by throwing her against that wall.

Ian hadn't wanted to do that.

But he sure as hell didn't want to explain that to Landon right now. Especially when he didn't understand it himself.

It was something about her smile.

Ian didn't know why, but on some instinctive level, his body hadn't wanted to do what it had been trained to do. And in the split second he'd realized it was her, He'd stopped himself.

"Maybe I was being a gentleman," he finally muttered.

Landon let out a sigh. "That would actually make me feel better."

"Why?"

"Better to be a gentleman who doesn't want to hurt a lady than be unfocused because of who we're going up against."

"I'm fine," Ian protested.

"You still haven't dealt with all the ramifications from your last battle with Mosaic, and you know it."

"I'm not going to let it affect me."

"Ian, you died multiple fucking times. There's no way that's not going to affect you now."

"It's not the same. That part of Mosaic is dead. So let's leave it alone."

Landon wanted to say more. Ian knew he did. But they didn't have time for a therapy session. And God knew, he'd been through enough of those over the past three years since his first bout with Mosaic. He'd clawed his way back to mental stability while making sure nobody knew he woke up sweating and panicked nearly every night.

Landon was concerned, and he didn't know the worst of it.

"And I *was* being a gentleman," Ian insisted. "Or at least I didn't want to be the asshole who hurt her."

Landon grinned. "In that case, let me explain the finer nuances of the move known as *Wax On, Wax Off.* You might want to try it on your waitress friend."

"I'll leave that one for you and Sarge. Let's focus on the mission."

Because he sure as hell would not be dating Wavy Bollinger despite whatever there had been in that moment between them as he'd pushed her back against the wall. He hadn't been sure what he was going to do as he'd stepped into her personal space.

Warn her that he was dangerous and she should keep that smile far away from him?

Tell her that her instincts hadn't been off—Ian wasn't Mosaic, but he was definitely dangerous to someone like her?

Drown in those ridiculously green eyes while he kissed her senseless?

Instead, he'd given her advice on how to more effectively attack him next time. All in all, probably the smartest thing he could have done for either of them.

With who he was and what he did, contact with another person was never casual, especially not with a woman. But that honest appreciation in Wavy's eyes—before she'd wanted to knock him unconscious—had caught him off guard.

She'd had no idea who Ian was.

Some women were attracted to the power that came with his position at Zodiac. Some liked to know they were with a former Navy SEAL. Damn near all were attracted to his bank account.

Wavy had been attracted to the guy at her diner to get coffee.

It didn't matter. Nothing was going to happen.

"Let's just get the info we need and get out of this damn state," he said.

"Roger that, boss. But if we can't talk about your past with Mosaic, can we at least talk about you smiling this morning at the diner?"

Ian shot Landon a look. "I did not smile at Wavy this morning."

He had been very careful not to smile at her. One, he wasn't a big smiler, and two, he didn't want to give anyone the impression that he was there for anything other than business.

But hell if it wasn't hard not to smile at Wavy Bollinger. She smiled at every fucking person she saw whether she knew them well or not. She made jokes, made people feel comfortable and at ease. Everybody liked her.

"You didn't smile *at* her," Landon said. "You smiled when we walked into the Frontier Diner and you saw she was working. This cutest little, *OMG, my crush and her tray are here* smile."

Landon wasn't wrong. Ian had smiled. Because he had been glad Wavy had been working this morning so he'd been able to see her. Crazy as it sounded, there was something about her presence that…soothed a part of him.

She'd chatted with them for a long time, despite being a little embarrassed about the tray incident.

She'd brought him a slice of pie. Even though it had been breakfast time. But when his eyes had met hers, the only thing Ian had been able to think about was the feel of her fingers wiping pie off of him the night before. And how it would be worth having pie staining another set of clothes to feel them again.

"Yeah, *that* smile. You're thinking about her now, aren't you?"

Ian definitely wasn't going to provide Landon with that intel. "I should have fired you years ago."

"You can't fire me. I know too much. You'd have to kill me."

"That can be arranged," he said.

But they both knew Ian couldn't run Zodiac without him. Landon, Sarge, some of his other core team members…he trusted them with his life. If he died, his fortune and the Zodiac Tactical company would continue on in their very capable hands. They were his family. The ones he trusted above all others.

Family wasn't always blood, and blood wasn't always family. Ian had learned that lesson the hard way.

"If you bring up Wavy Bollinger or my past with Mosaic again, I'm going to make good on my threat to put a cap in your ass."

Landon blew a kiss at him in the way only he could, but he grew serious as they got closer to the Hemingway building. "You sure this plan of ours is a good idea? You did hear the nerds tell us that the technology they gave us might not work, right?"

"Yeah, all five thousand times they said it." Ian knew it was a risk, but at this point he was not willing to give up any lead that might give them the upper hand with Mosaic. Kendrick and Neo had discovered that this building, with its huge underground bunker, had ties to Mosaic. They had to move quickly if they wanted any details.

"I still think you should let me head down into the underground section and you stay and pretend to be the interested party."

"I can do it. I'm not sending anybody I care about into a situation where they could get captured by Mosaic."

Even if the thought of entering an underground, windowless set of rooms already had Ian's entire body tense.

"You can't protect every single person every single moment," Landon responded. "Putting yourself at higher risk in order to make sure everyone else is safer is not the way to go. Like setting yourself on fire to keep everyone else warm, that sort of thing."

Ian shook his head. This was nonnegotiable. "They have Bronwyn. I'm not taking a chance on them getting you too."

Landon didn't argue further. He was his friend, and Ian trusted him with his life. But ultimately, Ian was the boss, and he was not going to budge on this.

"Besides," he added, "I'm too recognizable considering my history with Mosaic."

"Suit yourself. If you get killed, 'Landon Black, CEO of Zodiac Tactical' will have a nice ring to it."

Ian drove by the building. It was pretty nondescript on the outside—nothing to draw attention.

Landon gave a dramatic sigh. "Just once I wish someone would throw up a *Bad Guys Hang Out Here* sign so we know we have the right place."

He parked around the back of the building, close to the door, and they got out. "You just do your thing with people, and I'll see if I can get us any information."

Landon was good with people. Good at reading them, good at talking to them, good at giving them what they needed so they would trust him. He would have no trouble pretending to be a rich snob who wanted to rent out half of the building and expected everyone to pay attention to him as he toured the facilities.

They placed the comm units in their ears and tested them. Ian would be going in as Landon's assistant, keeping his head down and making his escape at the scheduled time.

"Ready," he said. "Finally, I get to be the boss for a while. As it should be."

"In your dreams."

They didn't make it ten feet inside the front door before they were met by a security guard and required to walk through a metal detector. His tech team had prepared them for that, so they weren't carrying any weapons, at least not any metal ones. they both had tranquilizer darts that could put a tango down for a couple hours.

Also, they could both kill the security guard with their bare hands before he had a chance to draw his weapon.

They made it through, and Ian kept his head tucked deep into the electronic tablet he was carrying as part of his cover as Landon—in Landon style—charmed the front receptionist. They waited as the building's rental representative made his way to the lobby.

"Mr. Ashton-Phelps." The guy rushed over to shake Landon's hand. "It's very nice to meet you in person. I'm so glad you could make it here this afternoon."

Ashton-Phelps? Ian rolled his eyes while keeping his head lowered. That was why Landon shouldn't be allowed to choose his own fake ID.

"My name is Gregory Simmons," the man continued. "I'll be showing you around today, answering any questions you have. Let's step right over here to the elevator."

Landon cut him off. "I assume there's some sort of secondary elevator or staircase I could take? I am not going to be riding the common elevator with everyone if I move my enterprise into this building."

Ian swallowed a laugh. Landon was laying it on like he was a sheik in Dubai, not a suit in the middle of Wyoming. But it seemed to work with Simmons.

"Yes, sir," the younger man said, suitably impressed. "There are two staircases, one on either end of the building, and there is, in fact, a private elevator down a secondary hall."

Landon nodded. "Then that is what I will use."

That's what they needed. That elevator was what led down to the subbasement. He wasn't sure if Simmons knew about the activity underneath this building or not, but it didn't matter.

His team was currently running every single person who'd set foot in there for the past six months. They would see if that led to any useful intel.

The only part of security the nerd team hadn't been able to crack remotely was the private elevator itself. If someone entered without a card, it would set off alarms. But once they were inside, they could override the system.

And Landon had gotten them access without asking.

Ian gritted his teeth as they stepped inside and Simmons activated the elevator with his swipe card. As soon as it began to move, he pretended to get an email on his tablet. "Mr. Ashton-Phelps," he said. "I've received a message, sir, about that emergency situation in Dubai." Since Landon was playing this over the top, he might as well join in. It helped him get his mind off the metal walls threatening to close in on him.

"Damn it, Struthers, I told you to handle that."

"Yes, sir. I will, sir. I probably shouldn't do it here in front of . . . others." Ian turned away the slightest bit from Simmons.

"Fine," Landon said. "Go back down to the lobby and don't come back up until it's handled. I don't want to deal with this anymore."

The elevator's doors opened and Landon and Simmons stepped out. Ian nodded.

"You won't be able to get back up in this elevator, so you'll have to use the regular ones near the lobby," Simmons offered.

"Yes, sir," he said. Simmons liked that. He liked not being the lowest man on the totem pole. That was fine with Ian as long as he left him alone in here.

He ignored the panic that wanted to swallow him and pulled out his tablet's specialized drive cord, then plugged it into the elevator's computerized control system. That was the first hurdle, and the entire mission was for naught if the nerds couldn't get the elevator to go where they needed it to without activating the alarm.

But it worked. He bypassed the ground floor altogether and headed deeper to a level that was definitely not on the elevator's keypad. Ian stayed to the side as the doors opened, squelching his need to get out as soon as possible, tranquilizer guns in both hands, knowing there would be guards.

If he couldn't take out any guards before they sounded the alarm, he'd be a dead man.

He stepped out of the elevator just as the doors started to close, when anyone watching would've assumed no one was inside. There were two guards. Ian took out the one closest to him with a fast roundhouse kick. As he came out of the spin, he let the tranquilizer dart in his left hand fly at guard number two. Two seconds later, he dropped to the floor. He then returned to the first guard and tranquilized him even though his kick had already knocked him unconscious.

They'd be out for a couple hours. If Ian and Landon were there longer than that, they'd have bigger problems than security guards.

He left them where they were, not wanting to waste precious minutes dragging them somewhere else. Not that there were many choices. The hallway was long and narrow with multiple doors.

"Landon, I'm in." He wouldn't respond but could hear his reports. "Took down two guards."

Ian pointed his tablet at each of the doors, sending the visual back to the tech team. They couldn't speak to him through comms, but they could message him over the tablet.

A message showed up a few seconds later. *Third door has the most potential for intel.* Instructions on how to bypass the electronic lock flooded in less than a minute later. He paid his tech team double the normal rate for a reason.

Ian followed their instructions, and seconds later he was inside. He looked around. The nerds had been right. This was it. This was what they needed. This was what they had been hoping for. He picked up the tablet and turned so the camera was catching the different computers and screens. He was sure his tech team was struggling not to orgasm just looking at the cutting-edge equipment around them.

They sent him to the computer console in the southeast corner of the room. That's not the one he would have chosen; it seemed more unassuming than the rest. But he wasn't the expert.

Ian could hear Landon babbling on to Simmons upstairs, so everything was okay, but they didn't have a lot of time. The nerds told him what to type, and he did so. Data started flying up on the screens all over the room.

*Can't download. Record manually.*

He set the tablet up so the camera was taking in as much of the information as possible, pulled out his phone, and began recording with that too. Once he got the footage back, the team would analyze it.

Hopefully, it would provide what they needed to take Mosaic down.

He'd only been recording about fifteen seconds when Landon's voice came in through the comm unit.

"Ian, do you read? Get out now."

"I need more ti—"

"Right fucking now."

# CHAPTER
# FOUR

"LANDON, talk to me. What's going on?"

"We tripped some sort of alarm. Simmons freaked out. I had to tranq him. You're busted."

Ian was still recording with the tablet and his phone. "I need a few more minutes."

Every second he stayed now would give them more data.

"You don't have a few more minutes, man," Landon said. "You need to get out now. I'm going to have to head up to the roof like Kendrick and Neo did, but there's no way you're going to make it up there."

The tablet pinged. Ian took it down to read it but kept his phone up recording.

*Second door in the hallway is an exit that leads underground away from the building. Go now. Incoming guards.*

"Do what they're telling you, Ian," Landon said. Evidently the same message had gone to him. "We won't get any intel at all if you get caught. Leave now."

"Fuck. Roger that," Ian told him. "I'm on my way."

He kept his phone up a few more seconds, but when an alarm blasted through the building, he really was out of time. He turned off his camera and ran out the door, pointing the tablet toward the door the team had said led to an exit. By the time he reached it, they were already providing a code.

Not a moment too soon. The elevator opened and the guards inside began firing at him as soon as they saw him.

Ian dove through the door and slammed it shut behind him, hoping his team of brainiacs was smart enough to know they needed to change that electronic combination if they could. If not, this wasn't going to end well.

He didn't stop. He ran through the dim maze, not sure which direction to go. And he didn't want to give up any speed while he figured it out. He looked down at the tablet but there was nothing—no signal. The tech team wasn't going to be able to help him down here, so he ran, trying every door he came to.

Behind him, a door slammed open as the guards made it into the tunnel. They weren't far behind him. He swung left and found a dead end.

*Fuck.*

These tunnels were old, built way before the building itself. Mosaic had probably realized it, and that's why they used this building. Ian shot back in the other direction as men yelled behind him. They were trying doors too, looking for him.

He finally found a door that didn't have an electronic lock and kicked it open. Inside was a small room with a metal ladder heading up toward street level. He had no idea what street, but that was fine with him.

He didn't care where he ended up, as long as it wasn't there.

He climbed quickly, not sure when the armed guards would catch up, and came to a grate at the top. He pushed on it as hard as he could but it barely budged. Damn it, those men and their guns were getting closer.

He couldn't get the leverage he needed while holding the tablet. He tucked it into his waistband and used his shoulder to push, gritting his teeth as it took all his strength to get the grate unstuck. But finally, it moved. He hefted with his legs and got it the rest of the way open.

Ian felt the tablet shift and start to fall, but there was nothing he could do. If he reached for it now, he wouldn't get the grate back open in time. The tablet crashed to the ground below him. He pushed the grate the rest of the way up and crawled through. A second later, bullets struck behind him.

Jesus, that had been close. Ian looked around. He was in the middle of Reddington City, but where exactly? He had moved west from where he'd started back in their computer room. That put him on the opposite side of where he and Landon had parked.

He touched the comm unit in his ear. "Landon, are you okay? Report."

There was a long moment of silence, and Ian let out a relieved breath when he finally responded. "I'm out, but I can't make it back to the car."

"Me neither," Ian said. "I'm on the west side of the building, a few blocks away."

"Shit. They're heading right for you. You need to get off the street quick. Don't try to blend. Run."

He did. He didn't know which way to head and veered right when he saw men dressed in suits running toward him. They weren't shooting, but he had no doubt they would if that became their only option. They'd spotted him.

He had no idea how to get away from them without running directly into innocents, and he wasn't willing to take the chance on collateral damage. So he cut down an alley, pushing himself for speed to get through to the next block. But when he came out of the alley, two more Mosaic guards were waiting across the street.

Shit, Ian had done exactly what they'd hoped he would.

And now they'd take the shot and nobody would be any the wiser. The guys up the block smiled with the knowledge that they had him trapped. They weren't even rushing anymore.

A car turned down the street. Could he get away if they waited to shoot until it passed? Ian kept his eyes on the men as the vehicle rolled toward him, knowing the guards from the tunnel would be coming up behind him any second. When the car passed, he would run beside it and take his chances. He already knew what happened when Mosaic took people alive, and he didn't want to experience that again.

*Time to run.*

Except the car didn't pass. It stopped right in front of him, and a window rolled down.

"Hey, Ian. Um, do you need a ride?"

What the hell? *"Wavy?"*

———

As soon as Ian got in her car, Wavy started driving. Reddington City wasn't a big crime haven but this alley felt pretty sketchy. She'd been a little surprised a couple of minutes ago when she'd seen him cut through it. She'd circled around the block and tried to seem casual, pulling up next to him and offering a ride.

She didn't want to ask him what he was doing here because he might turn around and ask her the same thing.

"What are you doing here?" he asked.

Or he might ask anyway.

"Um." She'd practiced this. "I was picking up some supplies at the art store." That was relatively close to the truth. "How about you? Out saving the world?" Wavy's laugh was so awkward, she wanted to cringe. "Or maybe doing some shopping?"

She wasn't sure exactly which way to go now that she had him in the car, so she took a left at the next light. She hadn't been sure she would actually find him. It had been a stupid plan from the beginning, to go to Reddington City on the off chance that she'd run into Ian there.

She'd dreamed of painting him last night. Which wasn't unusual for her—she dreamed about painting nearly everyone and everything. Ian DeRose had been naked, but that wasn't the problem. That sort of painting would be classified as acceptable dream fodder for any artist.

In Wavy's dream, instead of him posing and her painting him at her easel, she'd been using her brushes all over his body. She'd been painting *him*. He'd stood there watching her with those smoldering brown eyes as she'd painted him all the colors and patterns flowing through her mind.

All the colors. All of *him*.

Then he'd showed back up at the diner this morning. She'd tried to be friendly and talkative—although his friend Landon was much more talkative than Ian himself—but Wavy couldn't stop thinking about painting him. About the hard muscle she'd felt under her fingers when she'd been brushing pie off him the night before.

How it had felt when he'd backed her up against that wall in the alley.

So when she'd found out Ian was going to be in Reddington City, she decided to go there and see if she could "accidentally" run into him.

He wasn't talking. He was looking out the side-view mirror behind them. Oh crap. What if he really *had* been on some sort of world-saving mission?

She was such an idiot.

"Is there anywhere I can drive you?" She glanced in the rearview mirror, but no one seemed to be following them.

He looked over at me. "Where are you heading?"

She shrugged. "I guess back to Oak Creek now that I'm done shopping."

"Okay, Wavy Bollinger. I will go back to Oak Creek with you."

All right, that was a bit weird. She glanced over at him, but he was still looking in the mirror. "Yes, Ian DeRose," she said in the same serious tone, "I will give you a ride back to Oak Creek."

She gripped the steering wheel tighter and got on the road that would lead them out of town. This had been a mistake.

Could things be any more awkward between them? As they got farther out of town, he stopped looking in the mirror so much. Instead, he was looking at her.

But not in a *Wow, how fortuitous is it that we ran into each other?* sort of way like she'd been hoping. Instead, those endless brown eyes were pinning her. Studying her.

"What sort of supplies were you picking up again?" he asked.

"Oh, some art stuff. Stuff I didn't need. I like to come to the shop here in Reddington City. It's the biggest one around. A great shop." Shit, she was babbling.

She didn't so much as glance at him because as soon as she did, he would know the truth. That she was there because of *him*. Wavy drove past the on-ramp for the highway, planning to take the back roads to Oak Creek. It would give them a little more time together—although right now that might be prolonging the awkwardness. He wouldn't notice the difference.

Of course he noticed. "Something wrong with the highway?" he asked.

How exactly was she supposed to answer that? That she wanted to spend more time with him, so she thought she'd take the slower route?

Her slight laugh couldn't be described as anything but awkward. "Yeah. I don't like driving on fast roads. They make me nervous."

He seemed to relax a little. "Sure. I understand."

He pulled out his phone and typed something. Great. Maybe he didn't want to talk to her at all and this had all been a stupid mistake on her part. That seemed to keep happening when it came to him.

"That art store you were at." He glanced at me. "Would that be Brickman's?"

"Yeah," she replied. "Have you heard of it?" Why would he have heard of it? It was a small chain store that sold basic supplies.

"No, but I see it here on my phone. My signal seems to be going in and out."

"Oh yeah." She laughed that stupid nervous laugh again. "We're kind of entering a dead zone for about twenty square miles. No cell phone coverage at all."

"Right." He relaxed a little bit more, which was good since she was getting more nervous and stupid with each minute. "Got to love Wyoming mountains."

"Yes, exactly." He did understand. He did—

She let out a scream as he grabbed the steering wheel, jerking them off the road. She slammed on the brakes. "What are you doing?"

"Turn off the engine, Wavy."

Oh God. The calmer he got, the more dangerous he was. She saw that now. She turned off the engine and immediately found her head pinned against the window—his hand on her neck, long fingers spread out across her skull. She let out a whimper at the feel of the cold glass against her face.

"What were you doing in Reddington City?"

"I told you. Art supplies."

"Okay. Let me rephrase. What were you doing *near me* in Reddington City? Brickman's Art Supply is on the opposite side of town."

Oh God. She didn't want to tell him. "It was just a coincidence. Really."

His hand pushed her more firmly against the window. Not hard enough to hurt, but hard enough to know that if he decided to smash her face through it, it wouldn't require much effort on his part. "In my line of work, I don't believe in coincidences. So, you're going to have to be more specific. What were you doing near the Hemingway building?"

Maybe if Wavy stuck to her original line, he might believe her. "I was there by accident. I got turned around."

More pressure against the window. "Are you working for them?"

"What?" He was firing off questions too fast to understand. "Who?"

"Mosaic, Wavy. I have to admit you had me fooled with the whole tray and all the friendly talking this morning at the diner. But there's no way I can believe that you just happened to be near the Hemingway building today."

God, she was going to have to tell him the truth. She'd almost rather be branded a part of a terrorist organization than tell him the truth. But more pressure against her head and neck told her she didn't have any choice. "I was talking to my brother Finn. I asked him where you were staying, and he mentioned that you were going into Reddington City."

"And Finn spilled my plans to you?"

She tried to shake her head but couldn't move. "No, all I could get out of him was Reddington City. But then I snooped on his phone and saw the address. I decided to take a chance."

"*What?*"

She knew it sounded preposterous. "I decided to come out here to get my art supplies early and thought maybe if I found you, I could pretend like it was happenstance and see if you wanted to go to dinner."

The pressure against her head eased the slightest bit. "*Dinner.*"

Wavy wasn't sure she'd ever felt more like an idiot in her entire life. "Look, I live in a small town. I've lived there my entire life. I know every single person. So I meet this guy who's pretty interesting and isn't threatened when I nearly knock him unconscious. So yeah, dinner."

He released her.

She turned as he shook his head. "I'm sorry. It's that you're… never quite what I expect."

"Well, that's a first because I feel like my life has become stagnant and I never—"

The windshield shattered in front of them, and she screamed.

# CHAPTER
# FIVE

IAN GRUNTED before he grabbed her head once more, pushing Wavy down this time. Then he reached past her and yanked the handle for her door.

"Shit. They found us. We've got to go right now. Get out, stay low. Head for the trees."

Another shot rang out. The headrest of her seat exploded where her head had been a second ago. If Ian hadn't pushed her down, she'd be dead right now.

"Go!" he yelled, and she crawled out the door, struggling not to panic. Someone was shooting at them.

Ian crawled out right behind her. "Low and fast. Trees. *Now.*"

He grabbed her hand, and they both ran. Despite her terror, she realized that Ian was keeping himself between her and the direction the bullets were coming from. He jerked her to the left and then the right as they dove for the trees, trying not to make themselves easy targets.

As soon as they hit the tree line, they straightened, and he pushed her in front of him. "We have to keep running. They're going to come after us."

Wavy didn't argue with him. She had pieces of the headrest

all over her clothes, and it should've been her brains. Another shot rang out a few seconds later, confirming they were still in pursuit. Worse? They were gaining on them.

Damn it, she spent too much time in her studio and not enough time doing cardio. She was slowing him down. "You need to go without me. They're going to catch us." She had to stop for a second to get enough air to continue.

"I'm not leaving you." But he was looking around for an Option B since running wasn't going to work. "I don't have any weapons, so I can't eliminate them from a distance. I can probably take each of them one-on-one in close combat, but it will be risky."

"What's the primary objective here?" She'd been around her brother, the Special Forces soldier, and the Linear guys long enough to know the lingo.

"Getting you out. Survival, always survival."

"I can't outrun these guys but I've been hanging out in these woods my entire life, so I can out hide them, if you'll trust me."

She didn't pose the statement lightly because she knew he wouldn't take it lightly. Somebody like Ian DeRose did not trust people easily.

But he just said, "Lead the way."

Okay. She needed to treat this as the most important game of capture the flag ever. And the key was letting the bad guys get in front of them while thinking that Ian and Wavy were still ahead of them. And then finding somewhere to hide. Most of the trees weren't big enough to provide cover. She started back the way they'd come.

Ian probably didn't like the fact that they were doubling back toward danger, but he didn't slow down or resist. He stayed with her. More importantly, the bad guys wouldn't think they'd head back in their direction.

She could tell when Ian's instincts told him they were getting too close to danger, and he was right. But she knew where she was going. They had passed a fallen oak a few minutes ago, and she wanted to get back to it. It was as good a place as they were going to find to hide and let them pass. But getting there before they did was going to be close. She pushed herself for more speed, knowing Ian would keep up.

Ian saw the big fallen tree and knew her plan. He took the lead, pulling her along with him. They'd barely gotten behind it, pulling shrubbery around them, when Ian pushed her up against the tree. People were talking.

"We're gaining on them. The woman is slowing him down," one of the bad guys said.

"Remember, bring in the man alive," another replied. "The woman is dispensable."

Ian pulled her closer, his big body engulfing hers. He was pressed up against her, literally from head to toe. But he was stiff against her, and not in a good way.

"All we have to do is wait for them to tire and then take them. Let's go."

Ian and Wavy stayed where they were as the men took off. There was nothing in front of them but thinner trees—nowhere for them to hide. They stayed silent for another couple of minutes before Ian stepped away from her.

As soon as they'd disentangled themselves from all the branches, he relaxed a little. "It's not going to take them long to figure out we doubled back."

Wavy nodded. "We need to get down to the river. It runs parallel to the road we were on. There will be a lot more places to hide. A lot more mature trees."

They moved silently in that direction, putting as much distance as possible between themselves and the bad guys.

But after a few minutes, she couldn't help asking, "Is there a reason people are trying to kill you, or is this a normal day for you?"

"I broke into one of their buildings. Got some data I'm sure they don't want me to have." He shrugged. "Not to mention Mosaic doesn't hesitate to kill people whether they have a good reason or not."

"Where's my handy tray when I need it?"

He grimaced. "I'd take that weapon or any other right about now."

"You don't strike me as someone who's without a weapon very often. My brothers are like that too."

"Normally that would be true, but there was a metal detector in the Hemingway building, so Landon and I had to go in unarmed."

She increased her speed to keep up with him, ignoring the ache that started in her feet. "Does Landon have someone chasing him too?"

"He didn't when we last spoke. We were separated. But our comm system is short-range, so I can't reach him now."

That was why he'd made that strange statement about riding back to Oak Creek with her using her full name. He'd been letting Landon know what was going on.

They both checked their phones, but there was no signal. There wouldn't be until they were a couple miles from Oak Creek, which was probably fifteen miles north of them.

"Following the river will take us to Oak Creek, but if you want to circle back to the car, we should probably head in the other direction."

He shook his head. "No, the car is a known location. We can't go back there. Can you make it?"

It wouldn't be pretty, but she could. "We're going to need to move quickly because not only are your killer friends going to circle back around once they realize we're not ahead of them, but there's a storm coming this afternoon."

He looked up. There were clouds in the sky, but they weren't bad yet. "How can you tell?"

"I've lived here all my life. I can taste it when rain is coming."

He slowed down to look at her. "Really?"

She rolled her eyes. "No, not really. I had a hair appointment scheduled for this afternoon but cancelled it this morning when the weather channel reported a storm system was coming in. Storms and blowouts don't mix."

"I'm not going to pretend to understand what that means."

They picked up the pace. "But storms will work in our favor because I'm not lying when I say I have experience out in these woods. Even in weather that would make other people cry."

"Then lead the way," he said. "Let's make use of your expertise. And your missed blowout."

———

Two hours later, the rain started.

But long before that, Wavy was cursing her choice of shoes. When she'd tricked Finn into telling her where Ian was, she'd decided to put on new, cute little flats with her jeans.

She would give anything right now for her hiking boots or a pair of tennis shoes. Hiking through the wilderness in flats was not fun. Doing it in the rain was downright miserable. She knew she had blisters. She didn't bother to look.

They moved steadily along the river bank toward home. Normally fifteen miles wouldn't be daunting. She could cover it in a day's hike if she wasn't wearing cute little flats.

But she'd rather have blisters than a bullet in the head, so she kept walking. She kept walking when the pain should have made her stop. She kept walking when she was pretty sure that some of the liquid she could feel was blood, not rain. She kept walking.

She kept going until Ian reached out and grabbed her hand. She spun, startled. "What, do you see them? Are they here?"

Wavy'd been so focused on putting one step in front of the other as quickly as possible that she had no idea if the bad guys had caught up to them or not.

"We need to stop. You're hurt."

"I'm okay. It's just some blisters."

"Fine, then we need to stop. I'm hurt."

"You are?"

He nodded. "That first bullet grazed my shoulder."

She'd had no idea. He hadn't made a single complaint in the hours they'd been walking. She looked at him more carefully, her aching feet forgotten. "Are you okay?"

"I'll be fine. It's a burn from that first bullet that shattered the windshield. But I think it would do us both some good to get out of this weather."

That sounded like heaven, but she wasn't sure if it was the best plan. Better to be uncomfortable than dead. "I think the rain is supposed to last all night. We're still another seven or eight miles from Oak Creek."

"Yeah, I keep trying my phone, but there's no signal."

She rubbed the wet hair away from her face. This was her fault. "I'm sorry. I shouldn't have taken us this way. If I had gone on the highway—"

"Hey." He reached out and grabbed both of her arms. "You've gotten us this far. You got us away from the people who were chasing us. You've been in pain for at least the past two hours, and you haven't said a word."

"You knew?" She whispered.

He leaned his forehead against hers, a show of camaraderie. "I expected you to call a halt long before now."

Wavy nodded. "It's going to be dark soon, and this isn't going to get any easier after dark."

He stepped back, and she wished he were close again. "Then let's stop and find shelter, at least until the storm passes. Maybe until the morning. I haven't seen any sign of the Mosaic guys after us. I'm pretty sure they turned back toward their vehicles when the storm started. They're probably waiting for us to do the same."

"We should be able to find shelter. I can make something if I have to, but there are all sorts of crannies and caves along the river."

They trudged along for another twenty minutes. Every step was agony now that she was aware of the blisters. When she saw a break in the river causing a small waterfall, she led them toward it. There was a slight overhang near some boulders. It wasn't great, but it would at least allow them to get out of the rain.

She shined the light from her phone inside, and when she didn't see any scary-looking critters, she didn't hesitate to crawl in and lie down. There wasn't much room, barely enough to sit up, but it was dry. Ian wasn't so quick to follow her inside.

"Is this okay? Did you decide we should keep going?" Oh God, she hoped not. She really didn't think her feet could take it. It felt so good to sit down.

"No." He finally scooted in next to her. "No, this is fine."

She turned her phone light back on so he could see. He wasn't from Wyoming, so he probably didn't like crawling into dark caves that might have all sorts of creatures inside.

Or maybe he was hurt worse than she'd thought. He was unnaturally stiff. No sigh of relief to be off his feet and out of the rain. No quips about being attacked by bears.

"Do I need to look at your arm?" Not that there was much that she could do about it.

"No." His voice was tight. "I'm okay."

He didn't sound okay at all. Maybe he thought they should keep going. She didn't know how she'd do it, but she would if she had to. "I'm pretty sure my feet resemble ground beef. It's not pretty. But I can keep going if you think we should."

He sucked in a breath, then let it out. "No. You need to rest. Staying here is the smartest move. If one of us turned an ankle, it would be worse."

Thank goodness.

He sat up as much as the cave would allow. "Let me look at

your feet. We should treat those. Otherwise, you're not going to be able to walk on them tomorrow. And like you said, we still have quite a few miles to go."

"I have no clue how to treat blisters like this."

"Puncturing each one is the best thing for them. Normally, I would have a knife. You don't happen to have a safety pin, do you?"

She did. Oh Lord. Every time she was with him, she thought she couldn't say or do something more mortifying than the time before, yet here she was about to top it again.

"I do have a safety pin. It's holding the back part of my bra together." She'd changed into cute flats at the possibility of seeing Ian, but that he might get up close and personal with her bra had never occurred to her.

For the first time since they'd entered the little cave, he relaxed the slightest bit. "That will work fine if you're willing to sacrifice it."

She peeled her gross, wet blouse away from her as best she could and reached around to try to unhook her bra, but it was stuck in the fabric. She couldn't do it.

He chuckled. "Can I help?"

Despite her mortification, she liked the sound of that soft laugh. "I think you might have to."

She didn't know how his hands could be warm in all this, but they were as they moved against the skin of her back and found the safety pin holding the bra together. Damn it, she had meant to get a new one for the past three months but had never gotten around to it.

"Got it," he said.

Was it her imagination or did his fingers trail along the skin of her back as he pulled them away?

He slid down to her feet and eased her shoes off. He switched on his phone light. "Those look pretty rough."

"I probably shouldn't look at them. It's better if I can't visualize it."

"I understand. Hang on. I'll puncture the worst ones and drain the fluid. It would be best if we had some sort of bandage, but this is better than nothing. Better than them rupturing."

"How do you know all this?" She wanted to keep him talking. Anything to take her mind off fluid oozing from her feet.

"I've had plenty of blisters during my Navy SEAL years."

Wavy shouldn't be surprised. Finn had been Special Forces in the army. A lot of the Linear Tactical guys had served with him. It was no surprise Ian had that same sort of training.

He had punctured the first blister as he spoke. She couldn't feel any pain since the skin was dead, but she could feel the pressure.

His hands were gentle on her feet. "You're pretty tough to keep moving on these. I've seen full-fledged soldiers roll over and cry with less."

"That might still happen. I'm such a visual learner that not seeing them is probably the best possible thing for me. If I saw them, I'd be convinced I was about to die."

The pin lanced the second blister. But again, his hands were so gentle, she couldn't say that it hurt.

"One more," he said softly. His thumb trailed over the arch of her foot, and she shivered a little.

When she'd taken off for Reddington City a few hours ago on her ill-planned attempt to spend time with him, this was not what she'd had in mind.

But it was sort of nice. He was gentle. Soothing.

"Okay, done. You get an A plus as a patient."

"Well, you get an A minus as a doctor since you didn't wash your hands. But that's not bad."

He chuckled again. She loved that sound. It was so rusty and disused. She liked drawing those little laughs out of him. He pinned her bra back in place, and she could swear his fingers trailed over her skin again.

But when he laid down beside her, he was tense again. She

almost asked him what was wrong, but she'd have to be an idiot not to know the answer.

They were spending the night in the wilderness with armed thugs after them. Both of them were injured and they had no food or water. Any normal person would be tense.

So yeah, she was an idiot for enjoying herself a little. She should be as tense as him.

WAVY FELL asleep in the middle of a sentence.

It was like nothing Ian had ever seen. She'd talked to him for hours inside that hellish little cave once she found out that he liked it. And he did like it.

It wasn't so much her stories, although those were pretty interesting—tales of growing up in Oak Creek sandwiched between two brothers, the younger who'd thought his name was actually Baby until he was well into elementary school.

It was the sound of her voice. It gave him something to focus on, to steady his breathing around. It gave him a reason not to give in to the panic clawing to get out, trying to convince him that he was once again trapped. That he was once again going to die.

If it had just been Ian out there in the wilderness, he would've gladly sat out in the storm. But it wasn't just him.

At one point, she'd stopped midstory, something about the time that, as kids, she and her friends had started a cookie baking company and decided it was a good idea to call it the Chocolate Spit Cookie Company. A little bit of spit would be the "secret ingredient."

"This must all sound so stupid to you," she'd said. "I'll stop."

"No," He'd responded, probably too quickly, but she hadn't seemed to notice. "Please keep going."

There wasn't actually much more to the story. Not surprisingly, the Chocolate Spit Cookie Company had not been as big a success as the kids had hoped it would be.

But she'd kept on talking. Kept giving Ian her voice to focus on. It was amazing that someone could talk so much after having been so heroically silent for miles while they had run.

Her blisters were no joke. He was glad she couldn't see them. They had to have hurt like hell, and they weren't going to get any better once they started going again. But at least they wouldn't rupture and make walking almost impossible. Not that he was sure Wavy would tell him even if the pain got that bad.

Wavy Bollinger, patron saint of restaurant trays, was pretty fucking amazing.

She'd traveled miles without complaint, not losing her cool, keeping focused on getting them closer to Oak Creek. Given that she'd been one second away from having her brains splattered all over her car's interior, it was amazing she'd kept it together so well.

And then she'd talked to him for hours in this overhang. He wasn't sure if that was for his benefit—that on some level she'd recognized he needed it—or hers. Or both.

At some point, Wavy's hand had reached out to rest on his arm. It had stayed there after she'd fallen asleep midsentence. Ian covered it now with his own. He could feel the calluses on her fingertips, maybe from waitressing, but undoubtedly some of it was from her painting.

Interesting that in all her talking, she hadn't told a single story about that. She had a rainbow of paint on her wrist at any given time, but it didn't warrant any stories. What she wasn't saying said something pretty damned important.

And he wanted to know what. Almost as much as he wanted to touch the smooth skin of her back again like he had when he'd gotten that safety pin. Concentrating on her feet and not the fact her undergarment was completely unhooked had taken all his focus.

He needed to shut this down. Whatever it was that had him fascinated with this woman couldn't sway him from his primary objective: eliminating Mosaic. He couldn't allow any distraction, no matter how fucking tempting, to shake him from that goal.

He forced himself to take her hand, still resting on his arm, and move it so she was no longer touching him. He focused on keeping his breathing steady, which was infinitely more difficult without her voice and touch to calm him.

There was plenty of air in here. This was a cavern he could crawl out of at any time. Not something he could slam his hands against until they were bloody without any help coming.

He concentrated on the storm outside. If he could hear that, then he had air. He could breathe. He was alive. When the rain stopped, it became harder once again, so he focused on his breathing.

He knew the second she woke up.

"Hey," she whispered. "I fell asleep. I'm sorry."

"Why are you sorry? You traveled miles with people trying to kill you on your heels. I think you deserved some rest."

"But I was talking to you."

"Was talking to me making you feel better?" He had to know.

She was quiet for a long minute.

"What?" He finally asked.

"I don't know. I somehow thought that me talking was helping *you* for some reason, but that seems stupid now that I say it out loud."

She'd been comforting *him*. She'd recognized he'd needed it, despite the fact he prided himself on not letting his weaknesses near the surface. There were people he worked with every single day—men and women trained to observe and take in data—who didn't recognize that he got clammy in closed spaces, that he never talked while he was on the elevator, that sometimes being inside a car was difficult for him.

Yet this woman had been attuned to it when she'd had no reason to be. And she'd done what she could to help, probably continuing to talk long after she would have liked to have gone to sleep.

"Thank you," he whispered.

"Is it the Mosaic stuff? Is that what has you so strung tight?"

"Yes." That wasn't the complete answer, but it wasn't a lie either. "Do you think you're up to getting started again soon? We don't have any food or water. So the longer it takes us to get back to Oak Creek, the more difficult it's going to be on our bodies." Ian didn't want to bring up her blisters again, but those were going to get worse too.

"Yeah. We're at least a little drier now."

Still, she wasn't complaining. Anybody in their right mind would bitch about these circumstances, but she was soldiering on without complaint. Again, damned impressive.

A few minutes later, they eased out of the cave. He couldn't deny that being out in the fresh air was a relief. He must have done something that gave him away.

"Better?" she asked.

"Yeah, I'm glad to get moving toward town and do what I can to stop these fuckers." That was true too. Although again, not the whole truth.

They moved as quietly as they could through the wilderness, much slower since there was nobody on their tail and it was still dark. It was much more dangerous to try to move fast than it was to take their time. Plus, now that Ian was aware of those blisters, he wasn't going to make this any harder on Wavy than he had to.

She did know this wilderness well. She was able to pinpoint almost to the minute when his cell phone would get coverage back.

As soon as it did, Landon was the first person he called. "I'm alive."

"Thank fucking God," he responded. "Where the hell have you been? I got your message about Wavy and then nothing."

He kept his voice low. "Wavy and I had to take an unexpected detour through the wilderness when her windshield was shot out."

"Are you guys okay? That was quite a storm we had."

"Yeah, we're all right. We found shelter inside a cave."

Landon let out a deep breath. "The Linear guys told me there were parts of Reddington City that didn't get good cell phone coverage. So I was giving you guys the benefit of the doubt, hoping maybe you were taking advantage of the whole . . . *smiling* situation."

Ian shot a look at Wavy, glad she couldn't hear what Landon was saying. "Let's just say I'm thankful that Wavy decided to come to Reddington City to ask me to dinner or else I would probably not be here right now. Please tell me you've been working on what we need for the Hemingway building."

"Yes. First thing was to use a Zodiac contact to get a warrant in the works."

That was why Landon was his right-hand man. He knew what to do without Ian having to spoon-feed him.

"Good. We need official access to that building immediately. I lost the tablet in my escape, so whatever I was able to record on my phone is all we'll have for intel until we get a warrant and get in there."

"We'll have it in the next six hours."

He grimaced. Six hours was a long time, but having to work inside the law meant a slower process. "Roger that. If I'm not mistaken, we'll be coming in from the southwest side of town. Can you have a car ready? Wavy's going to need a doctor."

"Is she all right?"

"I'm not going to need a doctor," Wavy called out from in

front of him. "I just have some blisters, but I'll definitely take a ride."

He smiled before he could stop himself.

Goddammit, that really was becoming a habit. Time to shut it down.

"Track my phone," he told Landon. "Meet us wherever you can get closest. I'll see you then."

Time to stop messing around and get to work.

# CHAPTER
# SEVEN

NEARLY EVERY MINUTE of the next twenty-four hours pissed Ian off.

Not a single damned thing went right. Landon got as close as he could to pick them up, but it was still a lot on Wavy's feet.

She was still insisting she didn't need medical attention when they dropped her off in front of the town's lawn and garden store. She insisted that was where she lived most of the time.

He wanted to know more about that—what the hell did *most of the time* mean?—but forced himself to leave her there on the curb with a thanks and a terse goodbye. Although she assured him she was fine, he still felt like an ass. The look Landon shot him made Ian feel ten times worse.

He was there in Oak Creek for a purpose. That purpose was *not* Wavy Bollinger, no matter how engaging and charming she might be.

Landon and Ian drove back to the Mayors Inn, one of only two hotels in town, where they'd set up rooms to use while they were there.

He showered, got checked out by the doctor one of his assistants had sent, then Landon cleaned and dressed the burn the bullet had left on his arm. Neither of them had to say how lucky he'd been. How lucky Wavy had been too. If those shots had been made by someone a little more skilled at long-distance shooting, both of them would be dead.

As soon as he was done, they began working the case. There was a shit ton to do. First and foremost, uploading what he'd recorded at the Hemingway building to the tech team to see if it provided any actionable intel. Every time he thought about what had been lost when his tablet fell to its death, he had to remind himself to unclench his teeth.

It had been the tablet that had fallen to its death, not him. Living to fight another day was always something to celebrate.

But bad news poured in as the hours went on. First, they found out that Kendrick and Neo hadn't made any progress on the drive.

Silas Varela, a low-level Mosaic goon, was holding something over Neo's head to make her sabotage the process. He had evidently hurt her pretty badly—leaving bruises all over her body but only in places no one could easily see. Kendrick found out and was nursing her.

Ian had offered to take Varela out of the picture. They could relieve the pressure on Neo and throw him in a holding cell somewhere until this was all finished. But whatever the man had on her, she wasn't willing to risk it and wasn't sharing what it was. Kendrick was still trying to figure it out and needed more time.

Time, one thing they didn't have.

If this Varela bastard was willing to hurt Neo, then he was willing to hurt others. They needed to do something about that. Kendrick promised to keep reporting back as they made any new progress.

Dead end number one.

"You ready to go back to the scene of the crime?" Landon asked him a few hours after he'd gotten off the phone with Kendrick. "I've heard from our law enforcement connection. The warrant to search the Hemingway building has come through.

They're willing to let you walk through with them in an advisory capacity."

"Contact must be Omega Sector."

"Yep."

His interaction with the federal task force had been short-lived. For the past few years, they'd stayed out of each other's space. That had worked better for all parties.

Of course, for the past few years, they'd thought Mosaic was gone. Interacting with Omega Sector now was inevitable.

Ian stood, leaving a mass of paperwork around him on the small hotel desk. "Let's go. I just hope we're in there soon enough that Mosaic hasn't been able to wipe everything."

They both were on the phone as they headed out of Oak Creek back toward Reddington City. The Zodiac tech team was still poring over his phone footage. But if they could get what was actually *inside* the building, that would give them so much more data about Mosaic.

Landon and Ian were each talking with different contacts as they arrived in Reddington City. He let out a curse when some sort of police blockade had them circling around the south side of town to come back up to the Hemingway building. Any sort of delay now added to his frustration. Every second gave Mosaic more time to hide their tracks.

When they stopped more than a mile away from the building, he knew that there was a bigger problem. Nothing was moving, at all.

Landon and Ian got out of the car. As soon as they did, they saw it.

Smoke. A shit ton of smoke farther ahead of them.

People were lined up along the block, watching. Landon walked over to an older lady and gave her one of his charming smiles.

"Do you know what happened here?" he asked her.

She shook her head, tsking. "There is a huge fire in some office buildings up the street. I heard a lot of people died."

Landon and Ian looked at each other, then took off running toward the Hemingway building, dodging people as they went. It didn't take a genius to figure out what was going on, although Ian hoped he was wrong.

They were able to get past the first set of barricades with a little stealth. But as they got closer, they were stopped by policemen.

One grabbed him by the arm. "Hey, you can't be here. This is for emergency personnel only."

Ian shrugged him off. He and Landon weren't emergency services. Hell, they didn't even have a badge. But he could see that it was, in fact, the Hemingway building that was burning.

He needed to get inside to see if there was anything to salvage. He had given nearly everything to stop Mosaic the first time. He wasn't going to let a uniformed cop who had no idea what was really going on stop him from getting inside. The officer grabbed him again, and he spun, a growl on his lips.

Landon's hand clamped down on Ian's shoulder. That was the only thing stopping him from doing something that might've gotten his ass thrown in jail, like taking a swing at a cop.

Landon pulled Ian behind him and shot the officer a smile. "We're part of the investigative crew. What exactly happened?"

The guy shot him a look but then shrugged. "Buddy, I don't know, but you can't be here. I've got strict orders. There are a lot of dead people."

"Thanks, Officer. These two are with me. I'll take it from here." A voice came from behind them. Ian turned to find a man he'd never seen holding up a federal badge. The cop nodded and walked off to go stop someone else from getting too close.

"Callum Webb. Omega Sector sent me as your liaison."

They shook the man's hand. Webb was tall, standing eye-to-eye with Ian's own six-foot one, with dark hair and eyes. Early-thirties and fit—and an awareness in his eyes like every Omega Sector agent he'd met, like his Zodiac team did. His suit may have been off the rack at a relatively inexpensive store, but he was ready to move if needed.

"I'm Ian DeRose. This is Landon Black."

Callum nodded. "I know who you are. I was actually around when you went up against Mosaic the first time, but you wouldn't have known me."

"We need to get into that building." Ian pointed towards the smoke.

He shook his head. "Nope. I've already checked. Firefighters only. Too crispy."

Goddammit. "What the hell happened?"

Callum led them a little out of the way as more emergency personnel ran forward. "I'm still finding that out. Official word is catastrophic electrical failure, which caused a pretty massive explosion. So far, we have at least eight dead bodies."

He scrubbed a hand down his face. Mosaic had burned the entire building down to keep them from accessing what was inside. "Fuck."

Callum nodded. "They didn't just blow up that one building, they took down the one on either side."

This kept getting worse. "I was inside there two days ago. There was a massive amount of info about Mosaic in that building."

Callum crossed his arms over his chest. "I'm going to assume you got caught?"

Ian turned to him. "I'm not dead, so I didn't get caught."

"Had you used proper channels, brought us in on your plan, we could've caught Mosaic by surprise before they had a chance to erase everything and kill innocent people in the process."

He mimicked his posture, crossing his arms over his chest. "Last time I went through *proper channels* with you guys, it almost got me killed."

He winced. "I read the report about that. I'm sorry."

Ian nodded. "We didn't have time to take this through a committee, so Landon and I went in. Once we knew there was something, we called for a warrant. The warrant was probably what tipped them off."

Callum had the good sense not to argue that. "If Mosaic is back in play, we want to take them down."

"Based on what I saw, they're not only back in play, they're pretty damned organized and widespread. I got some of the data on my phone. My tech team is going through it. I'll let you know what we find."

Callum nodded. Ian was a little surprised he didn't insist on letting his people handle it. Good. His people were better and faster than anyone working for law enforcement.

It didn't take long to realize that staying there was going to be a waste of time. There was nothing they could do on scene, and it was going to be hours if not days before anyone could get into the building. By then, there wouldn't be anything usable about Mosaic. He already knew that for a fact. Callum was staying and agreed to keep them in the loop if he found anything. Landon and Ian drove back to Oak Creek.

Dead end number two.

They made it back to Oak Creek, and Ian crashed for a few hours. The report he woke up to from Callum confirmed what he'd already known would be true: there was nothing left in that building after the fire. Not a single computer or so much as a sheet of paper had made it out in recoverable condition. And the final body count was eleven. Dozens more injured.

"You want to go get a bite to eat at the Frontier?" Landon asked as they both sat back, trying to process the loss from the fire.

"No. Bring me something back."

"You sure?"

Did Ian want to see Wavy? Yes. For multiple reasons. To find out if her feet were okay. To thank her one more time for saving his life.

To see her smile.

But nothing had changed in the hours since he'd dropped her off. She was still a distraction he couldn't afford.

"I'm sure. I'm going to touch base with the tech team, see what they got from my footage."

He didn't expect Landon back for a while. He figured he'd be chatting with the good citizens of Oak Creek—one waitress in particular, which had Ian more pissed at everything because he wouldn't be the one there talking to her—rather than rushing back. But he proved him wrong, walking in with coffee and a lunch plate before he'd had a chance to get all the details from his tech team.

"Jenna, Landon just walked in. I'm going to switch to video."

Jenna Franklin, cohead of the tech department, made the transition without missing a beat. "We're working all angles with what you recorded, including a possible side channel attack to root up data—hey, Landon—and should have the results of anything viable within forty-eight hours."

"Hey Jenna," Landon replied, setting coffee down in front of him. Ian nodded in thanks.

"Is there anything usable right now?" he asked. He wanted to take some sort of action. Mosaic had almost killed Wavy and Ian and had killed nearly a dozen innocents.

His trigger finger was getting antsy.

"Erick Huen," Jenna said.

He had to put his coffee down before he crushed the paper cup. Landon's eyes shot to his. "What about him?" Ian asked.

"He's definitely part of this new Mosaic. His name was found in your footage in at least two different places. We're still trying to see what else we can find about him. Do you know him?"

"Yeah," he muttered. "He was my brother's best friend. And was presumed dead."

Landon whistled through his teeth. "Last few months are starting to make a lot more sense now."

"I'll take this conversation as instruction to focus on Huen," Jenna said. "We'll get you all relevant info ASAP, boss."

"When it comes to Erick Huen, give me *all* info, whether it seems relevant or otherwise."

Jenna nodded. "Will do."

They finished the call, and Ian turned to Landon. His food was growing colder, but he couldn't stomach it right now.

"Erick Huen." he leaned back in his chair. "No wonder all this Mosaic shit has felt so personal. He hates me because I killed Grant."

Landon shrugged. "Grant deserved to die."

"This changes things. If we're dealing with Erick—" he broke off when his phone rang. "Sarge. What's going on?"

Ian put it on speaker so Landon could participate.

"One of our facial recognition software programs pinged an ID for Bronwyn eighteen hours ago."

"Where?"

"New York. I'm going after her."

Landon and Ian rubbed their eyes, not responding. By the time Sarge made it to New York, Bronwyn would be long gone.

"You don't need to tell me anything," Sarge said. "I know the chances of finding her are slim. But I also know the chances of me sitting in this office here in Denver without going fucking crazy are even lower. So, I'm going. I'll take personal time if I have to."

Ian let out a sigh. "You don't have to take personal time. Just . . . watch your back. We found out that Erick Huen is part of Mosaic, which means this is more personal than we first figured. Take somebody with you to New York if you want backup. Report immediately if you have any info."

"Roger." Sarge disconnected the call without saying goodbye.

"That dude really has to work on his people skills," Landon said.

"I don't think Sarge considers *people skills* a skill at all. People are nothing more than a necessary evil for his job."

Sarge was older than them. Set in all his ways. Wasn't interested in being friendly. Although there was no one Ian would rather have at his back in a fight. He would die for the people he cared about.

But was his obsession with Bronwyn because of that need to help one of his teammates, or was it more personal?

Sarge wasn't ever going to sit around and talk about his feelings, so they might never know.

He forced himself to eat the cold hamburger. "I guess we're a man short for the time being."

Not a good time for it. Dividing was the quickest way to get conquered.

Ian sat at the tiny desk on the crappy chair for a few more hours poring over the footage Jenna had sent to him for any relevant details they might not recognize.

Except for Erick's name, he didn't find much. He'd had enough.

"I'm going over to the Linear facility. I've got to work out some of this shit either in their gym or their ring before I rip my own hair out."

He couldn't stay in that hotel room any longer. Mosaic was pulling farther and farther away from them, and he had to get the pent-up frustration out of his system.

A knock on the door stopped him.

He looked at Landon. "Expecting someone?"

He shook his head. They had their weapons out and in hand when Ian looked through the security hole in the door.

Wavy.

He didn't want to see her. Not right now, not in the mental state he was in, but he opened the door anyway.

"Hi." She said, big smile on her face as always. "I brought you some pie as a midday pick-me-up. I promise I won't throw it at you."

"Thanks," he said. "I appreciate it."

She shifted from one foot to the other. He could tell she wanted to talk to him, to try to ease him out of the dim hotel room and into the light.

Into *her* light. The light of her smile.

He couldn't. He couldn't do that with her right now.

"Thanks for coming by with the pie." His voice was harder than he meant it to be. Too curt. Damn it, he was handling this wrong. He was frustrated, but he didn't need to take it out on her.

"You're welcome. Would you like—"

Ian cut her off. "Now is really not a good time. But thanks again."

"Oh, okay." She paused. "Well, you're welcome. Enjoy." She gave him an awkward wave, her smile falling as she turned to walk away.

He closed the door, wanting to throw the box across the room.

"What the hell is wrong with you?"

"What are you talking about?" Ian knew what he was talking about. He was an asshole. "She brought some pie. I took the pie. I said thank you."

"Jesus. You think *Sarge* doesn't have people skills? How about asking her how her feet were? How about inviting her in to chat for a second? How about going out with her?

He shook his head. "It's not like that. This is not what I'm here for. *She* is not what I'm here for."

"*She* saved your life. Then you couldn't take two minutes of your precious time doing *nothing* to make her feel a little welcome? You're right. You do need to go to the Linear Tactical facility. And if you want to get in the ring, I'll be glad to kick your ass."

"You're welcome to try." Landon and Ian were evenly matched in the ring. Ian was bigger and stronger, but Landon was quicker.

"Fine, asshole. Why don't you take out your aggression on someone who deserves it?"

"Like you?" His eyes narrowed at him.

He pushed by Ian and out the door. "Like yourself. Let's go."

Landon didn't say a word to him the entire way to the Linear Tactical property. They parked in front of the office and went inside. Zac Mackay and Finn Bollinger, Wavy's brother, were sitting at their desks.

"Can we use your sparring gear and ring?" Landon asked without greeting as he walked through the door.

Zac didn't miss a beat, although he shot a look at Finn. "Sure. You guys need a referee?"

"No, I'm going to kick his ass. No referee necessary." Landon spun back around and headed out the door toward the training facility.

Zac and Finn studied Ian with almost comically wide eyes.

"I don't think I've ever seen Landon that angry," Zac said. "He's always so easygoing, I didn't think he ever lost his cool."

Ian watched his friend through the door. "He doesn't normally. He thinks I'm being an asshole."

"Are you?" Finn asked.

"Yes." He didn't tell him that it was his sister he was being the asshole to, or else he'd probably be fighting two people.

Zac stood up. "I think I want to see this."

Finn was right behind him. "Oh, me too."

Great. Now they got to have an audience as Landon rightfully beat the crap out of him.

Ian had wiped the smile from Wavy Bollinger's face. No matter how shitty the news he'd gotten had been or how bad the situation was with Mosaic, he'd had no justification for doing that.

He deserved whatever he had coming.

# CHAPTER
# EIGHT

WAVY HAD THOUGHT that spilling pie all over Ian DeRose, and then wiping his crotch, had been the most mortified she would be in front of him. She'd thought the same thing again when she'd attacked him with the tray. And one last time, when he'd had to unhook her safety-pinned bra, proving she wasn't adult enough to remember to buy undergarments when she needed them.

Turns out, she felt most idiotic just by trying to do something nice for him.

She couldn't say that he'd been rude to her when he'd taken the pie. He'd taken it, thanked her . . . and then promptly shut the door in her face. Not rude, but definitely not a recognition of any closeness between them.

No sign of the man who'd treated her feet so gently. Or who'd been struggling in that little cave with some demon she hadn't been able to see.

Ian had bigger things on his mind. Wavy knew that. Hell, the bullets flying at them had proved it. But she'd still felt like an idiot when he'd shut that door in her face. She'd kind of wanted to cry, but she'd forced herself to keep it together, and gone and done what she always did instead.

Paint.

Her studio over the lawn and garden store couldn't be called an apartment by any stretch of the imagination. It was a massive space, which was great, but it wasn't zoned for residential living. It happened to have a sink in one corner, and she'd set up a cot on the other side. There was a toilet, roughly functional, but with only a thin screen separating it from the rest of the room.

She'd been told by the fire marshal that no one was allowed to live here, so she didn't claim this as her permanent address, although this is where she spent pretty much all her time when she wasn't working. Legally, she still lived with her mom. Even more pathetic than living in a not-zoned-for-humans building.

Wavy couldn't say that she loved the space—the lighting wasn't great, plus it was hot in the summer and freezing in the winter—but it at least allowed her to do what she loved to do. And what she was going to do now.

She grabbed a new canvas and put it on the easel. She tried not to think about the tiny little painting she'd left for Ian in the box with the pie. It was about the size of a sticky note. Something she'd painted for him earlier today and wanted to give him.

She loved colors, and he needed more color in his life. What he didn't need, evidently, was *her* in his life. That's what had hurt about him closing that door in her face without a personal word.

She looked at the blank canvas in front of her. She knew she should practice painting more classic pieces. Things that might actually make a living for her eventually. But today, she wanted more colors.

She grabbed her paints and started. Her brushstrokes were timid at first, with softer colors. But that wasn't right. It wasn't what she wanted.

She grabbed her reds, purples, and made her strokes bolder. Screw the soft, gentle colors and strokes.

Wavy was *pissed*.

She didn't get angry very often, but right now, it was all she could see, and definitely all she could paint.

Ian DeRose wanted to close a door in her face when she was being kind? Fine. His choice.

This painting was hers. At least it wasn't hurting anyone.

Her mom called; she could tell by the ringtone. But she ignored that. Lexi called too, but she didn't answer. It didn't happen a lot, but she didn't want to talk to anybody right now.

More of the deep colors swirled onto the canvas, covering the pastels she'd started with.

It didn't take her long to realize she was mad at herself too. Ian hadn't done anything wrong—why should she be so upset? Why should she care what he did? He didn't owe her anything.

But logical or not, her emotions were churning because of him. She realized the deep-blue burst she'd created at the center of the canvas was Ian—his ice. His control. Then all the strokes dancing around it were the emotions she couldn't seem to contain around him.

Wavy didn't know how long she was at it. Long enough that her arms were getting heavy and her strokes were becoming less bold, less angry.

Banging on the door finally caused her to turn away from her canvas. She looked out one of the small windows. It was late afternoon already.

"I'm coming," she called out. That had to be either one of her brothers, or . . . Actually, it had to be one of her brothers. Besides her mom and Lexi, they were the only ones who knew about this place. And neither Mom nor Lexi would be banging like a crazed chimpanzee.

Another bang. Good Lord. Wavy snatched the door open. "Why in the world are y—"

Ian.

He was a little bit sweaty and had the start of a black eye. He was holding up the tiny painting she'd slipped into the pie box.

"What is this?" he asked.

She tried to grab it out of his hand, but he snatched it back too quickly. "Nothing. Give it to me."

"No. Tell me what it is."

"What does it look like, asshole? It's a painting. I must have accidentally slipped it into the box. It happens." That was much better than telling him that she had thought he needed more color in his life. "Thanks for returning it."

She held out her hand for him to give it to her but he didn't. She tried to shut the door.

He held out his hand to stop it. "I'm sorry, Wavy."

"You don't owe me an apology. You don't owe me anything, DeRose. I don't know how you found me here, but thanks for stopping by." She tried to shut the door again. Again, he wasn't letting it budge.

"May I come in?"

"Why? There's no need. I get it. You're not here for me. You're here for the job. You're here to shut down Mosaic."

He looked surprised.

"What?" she asked. "Did you think I didn't get it?"

"You basically said the same thing I've been repeating to myself for the past thirty-six hours."

"Great. Then we're both saying it, so that must make it doubly true. Thanks for bringing the little painting back. Hope you enjoyed your pie." His arm wasn't budging from the door, keeping it open with remarkable ease considering she was putting a ton of effort into trying to close it.

"Wavy, I'm sorry. You did something nice for me, and I acted like a jerk."

She let out a sigh. "You didn't act like a jerk. You were polite. You didn't do anything wrong."

"I did do something wrong, and we both know it. PS, Landon knows it too." Ian reached up and gingerly touched his eye. "He and I have been in the sparring ring for the past couple of hours. Your brother and Zac Mackay got quite a kick out of watching us go at it."

Wavy stopped pushing at the door. "You were fighting?"

He shrugged. "Sparring. There's a difference. We needed to work out a little bit of our stress. Nothing has been going right since I saw you last. We've had one hang-up after another with Mosaic."

He was stressed. He took this stuff with Mosaic seriously. Who was she to be upset about him not wanting to spend time with her when he had so many other important things he was trying to do?

"Look." she let out a sigh. "Really, it's okay. There's no harm done. I hope you enjoyed the pie."

"Landon wouldn't let me have any of it." Ian actually looked sheepish. "He said I didn't deserve it after how I'd treated you."

"Wow. No pie. Harsh punishment." She couldn't stay angry; it wasn't in her DNA. She stepped back from the door and gestured with her paintbrush for him to come in.

"I made the smile fall from your face. That was a bitch move. Smiling is your natural state of being. And for me to have taken that . . ." He walked forward a few steps, running his fingers through his thick hair, standing it on end, before turning to look at her with a shrug. "I'm not good with gentle. I'm not good with fragile. Landon is great."

She pointed the end of her brush at him, some of her heat back. "Gentle and fragile are not the same thing."

He nodded. "You're right. They're not. And you're not fragile, you've proved that already, but you *are* gentle."

"I'm not going to apologize for that."

"I would never want you to."

"I like to laugh, to smile, to live. My life has a lot of color to it."

He took a step toward her. "I know that. I've known that from the moment you tried to clock me with that tray."

He took another step closer, and she instinctively took a step back. Not because he scared her, but because . . . she didn't know why.

Because him being close to her was overwhelming. She didn't know what it was about him. She'd been around alpha-male-type guys her whole life, but Ian DeRose was different. How she felt around him was different.

It was time to get this conversation back on track. "Thank you for the apology. I appreciate it. But I know you're not here because of me. You have bigger things on your mind."

Damn it, he took another step closer. Wavy was caught between the need to back away to protect herself and the need to touch him, to let him know what gentleness felt like. What color felt like.

"I may not be here in Oak Creek because of you," he whispered. "But I'm very definitely in this building right now because of you."

"Why?" The need to touch him won. Her fingers stroked up his arm, feeling the tight muscles underneath. "Why are you here, Ian?"

"Because I can't stay away from you. Because I don't *want* to stay away from you. Because I want to ask you out. Because I had to see if you taste as sweet as you look."

His arm snaked around her waist, and he pulled her closer. There was no yanking. If she had stepped back, he would've let her go.

But stepping back very definitely wasn't what she wanted anymore. She wanted to touch him, not just to let him feel her touch, but because she wanted to feel his.

His kiss wasn't gentle. He'd obviously been fighting all day—with bad guys, with friends, with himself—and was at the end of his control. But skating the edge of his control made the kiss all the more enticing.

Her arms wrapped around his neck, brush still clenched in her fist, as he pulled her closer. The kiss deepened—hot, raw, honest. Everything the man was too.

"You do," he said, as his lips finally broke away from hers a few seconds later. Both of them were breathing hard.

"I do what?" She couldn't remember her own name, much less what they'd been talking about before his lips met hers.

"You taste as sweet as you are, Wavy Bollinger. That shouldn't surprise me. It *doesn't* surprise me."

"Oh." She tried to find something more profound to say, but there was nothing.

He stepped back a little, trailing his fingers down her arms, and glanced around. He was obviously trying to slow the pace a bit. "I want to take you out on a date. That's why I came here. To apologize and make it up to you with dinner. Soon. If you'll let me."

"You don't have to do that."

"I want to."

Wavy wasn't going to argue with him since it was what she wanted too. "Then yes, I'll go out with you sometime."

He smiled, and she couldn't help the smile it brought to her own face. "So, this is your studio. You live here too?"

"Most of the time," she said, "But don't tell the fire marshal. This isn't zoned for residential living."

"Do you mind if I look around?"

Wavy wasn't going to lie; it made her nervous. Eighty percent of the space in there was taken up by her paintings. If he said something negative, that would hurt her feelings. But she nodded. She needed to prove, probably to both of them: that her words had been true when she had said she was gentle but not fragile.

The pieces she had taken to the art agent who'd rejected her were still out, the most noticeable. Ian looked at those first, studying them for a long time.

"I'm not really an art expert," he said. "Do you like doing still lifes like this? Landscapes?"

No, she didn't. They bored her, but she also knew they were probably the most likely way to make a living as an artist. "That's what I learned to do and focus on in art school. It's generally the most commercially viable."

He nodded. "Understandable. Is that what you want—to make a living as an artist? I noticed that you didn't really mention your art the last few times we talked."

"I'd like to make a living with my art rather than waitressing, sure." While his attention was elsewhere, she spun the easel she'd been working on with her foot so he would be less likely to see today's work in progress. "But it doesn't seem like that's going to happen."

"But these paintings don't excite you." He pointed at the two in front of him.

"Honestly?" Wavy shrugged. "No, not really."

"What were you working on when I knocked on the door? It took you a while to answer, like you were caught up in what you were doing and irritated to be interrupted. Plus, you have your rainbow on again."

"My rainbow?"

He walked over and brought her wrist up, so that she could see the pattern of paint on it. "You also have some on your cheek too. Double rainbow."

"Yeah, I sometimes get messy."

"Will you show me what you were painting today?"

If he didn't like her still lifes, he surely wouldn't like her abstract stuff. "Sure. As long as you promise not to laugh."

"I promise." Those brown eyes fairly burned with sincerity.

She walked over to her easel and spun her blob of color so he could see it. Blob was really the only way to describe it. Oranges and reds, some purples thrown in with a splash of blue and some green.

He stood silently, staring.

"I don't know why I paint like this," she finally said when he didn't say anything. She had to give him credit, he didn't so much as snicker.

"I do," he responded, staring at the canvas. "This is you. On a canvas. Vibrant, alive. Passionate."

"Well, the only art agent I showed it to thought that people wouldn't ever be interested in buying it. That it was junk."

"Well then, that art agent was an idiot," Ian said. "I would buy this a thousand times over the most skilled landscape."

He walked closer, still staring.

"You were angry. It's obvious by the color choice."

"Yeah," she admitted, "I was pretty angry when I started this."

He looked at the purples and greens. Ran his fingers near them. "You were hurt too."

Now she was staring at *him*.

He saw *her* in the painting. In a few seconds, he'd seen beyond the blobbiness of it to what it really was: her. It was unnerving. It was . . . what made her nervous about him. He saw too much.

He turned to face her. "I don't like thinking about you being angry or hurt, but I can't lie. I like knowing I bring out this sort of passion in you."

The heat in his eyes couldn't be denied. What sort of colors would she choose if caught in the throes of making love to him? Her tongue dashed across her lip, and his eyes fell to her mouth.

It didn't take a genius to see he was thinking the same thing. He took a step closer, reaching toward her.

But then his phone rang. Ian kept his eyes pinned on her as he brought the phone up to his ear. "You better be about to tell me the world is coming to an end. Otherwise, I'm hanging up right fucking now."

Wavy couldn't hear what was said, but she had no doubt he was talking to Landon. His eyes dropped from hers at whatever Landon was saying. Maybe the world was coming to an end.

"Okay. I'll be right there." He disconnected the call.

"What happened?" she asked.

"Kendrick and Neo finally made a break in the Mosaic case with the computer drive they've been working on, but there's some sort of emergency. There's an all-hands-on-deck meeting at Linear Tactical."

# CHAPTER NINE

EVERY SINGLE MEMBER of the Linear Tactical team plus all their loved ones were on the LT property for the meeting.

These were good people. If there was something they could do to take down Mosaic, they all wanted to help. But it had been in a generic way, as all good people would probably want to do.

That had been before Mosaic's henchman, Silas Varela, had gone after some of their own—including one of their *children*.

Now the Linear team would do whatever it took to stop him. Varela hadn't been involved with the Hemingway building, but he was the one who'd hurt Neo. Hurt her so badly that she was still barely able to move days later.

Worse, Varela had gotten her to work for him by threatening to kill the little girl Neo had placed for adoption ten years ago.

Neo might not have lived in Oak Creek for long, but no one in the Linear Tactical family was going to let her suffer any more now that they knew she needed help. Ian stood there watching as all of them committed to that fact, in word and action.

Including Wavy. Her small hands had clenched into fists when she'd heard what had happened. Wavy might have the least amount of military and tactical training in the room, but he had no doubt she'd take on Silas Varela if she had to.

So much passion in one tiny package, and Ian couldn't wait to get closer to it. Closer to her. If it hadn't been for the call to come here, he had no doubt they'd be in her studio right now, but not looking at her impressive paintings.

He would still take down Mosaic, but he was done trying to keep away from Wavy Bollinger in the process.

He lent the Linear guys one of the Zodiac jets so they could get Neo's little girl to safety without Varela knowing. Neo would continue to pretend like she was working for Varela. But he thought she was in this alone and that he had her under his thumb.

He didn't, and he was going to find that out today when they took him down. It was just a matter of waiting for him to make a mistake.

An hour later, Varela made that mistake.

He got greedy and tipped his hand in the wrong direction, forcing Neo to an abandoned warehouse, planning to take the drive and probably kill her as soon as he did. He thought she would be alone.

He hadn't planned on her having a family to back her up.

He hadn't planned on her having Kendrick willing to rush into the building like a lovesick fool to save her life.

And he definitely hadn't expected Ian and the Linear guys to take him and his men out before they knew what hit them. Or the promise Ian made Varela as he lay on the warehouse floor trying to figure out how everything had gone to shit.

"You're going to work for me to help take your bosses down, or I'm going to make sure you're thrown into a dark cell that'll eventually become your grave."

The Linear guys around Ian went silent as he explained Varela's new reality to him.

"You can't do that," he sputtered. "I have rights."

He didn't have an ounce of sympathy as he pulled Varela to his feet and marched him out the door. "I'm not the law. I'm just the guy who's going to make sure Mosaic goes down and stays down this time."

———

Ian had done the right thing—or at least the *legal* thing—and taken Varela to an Omega Sector holding cell. He'd been telling the truth when he'd told him he wasn't the law, but that didn't mean he thought he was above it.

Callum Webb and Ian looked through a two-way mirror at Varela sitting handcuffed inside in an interrogation room. Ian rubbed at his arm where he'd been shot. The ache was still there. It would be for a while.

"We can't hold him indefinitely. You know that."

"I know," he told Callum without taking his eyes off Varela. He was getting to the point they needed him to be at—shifting, nervous, unsure what was going on or what his future held, but knowing it was all bad.

"Times have changed. Laws have changed," Callum continued. "Even somebody tied to a terrorist organization can't be held indefinitely without being charged."

"You and I both know that, but I'm going to bet that Silas Varela isn't up to date on the differences between the Patriot Act and the USA Freedom Act. Besides, I don't want to hold him without charging him. Between the beating he gave Neo and threatening to kill her daughter, you could have him facing prison time for the rest of his life. *That* he probably does know."

"I can give you twenty-four hours until I have to charge him. Forty-eight, maybe. But I'll have to answer for it."

"I won't need nearly that long. Did you get clearance to use him as a criminal informant? He does much more for us out of jail than he does inside."

Callum nodded. "Only because it's you, Ian, and because we all know we owe you one when it comes to what happened with Mosaic last time."

What had been done to Ian had been a personal vendetta, not the fault of any law enforcement agency.

"Whatever reason they're willing to let me use Varela, I'll take it. We need it."

"So we go in there and play good cop, bad cop?"

"More like pick your poison. You might want to make sure there's a momentary malfunction of the recording equipment."

"I can't let you hurt him," Callum said. "Any case we have falls apart if you hurt him."

He shook his head. "I'm not going to injure him. I'm merely going to explain his choices to him. Are you ready?"

Callum nodded, letting out a small sigh.

He gave him a tight smile. "Just follow my lead."

They entered the interrogation room. A sullen look fell over Varela's face as soon as he saw Ian.

"I want to talk to my lawyer," he said.

Ian didn't have to look back at Callum to know he was flinching. As an officer of the law, he was required to allow counsel if it was requested.

He wasn't and that's why he was doing the talking. But he didn't have much time.

"We haven't charged you with anything yet, Varela. As a matter of fact, nobody knows you're here. Mosaic doesn't ever have to know you were here."

The man blanched at the word Mosaic.

"That's right." He sat down across from him so they were eye to eye. "We know who you work for. And you and I both know that every minute you sit in this cell, Mosaic gets more and more suspicious. So, you want to call your lawyer? Fine. We'll make sure that Mosaic knows you were in here for hours before your lawyer arrived."

Varela stared down at his hands.

"How long do you think you're going to live once you get out?" He continued. "Or for that matter, how long do you think you're going to last in prison if we charge you for what you did to Neo and attempted to do to her daughter, and then make it known that you were in here talking to us before you were charged?"

"That's not fair, man!" Varela slammed his hands down on the table. "No matter what I do, you're going to get me killed."

"It doesn't have to be that way." He sat back with a little shrug. "You agree to work for us, report to us about your bosses, and we'll make sure they never know that any conversation with law enforcement happened."

Varela was smart enough to know that he didn't have many options here. Ian crossed his arms over his chest, relaxing like he wouldn't spend his last breath trying to take Mosaic down. "That's right. You either deal with me and live, or I turn you over to the good officer behind me. He'll read you your rights, charge you with assault and battery and attempted murder, and you'll take a chance with Mosaic with whatever word I put out on the street. I'll start with telling your men about how you betrayed them."

Varela narrowed his eyes at us. "What do I get out of it if I help you?"

Now Callum spoke up. "You don't go to jail for beating an innocent woman or threatening the life of an innocent ten-year-old. That's what you get, you fucking bastard."

Varela slumped in his chair. He knew he'd been beat. "Fine. What do I do?"

Callum handed Ian a key, and he unlocked Varela's cuffs. "Let's start by you telling me everything you know about Mosaic. And from there, we'll come up with a plan that keeps you alive and gets us the information we need."

# CHAPTER
# TEN

WAVY HAD GROWN USED to the fact that Oak Creek was always going to have more trouble than a normal town its size. The Linear Tactical guys, given their line of work and their pasts, were always going to be trouble magnets.

So when they'd gotten the call a week ago that there was an emergency, all-hands meeting—*everyone* needed—she'd gone also.

She might not have any special fighting or tactical skills, but those people were her family, and if they needed her, for whatever way she might be able to help, she was going to be there.

Ian, on the other hand, had *all* the useful skills. The type of person you definitely wanted around in an emergency situation. He'd been impressive—not a term she used lightly when talking about a group the caliber of her brother and the rest of the Linear guys.

Ian had stood out. He was definitely a leader. He'd made decisions quickly, not second-guessing himself. When it had been time for them to go after that Varela guy, he'd immediately jumped in and led the charge.

Impressive.

She hadn't seen or heard from him again in the week since. He'd helped save the day, then . . . left.

She shouldn't be surprised. And she *definitely* shouldn't be hurt. The man had stated repeatedly that his reason for being here in Wyoming—hell, his reason for *existence*—was to stop Mosaic. Varela was a key piece of that.

But after that blistering kiss in her studio, she'd thought she'd at least hear something from him. He'd said he wanted to take her out on a date.

He had more important things to do. Damn it, Wavy knew that. She didn't need to be coddled. The man had important stuff on his mind, but still, it stung.

She'd spent a lot of the past week painting. It had been all colors—none of her traditional landscapes at all. The rainbow paintings. Damn Ian for giving them that title she couldn't get out of her mind. They were never going to make her a living, but now she couldn't stop doing them.

Leeann had asked her to trade shifts with her. Wavy had worked the lunch shift today and was about to get off as she came in for the dinner shift. She needed to get back into Reddington City for more art supplies. Maybe she could make it before they closed.

She'd been painting so much she'd used up all her canvases. All she had left were the tiny pieces of canvas she'd cut up when she'd given Ian the baby rainbow painting with the pie.

She could make more of them, but who would she give them to? In her mind, they were only for Ian.

Ian DeRose. The man Wavy couldn't get out of her mind.

Ian DeRose. The man who probably hadn't thought twice about her since he'd left town.

Ian DeRose. The man who . . . just walked into the Frontier Diner?

She stopped, tray in hand, staring at him. He was tired, exhausted, more than the last time she'd seen him. His jaw was hard, dark hair on edge as if he'd run his fingers through it repeatedly.

She set her tray down and walked over to where he stood in the doorway. He looked so much less sure of himself than he'd been a week ago when directing an assault on a group of terrorists.

She nodded toward the door, and he walked back out. She didn't want to talk to him where their conversation would be monitored, then passed along to every single person in town. She pulled off her apron, stuffed it in the employee cubby, and said goodbye to Leeann.

Wavy walked outside and found him leaning against the hood of his rental SUV, long legs stretched out in front of him, strong arms crossed over his chest.

God, she wanted to paint him again, just like this. Her rainbows had been calling her all week, but right now, she wanted to do something realistic. *Him.*

He saw her and pushed off from the car. "Hi."

"Hi, yourself. You look tired." Probably not the best thing to lead with, but she was concerned about him.

Whatever reason he hadn't gotten in touch with her for the past week, it wasn't because he'd been blowing her off. It had taken a toll on him.

She wanted him to know she was concerned about him. He worried about everybody else. Maybe he needed somebody who worried about *him.*

He ran his fingers through his hair again—definitely *not* to style it. "It's been a long week. That doesn't excuse what—"

She held out a hand to cut him off. "You had things you needed to handle. I don't need to be coddled."

"I know you don't *need* to be coddled." Now he scrubbed the hand down his face. "But maybe I want to coddle you a little bit."

Wait, had he said coddle or cuddle? "Oh."

"We had to get Varela back into Mosaic. He's reporting

undercover to me. The longer he was unaccounted for, the more suspicious it was. So time was of the essence."

"Is he getting you the info you were hoping for?" She asked.

Ian nodded. "So far, he's doing okay. It's not an easy situation to be undercover with people who are going to kill you if they find out. But his other choice was to spend the rest of his life in prison. So, yeah, so far, it's going fairly well."

"I'm glad to hear it." There was an awkward pause between them, and she shifted her weight back and forth on her feet. "I didn't think you'd be back."

"Honestly, I didn't either."

Wow. That stung more than it should.

She swallowed her hurt. "Well, I'm glad that Varela is working out for you. Are you here to talk to the Linear guys?"

"No." He took a step closer. "I'm here to talk to you, Wavy. I'm hoping I can appeal to your kind nature and talk you into going out with me."

She shook her head. "You don't owe me anything. Not even a date. I don't want to be something you have to fit into an already full schedule. It doesn't matter that your schedule is full for important reasons."

He took a step closer. "I won't lie. My schedule is always full. But I don't care. I'm not good with words, but I'm here because, once again, I tried to stay away from you but couldn't. I'm here because if you're going to consume my thoughts every fucking day, then I want to at least be in your presence. Feel your light, your smile. Your rainbow."

"Wow." She couldn't stop staring at those brown eyes. "You're better with words than you think you are."

He stepped closer again. "I want to take you out on that date if you'll let me."

She'd never been the type of person to hold a grudge or refuse herself what she wanted in order to prove some kind of point. And she wanted Ian. He might be conflicted, but he wasn't playing games.

Wavy offered her biggest smile. "Sure, we can go out. When were you thinking?"

"Honestly, as obnoxious as this sounds, I was hoping we could do it right now."

She couldn't help it, she patted her hair. She knew what she looked like after a full shift at the diner. "You mean for dinner?"

"Yes. If you'll allow me, I have somewhere special I'd like to take you. No strings attached, nothing expected of you."

"Do I have time to go home to shower and change?" Shit, that meant driving all the way out to her mom's house.

"If you want to, absolutely. But you're fine in exactly what you're wearing."

What she was wearing was jeans and a button-down pink shirt. Not very exciting. At least he wasn't planning on taking her anywhere fancy. Which was fine with her. Fancy wasn't her style.

He lifted her wrist, so he could study it. "You've been painting."

"Yeah. A lot." She didn't need to go into any further explanation than that.

"If you want to go take a shower and do whatever, that's fine, but honestly, I'd rather have every second I can with you."

Wavy broke out into another smile. "Okay, at least let me change my shirt and shoes." She didn't want to go out on a date in her black working sneakers, although she had thrown away her cute flats after all the blisters. But she had some sandals in her studio as well as a lightweight sweater that at least accentuated what few curves she had. "Give me ten minutes, and I'll be back here."

Now he smiled. "Deal."

———

Wavy hurried. Like him, there was nothing more she wanted to do than spend the limited hours they had together.

She changed her shirt and her shoes—hopefully, she wasn't going to be running miles through the wilderness again, because those sandals were definitely worse than the flats. She freshened up her makeup but left her hair as it was, since her messy bun was still on the cute side, rather than the crazy.

He was waiting for her, just like he'd said he'd be once she got back.

"You look great. But you always do."

"Even running through the wilderness with killers on our heels?"

He opened the passenger door for her. "Especially then."

She wanted to ask where they were going, but forced herself not to. When he drove out of town, she thought maybe he was taking them to Reddington City. He was in jeans, too, with a button-down blue shirt that should have seemed mundane but brought out the olive tones in his skin. Her fingers itched for her paint brushes again.

When they stopped east of town at the regional airport, Wavy stared out at the sole airplane waiting on the runway. Not an airplane, a jet. His jet.

She looked over at him, one eyebrow raised. "Is this for us?"

He returned her stare. "Is that okay?"

"Where are we going?"

"Somewhere special." He lifted her hand to his lips. "I think you'll like it. If not, we'll go somewhere else."

"Lead the way."

She'd been on commercial planes before, but never a private jet. The pilot informed Ian that they were ready to take off whenever he was and that the flight plan had been cleared. There was one male flight attendant who also served as a co-pilot.

"This is yours?" She asked him as they took off into the late afternoon sky. The flight attendant served them drinks then went into the cockpit.

"Technically, it's Zodiac Tactical's, but since I own Zodiac Tactical, yes, it's mine."

"How did you get into the security business?" She liked that they were sitting across from each other and she could look into his face.

He shrugged. "Probably not unlike how Finn and Zac started Linear. Private security seemed like a natural extension of the work I did in the Navy SEALs."

"Zodiac is already established enough that you have a jet at your disposal?"

He leaned back against the headrest with an air of familiarity. He'd done that hundreds of times before, maybe tended to sit in that same seat when he was on this plane. "Technically, I owned the jet before I had the company."

"So you made your fortune and then decided to start a security company?"

He smiled. It always caught her a little by surprise. "Yes, technically. I made my money the old-fashioned way: I inherited it when my father, whom I hadn't talked to in more than ten years, died."

"Isn't that how everyone makes their fortune?"

He turned and looked out the small window without saying anything else. There was a lot more to his story, and she wanted to hear it, but it didn't seem like he wanted to tell it right now.

"So, you started Zodiac to have something to do? Because you obviously didn't need to do it for the money."

He shrugged. "I started it because there were things—jobs, missions—that needed to be done, and I knew how to do them. Or knew who to get to do them. My inner team is the best in the world when it comes to defense and security. No offense intended to your brother or any of the Linear guys."

She laughed. "Oh, I'm sure it would be a challenge to the death if they heard you say that, but they are all officially retired. Although, you wouldn't know it sometimes from the amount of trouble they get into."

Ian nodded. "I know they're good. I would hire every single one of them if they wanted a job. I have actually tried to recruit them multiple times. You know that Gavin Zimmerman's brothers work for me."

Gavin was one of the core members of Linear Tactical. Wavy'd known him for years. "Yeah, Tristan and Andrew. I know them, not well, but they are a pain in my ass every once in a while, like Gavin."

"That's the joy of small-town life, right?"

She nodded, taking a sip of her drink. "Yep. How about you? Where were you born?"

"I grew up in Baltimore."

Again, he fell back into silence. She tried to get him to talk more about his life, about anything, but he turned the conversation around to her art. She didn't know why he was interested, but she answered questions as best she could.

He asked her what she'd painted this week, to describe the colors and the strokes, like he was envisioning them in his head.

Nobody had ever done that before—been so interested in her art that they'd keep pressing for more details.

He kept her talking until they landed an hour later. She looked out the window, but she still couldn't tell exactly where they were. They were once again at a smaller airport, not one in a big city.

They got out, and she thought they would be heading for a car, but instead they got into a helicopter. He slipped a headset over her head so they could talk.

"Wow." She couldn't keep the wonder out of her voice, so she didn't try. "Your dates are pretty impressive."

"This isn't the date." He shot her another smile. "But we're almost to the date."

She grabbed his hand as they lifted into the air, staring out the window. All she wanted to do was take in the city below her.

"That's Denver, isn't it?"

"Sure is."

Of all the places she'd thought they might be going, this definitely wasn't it. "What's in Denver?"

"My home."

# CHAPTER
# ELEVEN

THERE WAS NOWHERE Ian could have taken her Wavy would have liked more.

It had nothing to do with the penthouse that she was sure was one of the most expensive in Denver. Out the floor-to-ceiling windows, she could see Coors Field, and also, if she wasn't mistaken, the Denver Art Museum down the block. On the other side with more windows, she could see the South Platte River, which flowed straight through downtown.

The penthouse was stunning inside and out. It appealed to all of her senses. The living room was stark, but not cold, the furniture leather and masculine, fitting for a Denver setting, fitting for the owner of the home himself.

She turned from the windows to find him watching her.

"It occurs to me that I probably should have taken you somewhere more impressive for a first date, but . . ." He shrugged one shoulder in an endearingly awkward fashion. "I wanted you to see where I live. I've seen your studio, and that's your most personal space. This is mine."

She gestured to the room around her. "This is perfect. There's nowhere else in the world you could have taken me that would have been as impressive."

He shook his head. "I actually doubt that very much, but thank you. I tend to eat at odd hours, so I have a cook who leaves me meals to heat up. But I asked her to leave me something fresh so I could cook it for you." He grimaced as he turned toward the kitchen. "To be honest, I don't know what it is, and it occurs to me that maybe you don't eat everything. Maybe you're a vegetarian. Maybe you don't like certain foods or are allergic to something."

She walked over and touched his arm. "I eat everything, believe me. Whatever your cook left, I'm sure is fine. Let's go find out what it is."

It was salmon, and the cook had left instructions that were so detailed, it was clear that Ian truly didn't cook for himself very often.

He gave Wavy a sheepish look as they finished and put it in the oven. "Sarah knows that I'm really helpless in the kitchen. She's been with me a long time, almost like a mother figure. I tried to get her to retire and go live out with her daughter and grandkids in Florida, but she won't do it. So she comes in a couple of times a week, whether I want her to or not."

Such a bemused look. He had no idea what to do with someone trying to take care of *him*—he was the one who took care of everyone else.

"She's worked for you for a long time?"

"I actually knew her before I went into the navy. She worked for my dad when I was a kid, then came to work for me when I started this business. She was the one who came up with the name Zodiac for my company."

"Really?"

He leaned back against the counter, more relaxed than she'd ever seen him. "She's obsessed with horoscopes. I'm an Aries, and she used to send me daily star readings. Now, she only does it every once in a while—usually when she's trying to get me to do something I don't want to do."

"Like what?"

"Mostly spend less time working. Take a vacation or something." He switched to a falsetto voice. " 'Mercury is in retrograde, and schedules are going to be botched all over the place. You might as well go sit it out on a beach for a few days, my little Aries.' "

"Little Aries?"

His low chuckle joined hers. "She's the only one in the world who can get away with that. But yeah, all of my inner team have zodiac signs as code names."

"Based on their birth dates?"

"Sometimes," he said. "But mostly on their personality traits. Sarah had a grand old time assigning them."

The fact that he'd let a retirement-aged mother figure have so much say in his business might be the most endearing thing she'd ever heard.

He opened a bottle of wine and poured them both a glass. "Landon is Libra. Of course, he's so charming and friendly, that's perfect."

"And you're Aries." She studied him as she took a sip of the wine. She didn't know a ton about Zodiac, but she knew enough. "Dominant. Leader."

He lifted his glass, studying the chardonnay. "Bullheaded. Tending to run roughshod over the feelings of others."

Wavy laughed. "So it's completely accurate."

He grimaced. "More often than not. Don't tell Sarah."

"Your secret is safe with me, little Aries."

They made the salad and cleared his stuff off the dining room table so they could eat in there. She told him the bar at the kitchen was fine, but he insisted that they have the view by the window.

She like that he worked there, surrounded by the gorgeous view. It made him feel more human.

The meal was everything Wavy could have wanted at a five-star restaurant, and better because Ian was at ease. He felt safe here, knew the security, knew the layout, didn't have to watch his back. That was why he'd brought her there, and that made her appreciate it more.

Plus, the salmon was damn delicious. And the wine was probably more expensive than anything she'd ever had in her entire life.

And while he wasn't exactly forthcoming with details about his life, he wasn't as closed off.

The subject of Sarah seemed to be a good talking point for him. "So, do you think that I could find out where Sarah lives so I could get stories about young Ian DeRose?"

He laughed. "I think she would be glad to talk your ears off. She worked for my dad in Baltimore for a lot of years, and she always looked out for me and my brother Grant."

Wavy stopped, fork halfway up to her mouth. "You have a brother? Are you guys close? How old is he? Are you younger or older?"

Ian shut down in front of me. "He's dead."

"Oh." Shit. Her and her big mouth. "I'm so sorry. It has to be hard, since you mentioned you were estranged from your father, to have lost your brother too."

Ian finished the last of his salmon and stood up with his plate. "Not as hard as you would think."

Okay. *Brother* was to be filed under touchy subjects for Ian. She stood up as well and followed him into the kitchen. "I'm sorry for your loss. My brothers are a pain in the ass but important to me. I hate to think of you not having family."

He shrugged. "I do have family. They're just not blood relations."

"Your Zodiac team?" she asked.

He nodded.

She understood that. "My brother feels the same way about the Linear guys. They're family in every possible way."

She helped him rinse off the plates, not sure what to say to get them back to the easy conversation they'd been having.

Thankfully, he helped them along. "I don't know that

there's any dessert. I didn't mention to Sarah that we would want anything, but I do know for a fact that there's some ice cream."

"Ice cream sounds perfect."

He dipped it into some bowls, and they walked out the sliding door to the small, enclosed patio where he showed her all the sights of Denver.

He went on to talk about the other branches of Zodiac Tactical with offices on different continents—some specialized in hostage and rescue, some in bodyguarding. All of it was fascinating.

As long as they didn't revert back to the subject of family, he seemed to be fine to talk, and she liked listening to him.

She wanted him to kiss her again. She wanted him to kiss her there in his home under the stars of a Colorado sky.

She knew it would be time to leave soon, and she wanted to feel his lips on hers again. They'd been inching closer to each other ever since they'd finished dessert. Outside, talking on his patio with nothing around them but the other buildings and the city, she wanted to be closer to him. She turned so she had her back against the railing and he was facing it.

He stepped so that he was in front of her, his arms braced on either side against the railing. It should have made her feel trapped, but it didn't. It made her feel protected, safe. "I've been thinking about this all week, wanting to do it again since the last time I kissed you."

But he still seemed hesitant.

"Well then, do it." She grabbed the front of his shirt and pulled his lips to hers. Whatever it was he was afraid of . . . getting too close to her, hurting her, thinking she was too gentle or fragile, he needed to get over that.

His jaw might be granite but his lips were soft and warm. Her hands slid up over his shoulders, behind his neck, and into that thick hair. He moved closer, pressed up against her like they had been when they were hiding from those Mosaic guys in the woods. Except this time, the tension wasn't the bad kind. This stiffness was the very, very good kind.

Wavy moved closer as his arms wrapped around her, but then something chimed in the night air.

Ian let out a curse against her lips. "I need to fire fucking everybody."

"What?" She asked. "What's going on?"

"That sound means that Landon and Sarge just turned on the express elevator. They're on their way up."

"This late?" It was nearly midnight.

Ian shook his head. "I didn't tell them you were here, but they wouldn't be coming up at this time unless it was something really important."

That bad stiffness was back. He wasn't pressed up against her, but all the tension he'd lost over the past few hours permeated his body once again.

"Look," She said, mourning their lost moment, "I can grab a commercial flight home. You've got stuff you need to do."

He shook his head. "No. I can have the jet fly you, but . . ." He looked torn.

"What?"

He leaned his forehead against hers. "I don't want you to go. Not yet. But this might take a couple hours, depending on what has happened."

"Want me to go hide in a bathroom?"

He gave her a half smile. "You are always so willing to roll with the punches. It's important. How do you feel about taking a nap in my bedroom while I talk to the guys? Then maybe a little more kissing under the stars before I fly you home?"

*Before he flew her home.* He said that like it was an everyday occurrence. But more importantly, he was making it clear he didn't expect anything from her if she wasn't ready. And while she didn't want to rush things, she was definitely interested.

"Okay, I'll stay," she whispered. "That would be nice."

His lips brushed against hers. "Thank you. I'm sorry about this."

He led her back inside. The elevator dinged in the foyer. Landon and a slightly older man—huge, with arms like tree trunks—walked into the penthouse.

"Boss, we got a . . ." The older man stopped midsentence when he saw her.

Both men stopped walking, unsure what to do. At least that meant Ian didn't have women up here all the time. Obviously, they didn't know how to react to her presence.

Landon recovered first. "Wavy, good to see you."

Ian put his hand at the small of her back. "And this is Sarge, one of my other right-hand men. Sarge, this is Wavy Bollinger."

"Finn Bollinger's sister?" Sarge asked.

"Yep. I claim him as my own, unfortunately." She smiled at Sarge, but he didn't reply in kind.

He nodded. "It's nice to meet you. I'm Harrison McEwan." He turned to Ian. "Sorry to bust in on you like this, boss, but we got new info about Bronwyn."

Wavy leaned closer to Ian. "No need to worry about me. Just point me in the right direction. I'll snoop through all your stuff."

He touched the side of her face. "Thank you for understanding."

And so she went into Ian DeRose's bedroom without him.

# CHAPTER
# TWELVE

THE GUYS DIDN'T SAY anything until Wavy was in Ian's room.

Landon turned to him, eyes comically wide. "There's a girl in your bedroom."

Sarge was a little more serious. "Sorry boss, I didn't know you had company, but we got another video about Bronwyn."

Ian squeezed his shoulder as they all walked into the living room. "It's okay. Wavy doesn't mind waiting."

He shot Landon a look before he could make a smart-ass comment. He wisely kept his mouth shut.

He turned to Sarge. He'd been back for a couple of days, but he hadn't had a chance to debrief him yet. All Ian knew was that the mission to find Bronwyn had been unsuccessful.

Sarge's jaw hardened as he opened his laptop. "I missed her by only a few hours in New York."

Ian nodded. None of them were sure what exactly had happened. Sarge had said he hadn't actually seen Bronwyn, but he wasn't convinced that was the complete truth.

From the report, he'd come back with bruises and cuts on his face, but no explanation for how he'd gotten them. If Sarge was keeping secrets, he had his reasons. He'd let it go for now.

"I've been up to my neck trying to get Varela resituated at Mosaic so that we could get as much intel from him as quickly as possible. I haven't had a chance to really look over the Bronwyn intel."

"She was in New York to case a place, prepping to steal something," Sarge said.

Ian looked at him. "You know that's her specialty, right? That's why we brought her into Zodiac in the first place."

Bronwyn Rourke was a chameleon—able to change her looks, her posture to appear as anything from a princess to a minivan-driving soccer mom. She could slip in and out of places no one else could get into. No one would think she was attractive at all unless she decided to play up her looks, and then it changed everything about her.

She'd come to work for Zodiac under unique circumstances, and nobody knew much about her. Except, evidently, Sarge.

"I don't think she was doing it of her own free will," Sarge said, massive arms crossed over his chest. "She was stealing something, but she was doing it for someone else."

"You think Mosaic is blackmailing her?" Ian asked.

"I don't think it's quite that simple. But I'm not sure what it is yet."

At some point, they were going to have to address the issue that Bronwyn might have gone rogue. None of them wanted to think that, especially Sarge, but it was the most likely possibility, that Mosaic had offered her a lot of money, and she was working for them now.

"Show me what you've got."

Sarge clicked on his computer. "This new footage is different. Worse than her robbery in NYC."

The footage wasn't great in terms of quality. It was grainy, taken from a distance, and enhanced to be usable. This told him immediately that Sarge was spending a lot of his own time looking at anything that could possibly be Bronwyn because no facial recognition software would have picked up her face based on this.

She was huddled on the ground in an alley, folded over on herself, obviously sick or in pain.

"How do you know that's her?" Ian asked.

"I got a shot of her face. It's her."

If Sarge said it was, he would believe him. Landon and Ian leaned in closer.

"Is she injured?" Landon asked. "It looks like it."

Sarge shook his head. "I don't know."

The footage wasn't easy to watch. The woman was in pain and alternating between holding her head and then her stomach. She vomited more than once, and then to make matters worse, some knife-wielding thug came up to her, kicking at her with his booted foot.

He evidently thought she was down for the count because the thug crouched and started patting her, looking for a wallet or valuables.

Bronwyn didn't hesitate. As soon as he was close enough, she reached up, grabbed his wrist, and broke it. The man howled, then got pissed. He jumped up and gave her a real kick, which she dodged.

Then he came at her with the knife. Bronwyn leapt up and with a speed that was almost blurry, the knife was buried in his own gut.

"Shit," Landon and Ian both whispered at the same time.

In a court of law, this would be considered self-defense. He would consider it self-defense too, but they all knew that Bronwyn had been more than capable of disarming him without killing him.

Whatever adrenaline she'd found fled from her body, and she slid back to the ground. That was when the camera caught a clear shot of her face, and he could see why Sarge was certain. It was her. It was definitely Bronwyn Rourke.

She stared down at the dead guy with an agonized expression. A couple of seconds later, she grabbed her head again like she was in pain and then stumbled out of the alley.

"Do we know where or when this was?" Ian asked.

Sarge reached over to shut off the footage. "It was taken off a security camera in Anchorage."

He ran a hand down his face. Alaska.

Landon plopped down in a chair. "This doesn't make any sense. First, she was in London. A couple weeks later, she's in New York, and a week after that in Anchorage. What the hell?"

Ian looked over at Sarge, waiting for him to tell him he wanted to go out there again to look for her.

He could read his mind. "I know the trail will be cold by the time I get there, like it was in New York. I was wondering if you could have Varela poke around inside Mosaic. See what he can find out."

"The Varela situation is sensitive." Ian let out a long exhale. "I want to find Bronwyn. You know I want to do whatever we can to help her, but Varela can't go in and start asking random questions about something he shouldn't know anything about without it making him seem very suspicious."

Figuring out how to use people like pawns had always been part of his job, but this time it wasn't something he wanted to do. Varela was a sadistic asshole, and Ian wouldn't lose any sleep if he got killed, but as a tool, he wanted to use him as strategically as possible.

Sarge crossed his arms over his chest. "There shouldn't be anything more important than getting one of our own back. The end."

"This is bigger than just one person. You know that. Bronwyn is part of this team, and I will do whatever it takes to get her back. But the primary objective is to bring down Mosaic."

Sarge stepped forward, eyes narrowed. "That's because of your personal baggage with Mosaic. I don't know exactly what happened when you went up against them before, but I know that taking them down is personal for you."

"Taking down Mosaic should be personal for *all* of us. You know what we've discovered—a new, multifaceted Mosaic. Four different leaders rather than one. Spreading their terrorist efforts across weapons sales, black-market technology, and now human trafficking."

"That's not what I mean, and you know it," Sarge said. "We all want Mosaic to go down. They're monsters. We've seen what they're doing to people. But you've got blinders on when it comes to them. You'll sacrifice Bronwyn to eliminate Mosaic because this is some sort of personal vendetta with Erick Huen."

Silence fell between the three of them. Sarge wasn't wrong. Ian didn't look at Landon, but he knew he would probably agree.

He didn't have his normal objectivity when it came to Mosaic, and definitely not when it came to Erick. The nightmares from two years ago demonstrated that. And Erick had had a front-row seat.

Ian ran a hand through his hair. "So, what are you suggesting?"

"We focus our efforts on getting our personnel back, and *then* we find a way to take Mosaic down. We don't have to sacrifice Bronwyn."

He crossed his arms over his chest and walked to the window. Talking to Wavy there this evening had been the highlight of his week, hell, his whole year. Just *talking* to her.

She would want him to get Bronwyn back. He would never drag her into this ugly situation by asking her opinion, but if he did, Ian had no doubt that she would say to start with saving the ones who mattered to her.

Ian spun back around to face his friends. "If I admit I'm not completely objective when it comes to Mosaic, will you admit that you're not objective when it comes to Bronwyn?"

"Yes." Sarge didn't hesitate. Didn't flinch from the truth.

"Are you going to tell me what's going on between the two of you? Is it a romantic connection?"

"Let's just say Bronwyn and I have history. You've always wanted to know why I was so obsessed with Prague? She's the reason."

His eyes narrowed as he studied him. He'd been almost...*haunted* by the city for years but would never say why. Ian had thought it was because some thugs had gotten a jump on him when they'd been there for a SEAL mission years ago. He'd had no idea Bronwyn had any connection to Prague at all. Then again, nobody knew much about the younger woman or her past.

Except, evidently, Sarge.

"Fair enough," he said. "Are you going to tell me the truth about what happened in New York? I know you saw her."

"Fine. I did see her. We had a . . ." He touched his cheek, which had been bruised and cut when he'd come back from the city. ". . . conversation. She needs our help. That's all that matters."

"Okay. I'll task Varela with concentrating on Bronwyn, finding out whatever we can. I don't know that it's going to be enough, but we'll try."

"That's all I'm asking," Sarge said.

"I want multiple teams ready to move on whatever intel we find," Ian told Landon. To Sarge, "I'll let Varela dig into it for three days. After that, I've got to pull him off. If Mosaic finds out he's working for us, he won't be useful. He probably won't be alive."

Sarge didn't like that, but it didn't matter. No matter what Sarge or Landon said, or what he thought Wavy would tell him, Ian was objective enough to know that they couldn't deviate from their primary purpose of taking Mosaic down for one person, even a member of the team. He would allocate more resources for finding Bronwyn, but Ian couldn't set them up to win one battle—albeit an important one—if it meant losing the war.

"Fine. We'll hope it's enough." Sarge left without another word, getting into the elevator without Landon.

Landon stood and slapped him on the arm. "Sarge's infamous people skills at work again."

"He has the right to be pissed."

"And you have the right to make the decisions you're making. Sarge knows that. Try to enjoy yourself with Wavy. You deserve time to be happy, Ian, and there's nothing you can do right now anyway. So enjoy yourself with a lovely woman."

Lovely she was. But Ian was pretty sure that wasn't going to happen.

# CHAPTER
# THIRTEEN

IAN POURED himself two fingers of whiskey and looked out at the skyline. He couldn't bring himself to go to Wavy in his bedroom. At least not for what he'd been hoping—a continuation of earlier. Good conversation. Laughter. Sweet kisses.

To kiss her now would be to taint her. Infuse her rainbow with the gray of his world.

She was probably asleep. It was after midnight, and she'd worked a full shift at the diner today. He would go in there, get her, and fly with her back home, explain to her that he wouldn't be around anymore. He couldn't drag her into his life. Not right now.

But the thought of walking away from her—*again*—ate at him. God, he wanted her, not just in a physical way, although hell, *definitely* in a physical way. He wanted her close to him. He wanted some of her light to fill the dark crevices that had overrun more and more of his soul.

But Ian wasn't bastard enough to keep her with him for his own selfish reasons.

He had to make hard choices all the time in his line of work. Sometimes choosing who lived or died. He would make the hard choice now, even though it ate at his gut.

But his intent to stay on the straight and narrow took a hard hit the moment he walked into his bedroom. Wavy was lying on his king-sized bed, her auburn hair fanned out on his pillow. She was on her side, curled up in the sweetest pose, one hand tucked under her cheek.

It shouldn't surprise him that she slept as sweetly as she did everything else. He would give a huge chunk of his considerable fortune for the right to crawl in beside her and wrap his arms around her. But it wasn't his right, and more importantly, it wasn't the right thing to do.

Using every bit of willpower Ian had, he crouched down beside her on the bed and touched her shoulder. He had to force his fingers not to trail along the skin her sweater had left exposed. "Wavy."

Those green eyes blinked opened. "Hi. Oh no. Bad news?"

Ian rubbed a hand down his face. "It feels like it's always bad news."

She reached out and cupped his cheek. "You're so tired. Your eyes are always tired."

He tried to give her a reassuring smile. "My body is used to running on very little sleep, so you don't have to worry about me."

"I'm not talking about sleep. You're tired *inside*. Fighting demons takes a lot out of anyone—even the strongest."

How did this woman see so much? "I should probably get you home."

"Do you need me to leave? Do you have to go somewhere?"

"No, I . . ."

He wasn't sure what to tell her. Was there work to be done? Yes. There was always work to be done. Did he want her to go? No. But she needed to.

She rolled over onto her back and patted the bed beside her.

"Come lie with me."

"Wavy, I—"

"Isn't it what you want?" She leaned up again to look at him.

"If it's not what you want, I understand. Is it what you want, Ian?"

He wanted it more than his next breath, but whether it was *right* was an entirely different story.

She let out an exaggerated sigh. "Ian DeRose, don't insult me by starting up with the *gentle and fragile* talk again. Just get in the damn bed."

How was he supposed to argue with that? He kicked off his shoes. "Sweet and strong," he muttered.

"Like a good rum punch," she said. "We make coolers of it and drink it down by the lake in the summertime. Small-town life."

"Sounds wonderful."

"I'll have to introduce you to Electric Smurfs sometime."

"What is that, a place?"

"No, a drink. A blue one."

"I was a sailor, and that still sounds a little scary."

She grinned. "Oh, it is. Stronger men than you have run in terror from the power of the Electric Smurf."

His arm wrapped around her as she rolled over onto her stomach along his side and planted her pointy little chin on his chest. Ian would endure the small ache the rest of his days if it meant having her that close. "Sounds like a formidable foe. Tell me more about the lake."

She started talking about a lake surrounded by cliffs on three sides, which the people from Oak Creek called Pikes Peak. Ironic, since Pikes Peak was an actual mountaintop outside of Colorado Springs.

But she stopped talking after a minute.

"Out of things to say?" Ian asked.

She looked at him with those green eyes. "I feel like I'm always talking around you. Like I never shut up. I usually only do that when I'm nervous."

"Do I make you nervous?"

"No." That little chin dug into him as she shook her head.

"You don't make me nervous. Me talking makes you more . . . at ease. I think that's why I never shut up around you."

"I like hearing you talk. It relaxes something inside of me." He wasn't sure why or what that meant. People talking was something he tolerated but didn't enjoy. Hearing Wavy was different.

"I'm glad you like hearing me talk. But I think I'd rather use my lips for other things right now, if that's okay with you."

"Wavy . . ." Her name came out as a groan.

"You came in here to say goodbye to me, I know."

This woman saw too damn much. "It's not that I don't want to be around you. It's not that—"

She put a finger over his lips. "You can say whatever you want, but ultimately it's going to come back to you thinking I'm too fragile for your world."

Ian couldn't stop himself. He rolled her underneath him. Their bodies were pressed together from shoulder to feet. He rested his weight on his elbows and looked down into those endless green eyes. "I don't think you're fragile. You've taught me that very well in the little time I've known you. But my world is ugly, there's no escaping that. You're right; I don't want it to taint you. I don't want it to touch you at all."

"What about you, DeRose? Do you want to touch me? I'm not worried about whatever evil it is you think surrounds you. I want to know how *you* feel."

Wavy Bollinger was enticing when she was sweet and smiling. But when she was spicy, she was damn near irresistible.

His lips crashed into hers.

All of their kisses had been explosive, but this one felt like it would singe them both to ash.

After a few minutes, he knew that this was going to lead to a lot more than merely kissing. He tried to pull back.

"Wavy." He leaned his forehead against hers. "This wasn't why I brought you here. It wasn't what I was planning when I came to Oak Creek today to ask you to go out on a date with me.

It's not what I was intending when I asked you to wait here in my bedroom."

"None of that changes the question, DeRose. What do you *want?*"

He wanted her. He wanted to bury himself inside of her until neither of them knew where he ended and she began. He wanted to breathe her into him. "I want you."

She dragged his head back down to hers.

When her tongue slid between his lips, Ian let out a groan that started deep in his throat. "You're going to be the death of me, Rainbow."

She licked at him with that little tongue, like a cat. "Maybe. But not tonight."

"Are you sure this is what *you* want?" he had to make sure. He lifted himself so she couldn't use that mouth to distract him. Because hell, this woman distracted him just by breathing.

"I'm very sure. But I need something from you first."

He kissed her forehead. "Tell me. Whatever it is." If it was in his power to give it to her, he would.

"I want to use that giant shower in your bathroom. I peeked while you were talking. It looks like there's room for two."

He was off her, on his feet, and scooping her off the bed before she could say another word. She squealed a little as he lifted her.

"That shower was definitely built for two. Be the first person I share it with."

Wavy cupped his cheek with her hand. "You don't have to say things to me to make me feel more comfortable."

"I want you to feel comfortable, but I won't lie to you to get you there. I haven't been a monk, but I don't bring women to this place."

She hooked her arm around his neck and used it as leverage to pull herself closer to his mouth. "I'm glad you brought *me* here."

"I am too."

Their lips met, and Ian was still kissing her as they made it into the bathroom. Still kissing her as he set her down on her feet. Still kissing her as he reached in to turn on the water, and they began peeling off their clothes. He wasn't sure he was ever going to be able to stop kissing her.

They only broke apart to kick off their few remaining pieces of clothing.

Damn, as much as he liked kissing her, looking at her naked body was running a very fucking tight second.

"You look like you might start drooling, DeRose." She stepped away from him and into the steamy water, then turned and beckoned with one finger.

Ian had never seen anything as sexy in his whole life. He couldn't get into the shower quickly enough. He walked right up to her, cupped her face with his hands, and pulled her in for another kiss.

He'd always liked this shower. It had two shower heads, but more importantly, it was big and open—nothing that gave him a bit of panic. Glass on all sides from the door leading into it to a slightly frosted full window on the side. It was clear enough to catch a blurred glimpse of Denver beneath them, but no one could see in.

Not even if he pushed her against it and eased inside her gorgeous body. If someone was looking closely enough, they might be able to make out a shape, but definitely no details.

The hot water hit them from both sides as they kissed. He reached up and aimed one of the heads down so it wouldn't hit Wavy in the face with her shorter height.

Then he trailed his fingers down the side of her neck, over her shoulder to run down her chest and cup her breast. She let out a breathy sigh as his fingers discovered what she liked and his lips soon followed the same path. Her breath caught, and she let out a shuddering moan as his mouth closed around her nipple.

"I want to take a whole bunch of time getting to know how

you feel. How you taste." Ian kissed his way back up her chest to her lips. "But if you keep making those sexy little sighs, I don't know if I'm going to last that long."

She wrapped her arms around his neck to keep his lips against hers. "I want all the slow and getting to know each other. I want hours in bed discovering all the things that drive us both crazy. But can that come later? Right now, I just want you."

Oh, thank God. "Let me grab a condom."

She gave him a small shrug. "I'm on the pill, if that helps. And it's been an embarrassingly long time since I've been intimate with anyone."

He kissed her again. "Same for me. If you're okay with it, believe me, I am too."

"I'm more than okay. Take me right here up against this window. I know no one can see, but it still feels naughty."

Ian bent his knees so he could slide his hands down her hips, then grip her ass. "You're naughty, are you?"

She laughed. "No. Never in almost my entire life. But it feels naughty, so I like it."

He lifted her up and pressed her hard against the glass. "You know, naughty girls get fucked up against the window, Wavy."

"Oh, God." Her breath caught, and her nails dug into his neck.

She liked a little dirty talk. He liked that she liked it. Her legs wrapped around his waist, and he eased closer, rocking his hips so he was rubbing against her, pinning her to the wall.

"Ian. Yes."

He pressed against her again, both of them grinding. Then, wrapping one arm around her hips and keeping her pinned, he reached between their bodies, feeling her wet heat. She thrust against his hand, and they both groaned.

"You shoot my control all to hell, woman."

She laughed, but it was different than her normal laugh— throaty and low. "I want you, Ian. Take me."

He entered her in one deep thrust. Her strangled cry blended with his moan as her heat surrounded him. He gave her a moment to adjust, then slid almost all the way out before slamming inside of her again.

"Yes." Her head fell back against the window, her fingers gripping hard at his shoulders. He looked down to watch their wet bodies where they were joined before thrusting once more.

He could've done that for hours, watching their bodies, listening to her groan his name, but instinct took over. He needed more.

He slid his hands down, holding her by the thighs so he could open her more fully, then rolled his hips over and over, hitting right where she wanted it. Her moans told him so and pushed him over his own edge.

His lips found hers again, keeping her pinned against him as he thrust again and again. It was her name he called out as his body tightened, and he let himself go.

# FOURTEEN

THE NEWEST OFFICE of Zodiac Tactical had opened somewhere Ian had never dreamed he'd have a branch.

Oak Creek, Wyoming.

About a month ago, Landon had dragged his ass onto the jet and taken him back to Oak Creek. He hadn't been sad to be heading there, but Ian had been surprised when he'd seen where he'd taken him. He'd made an office out of the small house at the edge of town, renovating it so one of the bedrooms was a full office and the other, well, the other was still a bedroom.

It had been six weeks since the night Wavy had spent with Ian in the penthouse. Not surprisingly, he hadn't been able to walk away from her. If he hadn't been able to do it before tasting her luscious body, there was no way he was doing it afterward.

But the distance had been hard. They tried to talk every day and see each other as often as they could, but life hadn't stopped for either of them. His goal of taking down Mosaic hadn't shifted.

But now that his mind and body knew what it was missing out on when he wasn't around Wavy, he craved her. When he wasn't around her, it was like the rainbow was missing from his sky.

He wasn't much fun for his team to be around.

The house had all the security and tech Ian needed to communicate with any of his other offices without having to rely on a single laptop in a hotel room. It allowed him to have a home base and still be close to Wavy at least two or three days a week.

Landon had said the Oak Creek office was vital for the survival of the company since one of them was going to kill him if Ian kept biting everyone's head off.

Being around Wavy was the only thing keeping him sane.

Especially since the entire situation with Mosaic was moving in fucking circles. Like he'd promised Sarge, he'd tasked Varela with trying to find out what he could about Bronwyn. He kept him on it for a week, but his intel about her had been scarce, and what he had been able to gather hadn't been timely enough to help them figure out where she was.

His questions were raising suspicions, so Ian had pulled him off Bronwyn detail. Sarge hadn't liked it. But it always came back to winning the war, not just the battle.

Sarge had gone to ground to see if he could find any intel about her through unofficial channels. He still reported in a couple of times a week, usually to Landon since Sarge and Ian almost came to blows every time they talked, so he was in essence gone for now.

Varela hadn't been as useful as they had hoped. He checked in with Callum and Ian every week. He'd been able to get them some names of leadership—two in particular, besides Erick. But ultimately, Varela was little more than a low-level thug. Maybe smarter than most, but not a part of Mosaic's inner circle. The more questions he asked, the more suspicious they became of him.

They would have to pull him soon. He was going to bolt— take his chances on the run. Ian was sure of it, especially after their last conversation two days ago. He'd been pretty shaken.

"Man, you've got problems."

"Varela, it's four o'clock in the fucking morning."

"I know. But I think they're watching me. Might know something's up."

Shit. "Then come in. Leave now." He was no good to them dead.

"I can't. I have to get proof. The stuff they're doing. You won't believe it." His voice went in and out like he was leaning away from the phone and back.

"Human trafficking. I know."

"This is a shit ton more than trafficking, man. They're—" There was silence for a second before he finally spoke again. "Listen, just know Erick Huen isn't your biggest problem."

"Then who is?"

"Not who. *What*."

"Fuck, Varela, stop talking in circles. If you've got something, come in and let's figure out how to move forward together. It's the safest thing for you."

"I'll be in at the normal time if I can."

Damn it. "Be there. With proof or without. What do you think is happening? The more you can tell me now, the better."

"It's the science. The drugs. They're— Shit, I gotta go."

The line went dead.

He'd contacted Callum immediately to let him know Varela was probably in trouble, not that they knew exactly where he was at any given time. Bugging him would've signed his death warrant. But Callum had received a couple of texts from him in the past forty-eight hours, so at least they'd known he was still alive. They'd all meet tomorrow and figure out where to go from there.

But now. Tonight was his night with Wavy, and he needed it. All his frustration melted away when he could see her smile, take some of her rainbow in for himself.

And she wanted to spend time with Ian DeRose the man, not Ian DeRose the billionaire or Ian DeRose the well-connected head of a world-renowned security company.

*Him.*

His jet sat a mere ten miles out of town, but she never asked him to take her anywhere. She knew he had contacts that could help her with her art career, but she never hinted at wanting assistance.

He hadn't told her that he'd sent a couple of her paintings to the office of an acquaintance of his, François Nester. François probably wouldn't look at them himself; he was basically art dealership royalty, but maybe the pieces would catch the eye of one of his assistants. They might be willing to talk further with her. And not because he'd strong-armed anyone. All he'd done was send a courier with her work.

Ian wanted to do that for her because she'd done so much for him by just being who she was. She'd brought so much light and joy and color into his life merely by being there.

She gave him what he needed to keep up the battle to take Mosaic down. The nightmares were fewer. The panic had lessened. He was able to see a little bit more clearly. If he had been this way six weeks ago when Sarge had first come to him about Bronwyn, it's possible he would've agreed to put all their resources toward finding her because saving one of their own was more important than anything.

There were little sticky note-sized paintings all over his desk there in Oak Creek and in his home office at the penthouse. Wavy gave him one almost every time he saw her, the hues on the tiny pieces of canvas matching whatever rainbow that had most recently stained her wrist.

And the more Ian had of her, the more he wanted.

Hell, he had turned off the security cameras there in that office because the last time she'd shown up with a spicy little smile and a painting for him, he'd had her bent over the desk and screaming his name within ten minutes of her walking through the door. Of course, she'd returned the favor, and he'd lost control embarrassingly fast when she got on top of him in bed a few hours later.

She had a couple of days off, and he was going to take her

back to Denver with him. Except for the meeting with Varela and Callum, he wouldn't be leaving her side for forty-eight glorious hours.

As if his thoughts had summoned her, a slight tap came at his door. A second later she peeked inside.

"Hi." He knew he had a goofy smile on his face, but he couldn't help it.

She smiled back. "I feel like I haven't seen you in forever."

He walked over and wrapped his arms around her hips, hiking her up close to him. "It's been two days, but I'm not pathetically counting or anything."

"Two days and six hours. Now who's pathetic?" She grinned at him. Her arms wrapped around his neck, and he knew he wasn't going to be able to wait until Denver to have her under him. Hell, he wasn't sure he'd be able to wait until the bedroom.

"I missed you," she said against his lips this time.

"I missed you too." When his hands slid to cup her ass and lift her, she wrapped her legs around his hips.

Her lips broke into a smile against his. "Do we have time for a quickie before we fly to Denver?"

"That is the most wonderful question I've heard all day. And yes, we do, even if I have to fly the damn plane myself." Which he could if he had to.

Ian had her perched on the desk when his goddamned phone rang.

"I'm going to ignore it," he said against her mouth. "If it's an emergency, they'll call back."

The phone fell silent, and he unbuttoned her blouse, kissing down her neck as he went. But a few seconds later, the phone rang again.

He wanted to let out a curse that would make his navy buddies proud.

"You're fired," Ian said as he grabbed the phone and put it to his face.

"Boss, we need you here at the office," Landon said. "Immediately."

He stiffened. "What happened?"

Wavy eased away, looking at him in concern. She could hear Landon too.

"It's Varela. He's dead."

He let out a low curse. "Are you sure? How do you know?"

"Mosaic mailed him to Callum Webb. In pieces."

# CHAPTER
# FIFTEEN

WAVY HAD SPENT every spare minute of the past five days painting.

Ian was still in Denver. She'd gone with him a week ago despite knowing what had happened to Varela.

She'd wanted to be there when he was done to try to help him with the mental and emotional fallout. Ian didn't let himself lean on other people very often. He didn't lean on her much, but however much he would, she would do whatever she could to support him.

Even if it meant most of her time had been spent hanging out in his penthouse waiting. She wished she'd had her paints. The lighting there was better than her dim studio any day. But mostly, she'd wished there was something more she could do for Ian.

He'd been silent and grim when he'd returned home after his meeting about Varela. He hadn't given her any details. She knew he would always protect her from things like that, but he'd said that it had been a direct message from someone named Erick Huen. She'd heard him mention that name before, knew that he was one of the key members of Mosaic Ian was trying to take down.

She'd just held Ian that night. She'd known he was conflicted about having her there at all—afraid he would taint her. Afraid the darkness of his world would bleed into hers. She wasn't putting up with that bullshit line of thinking.

Wavy had led him into the shower and washed his strong body as he'd stood there, stoic. She'd had proof right in front of her eyes that he wanted her, at least physically, but his mind and emotions had been trapped somewhere else.

After she'd dried him off she'd lain in the bed and held him, stroking his hair, holding him against her. She'd wanted to do that the first day she'd met him, to reach up and stroke the hair above his ear, to offer him some sort of connection. She'd scoffed at herself, but it ended up she was right, he did need it. And he accepted it from her. That was something to be treasured.

Deep in the early morning hours, she'd woken to find his face buried in her neck and him rolling her under him. Their lovemaking had been as silent as the rest of the night, but she'd known he was trying to connect with her, to hold on to her.

It was enough.

She stepped back from the painting she'd been working on for the past couple of days. It was more complex than her other rainbow paintings. There was something different about it, something much more engaging and intriguing. She liked it.

Since her relationship with Ian had started, she'd given up on any of her art except for her rainbow paintings. They were the only things she wanted to do, plus Ian always seemed so excited to see them. That played a part. A huge part.

Ian played a huge part. She didn't know where all of this was going with him, but she knew without either of them saying it out loud that it was something serious. Maybe not marriage serious, but neither of them took their blossoming relationship lightly.

When he'd first shown her his office in Oak Creek, Wavy couldn't help but smile. He was carving out a place in his life for her. That was Ian announcing his feelings. She didn't need flowery words or romance. She had the man. That was better.

She looked down at her phone and bit back a curse when she saw the time. Damn it, she was late for work *again*. Leeann was going to kill her.

She left all her painting stuff as it was and threw yesterday's clothes back on, rushing out the door a couple minutes later. Leeann shook her head when she saw her running in from the back, then pointed to the tables that still needed to be waited on.

There was something to be said for waitressing. It kept her body and my mind busy while she did it. It was a good, honest living. But she couldn't help but hope that maybe she could sell a few pieces of her art. It didn't cost a lot to live in Oak Creek, and she'd like to be able to back her hours down and spend more time painting.

Not to mention that making a living as an artist, even a modest one, would make her feel a little more on an equal footing with Ian. A little less like Waitress Cinderella being swept off her feet by the billionaire prince.

Ian had mentioned using some of his connections to get her an audience with some agents. She wasn't sure how she felt about that. On the one hand, she didn't want to use his money. She didn't want to ever use his money at all.

But on the other hand, if his connections could get her in the door, get those new paintings in front of someone she wasn't able to meet on her own, maybe that would be enough.

The lunch shift finally slowed down, and she only had a couple of tables left. It was midafternoon, and Leeann was about to leave. She was working a double, so her day had barely started.

She pointed to the back booth. "That guy asked for you personally."

Wavy spun around hoping it was Ian and she was playing a little joke on her, but it wasn't. It was a man she'd never seen. Sharply dressed—chinos and a collared shirt. Trim, late thirties or early forties. Not the type of person who visited their town or the diner.

She walked over to him. "Hi, can I get you something?"

"Just coffee. And I've heard that you guys have good pie?"

"Yes." She rattled off that day's available slices, still trying to figure out why he'd asked her to wait on him.

"I'll go with the lemon meringue."

She turned to get it for him. "Coming right up."

"Before you go, are you Wavy Bollinger?" he asked.

She spun back around slowly. "Yes."

"My name is Louis Noeya. I don't mean to be intrusive, but I noticed that painting on the wall over there and inquired about it and was told you painted it."

She raised one eyebrow. "Do you know Ian DeRose?" Had Ian contacted an agent without telling her? She wasn't sure how to feel about that.

"No. Should I?" He held out his hands in front of him. "Look, I'm a very small art agent working mostly out of Los Angeles, but I was coming through Oak Creek on my way to a meeting at one of your local ski lodges. I can see that I bothered you. Never mind."

She was being such an ass. She couldn't believe she had an *actual art agent* talking to her and she was being a jerk to him. "No, please, I'm sorry, I thought maybe one of my friends had put you up to a practical joke or something. What was your name again?"

"Louis Noeya." He slid a card across to her. Sure enough, there was his name, there was a Los Angeles address, and most importantly, there were the words *artist representation*.

"I'm sorry I've been so short with you. Yes, I do some artwork, but I've never sold any professionally."

He steepled his hands in front of him on the table. "I was wondering if you would like to come to my temporary office in Reddington City tomorrow and show me, say, five or ten of your best pieces? I can't guarantee anything, but I think it would be worth both our whiles. I'm usually not wrong when I have a feeling like this."

She stood there, staring at him. "Are you for real?"

He chuckled. "Sure am. Look, I really don't want to get your hopes up. I may only be interested in a few pieces, maybe none at all, But it's worth a try, right?"

Hell yes, it was worth a try. She quickly agreed and took a couple of his cards and promised to meet him tomorrow.

Wavy was walking on air the rest of the day. She couldn't sleep that night, trying to choose what pieces to take to show Mr. Noeya. She would bring a variety. A few of her older landscapes, like the one he'd seen on the Frontier wall. But also, some of the rainbow pieces. Particularly the one she'd been working on this morning that had made her late to work. It was her best yet.

She'd barely gotten any sleep, but she wasn't tired when Ian texted her to let her know he'd be coming back to town tomorrow evening. That would be perfect. By then, she would be back from Reddington City and hopefully would have some good news to share with him about her career taking off, even if only the slightest bit.

She decided to splurge and grabbed one of the latest tiny canvases she'd made for him, jotting on the back that she had a surprise for him. She would overnight it to Ian—hopefully, it would make his day a little brighter. He'd kept every single tiny painting she'd ever given him. Sometimes he had more than one on his desk when she wasn't around.

Like he wanted to have part of her close to him. It made her heart swell just thinking about it.

Hopefully, tomorrow night she'd have art representation for the first time ever. And she would have gotten it on her own. Ian would never have to worry she was using him for his connections.

And then they could celebrate together.

# CHAPTER SIXTEEN

IAN HADN'T SEEN Wavy in a week, and that was too damned long.

As if his whole body wasn't itching to touch her, one of her little paintings had shown up in the mail that day. He'd grinned like an idiot when he'd seen it. He thought all three of his assistants' eyes were going to bug out of their heads at his reaction.

Ian didn't care. Wavy had *mailed* him a painting. Sent it overnight so she was sure he'd get it before he saw her. This current one was made up of pinks and purples—happiness and passion blended together. He couldn't seem to stop running his fingers across it.

And on the back, in her delicate, flowery script, she'd said she had a surprise for him.

There weren't many people in the world who could surprise him, but he had no doubt she was one of them.

Because he had no idea what she was thinking when she said *surprise*. Could be a new type of pie at the Frontier Diner. Or a waterfall off one of the nearby trails that she wanted to show him.

Or it could be her naked in his bed with a pair of handcuffs to be put to creative use.

There was no telling. And he fucking loved it. This woman had gotten under his skin one laugh at a time.

A few hours later, his jet was setting down outside of Oak Creek, and he was getting into the vehicle he now left there full time. Continuing to spend so much of his time in Wyoming wasn't going to work long term.

Maybe he could talk Wavy into moving near one of the Zodiac Tactical offices—there were multiple places she could choose from. She'd mentioned being ready to leave her hometown, and if she picked somewhere near a Zodiac office, he'd be moving headquarters there.

Or if she wanted to live somewhere else, he'd open a new, *real* office there. Hell, if she wanted to stay here in Oak Creek, he'd do that too. The thought brought a smile to his face. Smiling . . . something he'd been doing more and more of. It didn't feel awkward anymore.

And who was responsible for that?

The package sitting at the front door of his makeshift office as he pulled up had him pulling out the weapon he kept in the glove compartment.

There should be no mail here. All mail was rerouted into town or to one of his other offices. He stepped closer. His name was written on the outside of the box and nothing else. Definitely suspicious.

Taking a step back, he got Landon on the line, placing his phone on speaker mode.

"What's up, boss? Did Wavy clock you with another tray?"

He didn't try to hide his concern. "I've got an anonymous package by the front door of my building here in Oak Creek." We both remembered what last week's anonymous package had held: pieces of Silas Varela's body. "Run the scanner and the cameras here. See if you can get any info on who left this thing."

"Roger that. I'm running it now," Landon said. "Give me a few minutes. And for God's sake, don't touch that box."

Being out here in a relatively unsecure location wasn't the

smartest way for him to run his business, so they'd put high-security measures in place. Cameras everywhere and infrared sensors to be able to tell remotely if someone was inside the building. He could've checked it from his phone, but he'd rather keep his weapon out and let Landon do it.

Because there should be no box here. No one outside Zodiac's inner circle should've known about this place at all.

As soon as Landon assured him the building was clear, Ian would grab the technology that would allow him to make sure there was no explosive inside the box itself.

"Boss, we've got a problem," Landon told me. "Building is clear, but the cameras were switched off manually at some point. I'll have to check into that further."

Fuck. There was no reason for him to check further. *He* was the one who'd taken the cameras offline last week because of what he'd been doing with Wavy. There was no way in hell he'd risk anyone else seeing her like that.

"No need, Landon. I took the cameras offline and forgot to put them back on." Because he'd pretty much forgotten his own name by the time Wavy had been done with him. "Reconnect them now and get them running."

He kept his weapon out as he went inside, but there was no indication anyone had been there. No doubt Landon was already sending a backup team, and they would check more thoroughly when they got there.

He scanned the package with their equipment. It was clear of any explosives, so he grabbed some latex gloves out of a crime kit in the back room.

"Okay, we're not working with explosives," he said. "I'm going to open it."

"Ian, you need to wait for backup."

"No." His gut was screaming that there was something really wrong. "I want to find out what this is all about."

"Fine." Landon let out a sigh, his fingers clicking on a

keyboard. "But I'm at least calling some of the Linear guys to come over as backup. This feels ugly."

It did feel ugly.

He crouched down in front of the box about twice the size of a shoe box. He slid on the gloves and used his pocket knife to cut through the tape.

Inside the box was another smaller box. Great. Someone wanted to play games. He switched the call to video and propped up the phone so Landon could have a closer view of what he was doing.

He opened the second box only to find a third, smaller one inside.

Ian gritted his teeth. "Mosaic is fucking with us. This is a Russian nesting doll in box form."

There were seven boxes in all. Inside the last box was a square envelope with writing on the outside.

*What price are you willing to pay to win this war?*

"Whatever price I have to, asshole," He muttered as he turned the envelope to open it.

"Ian, wait. I don't like this," Landon said, but he didn't stop.

He needed to know.

Whatever game Mosaic was playing with him now, he was ready, because he was going to win. They were going down. He didn't have Varela anymore, but he'd find another way.

He eased open the envelope with the knife. The first thing he saw was a photo of Wavy wearing a red polka dot dress and smiling. It almost brought a smile to his own face until he saw what she was doing, who she was smiling at.

She was shaking the hand of Erick Huen.

She was standing next to him, smiling at him, shaking his hand.

Ian stood and ran for his car.

"Jesus," Landon said. "Was that Wavy with Erick?"

"Yes." He peeled out of the driveway and headed into town.

What did the photo mean? Was Erick threatening her? Trying

to let him know he could get to her? How long ago had the photo been taken? He'd talked to Wavy that morning, and they were supposed to meet a little later that afternoon once she got off her shift at the diner.

He had to see Wavy for himself.

"Landon, we need to figure out why she was with him. I know she knows the name, but obviously she doesn't know the face." He hung up and slammed his foot on the gas.

Erick Huen had been around her. The thought made him sick.

He pulled up at the Frontier Diner a few moments later and ran inside.

"Hey there, honey." Leeann, the older waitress who worked with Wavy, smiled at him. "What are you doing here?"

"Where's Wavy?" He demanded, unable to be civil until he saw her with his own eyes.

"She's not here. Oh, that's right, she didn't tell you. She wanted it to be a surprise."

Ian's heart hammered against his ribs. Wavy wasn't here. Something about her *surprise*.

"She's gone into Reddington City to meet with an art dealer," Leeann continued. "Some agent who was interested in her work and wanted to see more."

Fear closed around his throat. "Where? When?"

"Here's the card he gave her yesterday when he came into the diner looking for her." Leeann grabbed a business card sitting by the register and handed it to him.

*Louis Noeya, Art Agent*

But the picture was Erick Huen.

"Wavy was all excited. Had her red polka dot dress on. Her lucky dress, she calls it." Leeann winked at him. "She said she hoped to get lucky twice today, if you know what I mean."

He couldn't breathe. He couldn't say anything to Leeann. He turned and ran back outside, the business card in his hand.

His phone rang again, and he answered, knowing it was Landon.

"Erick has her," he whispered, unable to say anything else. "Mosaic has Wavy."

Ian looked at the business card again, the letters that made up the name, Louis Noeya, morphing as the anagram became clear.

*Louis Noeya* spelled *You lose Ian.*

Mosaic had Wavy.

# CHAPTER
# SEVENTEEN

WAVY HAD MADE her way through the art dealers and agents in Reddington City, all three of them, years ago. Wyoming wasn't a huge hub for the art world. Mr. Noeya was only here temporarily, and she was more than happy to take advantage of it.

Her red polka dot dress had never let her down. She didn't know if it was a very professional choice, but it was her lucky dress with cute little red heels so she wore it.

She had ten selections of paintings in her portfolio. A couple of them were realistic still lifes, one was a portrait of a little girl from town, but the rest were her rainbow paintings. She was going to follow her gut and show this agent where she thought her career, if there was ever going to be one, was heading.

She could hear Ian's voice in her head about her work: passionate, inspiring, stimulating. All the things art should be.

Mr. Noeya's temporary office wasn't downtown like she'd been expecting. It was out closer to the warehouse district near the airport. But rent was much cheaper out there, so it was understandable. The man had made it clear he wasn't big in the art world.

But she didn't need a big income. If he would agree to represent her, to get a few of her pieces out and see if they could get any traction, that's all she wanted.

She made it to the office, rehearsing in her head what she would say, how she would explain her work. Of course, it ultimately was going to come down to his opinion, not anything she said.

Wavy parked in front of the studio, close to a small, simple sign: *Reddington City Artist Studio and Representation.* She got out and smoothed down her dress, reaching into her pocket to touch the tiny painting she'd put there. It made her feel like Ian was closer.

She could do this. Her paintings were good, especially the work she'd been doing the past few weeks. It was like the more emotion she had inside her system, the more they came out onto the canvas. She grabbed her portfolio from the back seat. Lifting her arm slightly to keep the large, thin briefcase from dragging on the ground, she fairly floated up to the building and opened the door.

The inside was almost as generic as the sign. Completely white walls, but at least there were quite a few paintings hanging up everywhere. If it weren't for them and the sign out front, she would've sworn she was in the wrong place.

Mr. Noeya walked out of a side door. "Miss Bollinger, I'm so happy that you made it."

"I wouldn't miss it."

He was once again dressed in slim chinos, a classic stone color. His leather loafers matched the brown of his belt. A lavender shirt was tucked in at his trim waist.

He approached a large, conference-sized table. "Shall we go ahead and get started? If you don't mind, could you lay out whatever pieces you've brought, so I can take a look at them?"

She sucked in a breath, then let it out. This was it. She took her pieces out of the portfolio and laid them out one by one, the different sizes taking up almost all of the conference room table.

He strode around the table, studying them, stopping every few seconds to lean in closer, probably to judge her brushwork.

He studied the still lifes as long as he did the rainbow paintings, which worried her a little bit. Maybe she should have brought more of them since that was the only direction she really wanted to go.

Watching him was making Wavy crazy, so she turned away to study the artwork on the walls. She needed to let him do his job.

"You really are quite good," he said a few minutes later. She didn't turn from the wall, but why did he sound surprised? If he didn't think she was any good, why would he have invited her there at all?

"Thank you."

The painting closest to the desk caught her attention. It was small. Smaller than a lot of the others. But as soon as she honed in on it, she recognized it. It was a Peter Paul Rubens—one of his landscapes. She rushed toward it. She'd studied the Baroque period in art school.

"Oh my God," she said, "Is that actually a Peter Paul Rubens original?" Why in the world would Mr. Noeya have this mundane office if he had a Rubens original? Hell, he could sell that and live the rest of his life very comfortably.

"Yes, it is an original."

She looked back at the other paintings. "And is that an Edmond Aman-Jean?" She couldn't believe it. That wasn't worth as much as the Rubens, but still worth hundreds of thousands of dollars.

"I'm actually surprised you recognize it. It's not like he's as famous as some of the others."

She rushed to another. "And that's an Isaac Levitan, right? How do you have all these?"

"I brought them from my personal collection."

Why would somebody who had millions of dollars in a

personal art collection be inviting her, a complete unknown, into an office on the airport side of town?

Wavy spun around to find Mr. Noeya looking at her with a smile. "Okay, you caught me. I'll admit it. I brought you here because I thought you would be more comfortable."

"More comfortable with what?"

"I actually have multiple offices all over the world."

She racked her brain. She had never heard of a Louis Noeya in the art world. Surely she would have heard of him if he had offices all over the world.

Should she be worried? The man wasn't very big, didn't look like he would do anything that might cause a wrinkle in his chinos.

"I can see I've made you uncomfortable. I'm sorry. Come over here and let me show you something in your own work. It's what brought you to my attention and why I had you come out here today."

He stared at her patiently, and she finally walked over. Maybe he was just some rich guy who also dabbled in representing artists.

"You really do have some talent," he said, pointing to my landscapes. "Your abstract expressionist paintings aren't to my taste, but admittedly that's not my style. Feels too sloppy."

She shrugged. It was time to stand up for herself. "To be honest, if you're not interested in those, then we don't have much to talk about. That's the way my creative mind is taking me. And I don't have much choice but to follow."

He nodded. "I understand." He squeezed her on the shoulder as if in consolation. She felt a little pinch but he moved his hand away before she could shrug him off.

"I like some of your art, Wavy. I'm sorry I won't be able to see more of it for a while."

"Yeah. I don't think this is going to work out." She stuck her hands in her pockets, grabbing the tiny painting for support. She wanted to get out of there. Ian wouldn't want her to stay.

"I think it might work out better than you expect."

Why did his voice sound funny? Why did all her art look blurry to her? What was going on? She grabbed the table to keep herself upright as the room began to spin around her. "I don't feel so good."

"I'm sure you don't, but that will pass."

She tried to focus on his face, on anything, but the room was spinning faster. She took a step toward the door.

"What did you do to me?" Her voice sounded funny to her own ears. She dropped to her knees, still trying to move toward the door. "Who are you? What do you want?"

He crouched down beside her. "My real name is Erick Huen, and you're my ticket to destroying Ian DeRose."

———

Ian had known true panic in his lifetime.

A person didn't asphyxiate inside a coffin, doing everything they humanly could to get out, without experiencing panic. Ian knew what it was to scratch and punch at something until he was bleeding and broken. He knew panic intimately—the taste of it in his throat, the coating of it on his skin.

But what he'd gone through in that coffin was nothing compared to his terror knowing that Erick Huen had Wavy in his clutches.

This was personal for Erick. There was no other tactical reason to bring Wavy in at all. She had no advantage in terms of money or connections or anything of that nature.

That made it worse. Knowing that keeping her alive or deciding to hurt or kill her was based on the whims of a man who felt like he had every reason to hate him struck terror into his soul.

Erick figured hurting Wavy would hurt him. He was right.

He broke every traffic law known to man driving from Oak

Creek to the address on the business card in Reddington City. Callum already had local police on the way to the building.

Erick obviously had no problem with them knowing where she'd gone—he'd printed fucking *business cards* for Christ's sake—which Ian knew meant he no longer had her there. Landon warned it could be a trap, but he didn't care. He could get there quickest. If there was any hope at all that he could get her back right away, he was going to take that chance.

Landon already had the tech team combing traffic footage and cameras around that area, as well as tracking Wavy back from when she'd left Oak Creek. They would follow the timeline with her. Hopefully, it would lead them somewhere. Lead them to *her*.

He found the makeshift art studio without any problem. The local police had already been inside and confirmed what they'd expected: there was nobody there. The cops had done as Callum had told them and left the scene alone as soon as they'd determined no one was on the premises.

He took a moment in his car before he got out. He needed to lock down his emotions. Neither fear nor fury would get Wavy back. A cool head and doing his fucking job would get her back.

He got out of the car and moved inside the building. None of the cops stopped him, so they must've been warned to let him in.

Ian could see why Wavy would've been excited to meet with an art representative at this place. He wanted to kick his own ass for not having used his contacts long before now to help her touch base with an agent, but he forced that down with the fear. Regrets weren't going to get her back either.

He would only have a little bit of time alone inside the room before anybody else arrived. He didn't touch anything, not wanting to mark anything with his own fingerprints in case forensics could help them. Landon and Isaac were on their way. He needed as many eyes there as he could get.

Zac and Finn were the first to make it through the door. He was surprised he'd had twenty minutes in the office by himself.

Finn didn't bother hiding his fury. Within seconds, the big man had him slammed up against the wall, fisting his shirt.

"Mosaic has Wavy because of you."

There was no way around that point. If he wanted to beat the shit out of him, he couldn't blame him. "Yes."

"What the fuck are you going to do about it?"

"I'm going to get her back. That's what the fuck I'm going to do about it." And that was the damned truth. "Why don't you let me go so we can make that happen."

"Why did they take her?" Zac asked as Finn reluctantly let go of his shirt and stepped back. Ian didn't blame Finn for his anger. If the roles were reversed, he'd be pissed too. But as mad as he was, it was nothing compared to the anger he felt at himself for allowing it to happen.

"This is personal," he told them. "They didn't take Wavy because she has any advantage for them as an organization. One specific person took her in order to get to me."

"Who?" Finn asked.

"His name is Erick Huen. He's high up in the organization. He has reason to want revenge from the first time I took Mosaic down."

"Business or personal?" Zac asked.

"It doesn't matter," Ian responded.

"It fucking well does matter," Finn snarled. "Everything started to matter the moment they took my sister."

"Fine. It's personal. I killed his best friend when I took down Mosaic the first time."

Both men nodded. That had appeased them for now, but it wouldn't be long before they pressed for more details. His secrets were about to come out. Both men looked around the room.

"Don't touch anything," he said. "I've got a forensic team on the way."

"You're not calling in law enforcement?" Zac asked.

"Not locals. I've got a federal agent who'll want to be in on this, but my team will be here first."

He wondered if they were going to argue with him. They didn't.

"Good," Finn said. "Going through law enforcement channels will slow everything down, and I am not playing by the rules when it comes to getting Wavy back."

He nodded. "Then we're in agreement."

Zac and Ian continued examining the room. Finn couldn't get past the conference table, where Wavy's paintings were spread out.

"These are hers? Wavy's?" he asked.

"Yes." It was a good representation of her work. The landscapes were technically solid but not as demonstrative of her true talent and passion as her rainbow works.

He'd seen all the paintings on the table before except one. It was new. And goddamn, it was breathtaking in its vibrancy.

Like the woman herself.

"I had no idea," Finn said. "I had no idea she was this talented. These are amazing."

"You've never seen her paintings?" Ian asked. "How is that possible? It's such a huge part of her."

Finn shrugged one big shoulder. "She doesn't show it. I mean, we've seen some stuff. She's painted stuff for our mom that's hanging at my parents' house, and she's always done some sort of art ever since she was a kid. But I had no idea she'd progressed to this level. Some of these are . . ." He trailed off.

"Amazing?" he asked. "Breathtaking, mesmerizing, should be hanging in a museum somewhere?"

Finn scrubbed a hand down his face. "When she came back from art school and didn't really have any contacts, we all assumed she wasn't talented enough to make a living with art. We all encouraged her to keep waitressing, that it was fine, that we loved her, that we wanted her here. But . . ."

But they'd all been complicit in holding her back. Home was sometimes the place that didn't allow you to change.

Finn didn't say it. He didn't have to. Ian knew what he meant. He knew what it was to have a family that kept you from the life you were supposed to lead. At least Wavy's family had good intentions and were trying to protect her.

His family hadn't had good intentions when they'd tried to keep him in the mold he'd always been in. That was why he had walked away and joined the navy at eighteen. It had changed the very course of his life.

He clapped Finn on the shoulder.

"We'll get her back, and then you'll let her know that it's time for her to pursue her passion."

They were going to get her back. They had to.

# CHAPTER
# EIGHTEEN

WAVY WOKE UP SLOWLY, her eyes gritty. They didn't seem to want to open. They hurt. Why did they hurt?

Actually, everything hurt. And it was hard to breathe. Did she have the flu? It had been going around a few weeks ago. Had she gotten it? No, she'd been at work yesterday. And then she—

*Oh, God.*

The art dealer, Louis. No, that wasn't his real name. Erick Huen. The man who hated Ian. He'd drugged her.

Now, she really tried to open her eyes. They were puffy, and everything still hurt. Her shoulders especially, but that was because her arms were tied behind her back.

Once her eyes were finally open, she still couldn't see much. It was too dark.

Where was she? How long had she been gone? When would Ian and her family start searching for her?

She'd been so stupid to meet with someone alone at his office. Leeann had seen him and known she was going, but how long would it be before anyone knew there was a problem?

She didn't know where she was. Was she still in Wyoming? Was she still in the *country*?

Panic pooled throughout her body, blanketing her, slimy and slick. She started to shake, and breathing became more difficult.

*Focus, Wavy.*

The voice in her head wasn't just one person. She could hear Finn, Ian, her parents, Baby. And they all wanted her to do the same thing: survive.

She forced herself to slow her breathing. It was hard with a gag in her mouth. But if she breathed through her nose, she could get enough air.

The panic receded a bit.

She tested her hands. They were tied tight at the wrists, but in her fingers she could feel the tiny painting that had been in her pocket. She rubbed her thumb against it.

It calmed her more. Enough that she could think.

If they had her gagged, maybe that meant that she was somewhere close enough that someone could hear her. She felt something cool against her legs. She realized she was in a van once she scooted her body over to the side and touched the cold metal walls.

They weren't moving, but maybe they were somewhere close enough that somebody could hear her. Nausea rippled through her as she shifted her body. She couldn't throw up. If she did with the gag in place, she'd choke and die.

She positioned herself so she could bang on the walls with her feet. She didn't have anything else that could make any noise unless she wanted to use her head, which probably wasn't smart. She slammed the side with her feet, the heels of her shoes breaking after only a couple kicks.

But without the heels she could kick harder. And she kicked as hard as she could, the exertion making it hard to breathe through her gag.

But she couldn't keep it up for long. Couldn't get in enough air for the energy she was exerting. One shoe fell off, but she still tried to kick with her bare foot until it was bruised and sore.

It was no use. Wavy fell to the side, just sucking in enough air to stay alive.

The last thing she felt was the tiny painting in her fingers as the darkness overtook her again.

# CHAPTER
# NINETEEN

SEVEN HOURS after Ian had left the building Erick Huen had lured Wavy to, they were sitting around a conference room table at the Zodiac Tactical's Denver office. He had all his key team members on a conference call with them. He wanted every single person he trusted working to get Wavy back.

Zac and Finn had come with them by his invitation, and because Finn was not going to be left behind when it came to anything having to do with his sister. Kendrick and Neo were also on the video call, prepared to help out in whatever way they could.

Callum was on the line too. They hadn't spoken since the debriefing concerning Varela's death. Ian knew he was on thin ice with his superiors over all of this.

Sarge was the only person missing that he desperately wanted there. He was still looking for Bronwyn.

It had now been nine hours since anyone had seen Wavy.

Everyone around the table and on the conference call knew that every minute that passed without clues or word from a kidnapper meant less and less chance of survival for the victim. He refused to acknowledge that data.

A picture of Wavy and her beautiful smile took up half of

everyone's screen. It was almost painful to look at. She looked so friendly and kind.

"This is Wavy Bollinger," he said. "She was kidnapped nine hours ago by Erick Huen, one of the heads of the new Mosaic. It was a personal attack against me. She's my . . ." Ian didn't know how to finish the sentence. ". . . girlfriend."

That seemed too trite and simplistic for what Wavy was to him. But in terms of explaining it to everyone else, it was the easiest term.

"Have you received any ransom notification, boss?" The question came from Tristan Zimmerman. He and his twin brother, Andrew, both knew Wavy.

"No," he responded. "If there had, believe me, I would have already paid it. If money could get Wavy back, there's not a single dollar I wouldn't spend."

Zodiac dealt with corporate kidnap and ransom situations all the time, mostly in foreign countries. Generally speaking, the most successful K and R cases were the ones where kidnappers wanted money for the return of their victims, and it was paid. A simple, albeit scary, business transaction.

Unfortunately, that wasn't the case with Wavy.

"Do you think this is a play to get you to back down from taking on Mosaic?" Tristan continued. "They know you had Varela working undercover, and they know you were responsible for taking down the group the first time, so maybe they want to keep you in check."

"That's a possibility," he said. "And if we get any word like that, I'll be sure to let you know. I won't be hiding anything." Not anymore.

Ian brought up Erick's picture on everyone's screen. "We know Erick Huen is who took her, and we know he's one of the four new heads of Mosaic. What you all may not know is that he blames me for killing his best friend two years ago when I was undercover with Mosaic. Erick's best friend was the head of Mosaic, Grant Saber."

He brought up a picture of Grant Saber. Given long enough, someone would eventually put two and two together, but he didn't have time to waste.

"Grant Saber's name was actually a combination of his real middle name and a nickname he'd had when he was younger, 'the Saber.' His legal name was Timothy Grant DeRose."

The room fell silent. Nobody said anything. Nobody breathed. Anybody who had been typing stopped.

"I killed my brother, who was Erick's best friend, right in front of him."

Grant had killed Ian multiple times first, but he left that part out.

Finn was the first to recover. "Your brother was the head of the original Mosaic?"

He nodded. "That's why I was originally sent undercover. It's public knowledge that I inherited my money from my father when he died. What you don't know was that a lot of that money was gained through illegal means. I walked away from the family business when I was eighteen and joined the military—I'd had no interest in being part of that. I didn't leave on good terms."

Everybody was listening and nodding, so he continued. "Almost three years ago, my father died. At some point in the ten years I hadn't been talking to him, he'd had a change of heart and cleaned up his act. My brother, Grant, had not. They went their separate ways, but when dad died, he left me all his money instead of Grant. You can understand how Grant was a little pissed at that, given how many years he'd served faithfully at my father's side. But by that point, Grant had built his own criminal network, the original Mosaic."

"That's why Omega Sector approached Ian to go undercover —not because of his new wealth, but because of his ties to Grant," Callum explained.

He rubbed the spot at the back of his neck where tension had been growing all day. This wasn't his favorite thing to talk about even under much better circumstances.

"Yes. I convinced my brother that I wanted out of the good-boy life and back into the family business. Since Dad had left the money to me, we could share it and control the world together, etc. Meanwhile, my plan was always to take him and Mosaic down. The plan worked."

Landon crossed his arms over his chest. Saying it had worked was truly too simple a phrase.

"It worked, but before I was able to take Grant down, he realized that I was undercover. I was . . . interrogated extensively."

Only Callum and Landon knew the specifics, but everyone else knew it meant he'd been tortured. They didn't need to know the details.

"Ultimately, I killed Grant in order to escape. The rest of Mosaic was dismantled. Erick Huen was injured when we moved in to make all the arrests and was presumed dead. But obviously, he isn't dead."

That was his mistake, one Wavy was currently paying for. He hadn't hunted Erick down the way that he should have because he'd actually tried to talk some sense into Grant every time Grant had put Ian back in that coffin until he died. But evidently, any goodwill Erick had had for him had ended when Ian had killed his brother.

His team was attempting to digest all of this—a history more complicated than they'd thought.

"Okay. Now you have the whole story. We know who has Wavy, and we know it's personal, and we all know that's the worst-case scenario. So let's work with actual data and get her back. This is top priority for everyone."

The forensic team reported first. They hadn't found any usable fingerprints besides Wavy's and Erick's. It turned out that he'd rented that particular building because it had attached garages. A nondescript, white van had been caught on a security camera leaving not long after Wavy had arrived, but it had crisscrossed around town, and the tech team had lost it. They were still searching for it.

Ian clicked on a few buttons to bring Kendrick up on full screen. "Kendrick, can you give us an update on the drive?"

He nodded, wrapping his arm around Neo. She still looked a little worse for wear from what she'd been through at Varela's hand.

"It was full of some pretty scary medical stuff. Means of human trafficking that relies on a cocktail of gene-editing, drugs, and neuro-inhibitors to brainwash their victims. Basically, Mosaic can make a perfect slave willing to do whatever they've been programmed for. Including thinking they're doing the right thing."

The room got quiet once again. Finn's hands curled into fists. It was all Ian could do to stop his from doing the same. The thought of Wavy turned into a mindless sex slave burned like acid in his gut.

Jenna Franklin, speaking for the nerds, outlined what their team was doing. Jenna had lived through a traumatic kidnapping herself before coming to work for him, so she took this very seriously. The tech team was deepening the search into Erick Huen as well as the other three potential Mosaic leaders Varela had reported. It was taking priority over everything else.

Callum assured them that his law enforcement task group would also be working all angles to find Wavy.

It was almost midnight by the time they were done. He had the best people in the world looking for Wavy. If she could be found, they would find her.

*If.*

———

A week later, they were no closer to finding Wavy than they had been at that meeting.

Ian stared down at the Denver skyline from his penthouse.

He hadn't slept for more than a couple hours since the moment Wavy had been taken. He had exhausted every option he had, used every contact any one of them had ever known to try to discover a scrap of information on her whereabouts. He'd offered money, threatened lives, resorted to physical violence . . . but nothing.

He kept waiting to hear from Erick Huen. Some sort of ransom note or demand or a smug call about how he was smarter than Ian—stealing Wavy right out from under his fingers. Or worse, a video of her being tortured.

As much as that would crush what was left of his soul, at least he would know she was alive.

Now, left alone with silence, he had no idea.

He had no idea if she would ever stand beside him again and look down on this view. No idea if he'd ever hear her laugh again, see those green eyes twinkle at something the rest of them missed because they looked at the world differently than her.

Landon had banned him from the office a few hours ago. Ian had told him he could go fuck himself, but then he'd pointed out the simple truth. He was hindering the process of helping Wavy by sitting there barking over everyone's shoulders and demanding information they didn't have.

He'd been right. At least Ian had been able to see it once Landon had pointed it out. So he'd left and come up here.

For once, the trip up the elevator didn't give him pause. He'd trap himself in a thousand elevators if it meant they got Wavy back.

His phone beeped, letting him know someone was coming up in said elevator. He didn't look to see who it was. He could only hope that it would be some bad guy who was stupid enough to try to rob him right now. At least that would give him an excuse to beat the shit out of someone.

Or hell, at this point, it would be a relief for someone to beat the shit out of him.

The balcony door slid open, but he still didn't turn.

"How are you holding up, boss?"

*Sarge.*

Now he turned around. "I thought you were gone."

Sarge shrugged. "I heard about what happened with Wavy. Spent the past few days chasing some possible leads."

Something inside Ian eased a little bit. He'd known Sarge would've heard about Wavy by now. It had hurt more than he'd admitted that he hadn't come back to help.

Of course, that tiny pain was like a pinprick on a ten-inch gash, but it had still been there. It was good to know he'd been helping from a distance. He reached out his hand, and Sarge shook it. "I hope you've had more luck than we've had."

"Maybe. I found out about a lab through a back channel."

He shook his head. "Given the medical background of what Mosaic is doing—gene-editing, neuro-inhibitors—we've already checked every lab and medical facility linked to any person with ties to Mosaic."

"Not this one. It does have ties to Erick Huen, but not in any way that's noticeable. It's a hidden lab. I have to warn you, it's not a good place to try to breach."

He pushed away from the railing. "I don't care. If it's a lead, we'll try it."

Sarge grabbed his arm when he tried to walk by him. "It's a shitty setup, Ian. We won't have tactical advantage. They will have all the advantages."

"I don't care." And then it occurred to him. "That's why you're here. You think Bronwyn is there, and you wanted to breach it, but you couldn't do it on your own."

"I won't lie. I got this lead while looking for Bronwyn, and she might be in the same location. But you made it clear that Bronwyn wasn't your top priority."

Ian rubbed his fingers over his eyes. He owed this man, his friend, an apology. Only now, when it was Wavy who'd been taken, could he see that so clearly.

"Sarge, about Bronwyn. I should never have—"

He held up a hand to stop him. "No. Right now we breach this lab, work the problem. We'll have time for hugging it out and kumbaya later."

Ian nodded. Apologies and fixing the broken relationship between Sarge and him would have to wait. "Let's get the team together."

# CHAPTER
# TWENTY

WHEN WAVY WOKE the second time, she wasn't in the van, and it wasn't dark. The lights were so bright, it hurt her eyes to squint the smallest bit. She blinked over and over, trying to open her eyes a little more each time. Harsh, fluorescent lights flooded this room.

She didn't have a gag. At least she could breathe easily, but it meant she was somewhere screaming wouldn't help.

Her arms didn't hurt like they had before. They weren't pulled tightly behind her back, but she still couldn't move them much. They were restrained. So were her feet. But she still had her little painting clutched in her fist. She didn't know how that had happened, but she didn't care. It was her only link to sanity.

She forced her eyes open, then immediately shut them tightly again. This time not just because of the lights.

She was on some sort of medical bed with railings on the sides. Her wrists and ankles were tethered to the bed itself. The bed could be raised or lowered, so she wasn't quite lying flat. She was propped up enough to look down on the rest of her body.

And her polka dot dress was gone. She was in a medical gown.

Panic blanketed her again, cloying and sticky. Someone had stripped her out of her dress while she'd been unconscious.

She clenched her eyes closed again. What else had they done to her that she had no idea of?

She tried to push down the panic, but it wrapped tighter around her.

She swallowed, her throat dry, and turned her head to look one way, then the other. Wavy wasn't the only one in this room. There were at least a dozen other people, all on similar beds, like this was some sort of hospital. They were spaced about ten feet apart.

Nobody was moving; nobody was talking.

All the beds had medical equipment by them. Her eyes flung back to her own bed. How had she missed the IV tubes coming out of both her arms? She tried to move her head, but she couldn't because there were wires attached to it too.

More panic. She tried to swallow it down before it swallowed her whole.

She looked over at the person next to her, a woman. "Help. Can you tell me what's going on? Hey. Hey, can you talk to me?"

Her eyes were open, but she didn't respond. Wavy turned to look on her other side a little farther down. A boy, a teenager. He also stared blankly. His head was shaved in different spots where nodes were attached.

Oh, God. Was that what was attached to her head?

"Hey, kid," she said. "Are you okay? Where are we?" She pulled at the straps on her wrists and ankles, but they didn't budge. "Can you hear me, kid?"

Still no response.

She didn't see any doctors or nurses or guards, and there was definitely no sign of Erick Huen. She was almost drowning in panic now. She pulled at her restraints, thrashing on the bed. But all that achieved was exhausting her and making her dizzy.

*Focus, Wavy. Work the problem.*

She counted to ten, forcing herself to relax. Panic wasn't going to solve anything.

What could she hear? What could she see? What could she control?

She closed her eyes and listened. Some of the people around her were making a sort of distressed sound—moans. But most of them were silent.

She opened her eyes again. Bright, fluorescent lights. No windows. Gray walls, white ceiling. Everyone was hooked up to at least a heart monitor and an IV, but that was all she could identify. There was a lot of other medical equipment also, but she didn't recognize what it was.

What could she control? That was scarier to answer.

Except for the people lying in the beds, she still hadn't seen anyone else around. Yelling couldn't hurt then, right? If just one other victim was lucid and could get loose, they could work together and maybe find a way out. "Hey—" her voice cracked and she started again. "Hey, is anybody awake? Can anybody talk to me? Hello?"

She heard someone from down at the other end of the long room. She lifted her head but couldn't see who it was.

"Hello?" she tried to make my voice louder, not sure why it wasn't working correctly. "Can you talk to me? Are you okay?"

"I-I think so."

"Okay. Good." Thank God. Hearing another voice ratcheted down her panic to manageable levels. "What's your name?"

"Janice," she said. She sounded young.

"Okay, Janice. It's going to be okay." Wavy pulled at her straps again. She had to get out of there. She had to get Janice out of there.

"You are not responding well to the medication. That's unexpected and unfortunate," a male voice said from behind her. She stiffened, then tried to turn her head to get a good look at him but couldn't.

"Who are you? Where am I? What's happening here? If you're a doctor, you need to understand that I do not want to be here. I was taken against my will."

Clicks on a keyboard. "I tried to explain to Mr. Huen that not everyone is a viable candidate, but he was insistent that you needed to be one."

"Erick Huen kidnapped me. Do you know that? You need to let me go. Just put me back in the van and let me go." She was trying to remain rational, but it was hard. She rubbed the painting between her fingers, seeking any semblance of calm.

"My work here is important, and he's threatening it by bringing you here if you're not a viable candidate. So right now, you need to go back to sleep."

A hand reached out and attached something to her IV drip. "No, wait. I don't want to go back to sleep. Can you just tell me what's happening right now? If you let me go, I promise, I won't say anything about where I was or what I saw."

That was a complete lie, but anything that got her out of this room got her closer to helping herself, Janice, and all the rest of the people.

"Right now, you sleep."

"Wait. Talk to me. Tell me about your w-work." Shit. She could already feel her words slurring.

"You're not a candidate, so you don't need to worry about it."

Not a candidate? Was that good—they'd let her go? Or bad—they'd kill her?

"Wait—" The world swirled. "W-what does that mean?"

"It means you'll never—"

Darkness.

———

It took Wavy multiple times of waking up, trying to talk to the people in the room with her, especially Janice, and being put back under before she learned not to open her mouth when she opened her eyes.

They put her back under every time she did.

But she found out a little information each time. First, that there was a girl named Janice. Second, that she was sixteen years old. The third time, Janice hadn't spoken at all, and she'd gotten a little hysterical. Someone else had moaned like they were trying to talk, but it had been on the wrong side of the room—so it couldn't have been Janice.

Could it?

Her mind was more muddied every time she woke up. And the pain—a throbbing through her temples that never seemed to quit. They were drugging her, with more than the drugs that knocked her unconscious. She had other aches too—they were doing things to her while she was unconscious, but she didn't know what.

The pain, the drugs, whatever they were doing to her was making it hard to remember . . . anything.

Why was she there? How long had she been there?

The only thing that seemed to tie her to reality was the tiny painting in her hand. There wasn't a lot of it left—it was barely larger than a postage stamp now. It had ripped when they'd tried to take it from her. Sometimes, she pressed it under her leg when the nurses or the man they called Dr. Tippens were nearby. She didn't want them to take it from her.

She wouldn't survive without it.

Wavy had to stay strong. She had to survive. Survival was always the most important thing. That's what her brother had taught her. That's what all the Linear guys taught in their classes. She knew it was what Ian would tell her now.

*Survive, Rainbow.*

She closed her eyes and listened to his deep voice. The pain wasn't so bad and the fear so immediate when she listened to his voice. She was tempted to stay inside her mind with him.

But she couldn't. She needed to think, to figure out a plan.

She had to focus on getting through what was ahead of her, on living through today's pain and the nausea that made her want to fold herself over and do nothing but vomit.

Erick Huen had been here earlier before they'd put her back under. He and Dr. Tippens had argued about her; Tippens saying she wasn't a viable candidate, Erick arguing it didn't matter—she would be one anyway.

What did that mean? Dr. Tippens had mentioned being a candidate before. Dr. Tippens was in charge around here. All the nurses call him by name when they asked questions or gave a report. Dr. Tippens was the boss.

Except for when it came to Erick Huen. That wasn't good.

Wavy cracked her eyes open again. Had she fallen back asleep? She never knew how much time had passed. There was something going on. Something was different than the other times she'd been awake.

There were a lot more people, more medical people, but also other people. People with guns.

Her head hurt, and she closed her eyes again. She had to swallow back the urge to vomit. That would only bring more pain. She rubbed her thumb along the portion of the painting.

But keeping her eyes closed made it harder to stay conscious. Her body knew if she would let it fall back under, she wouldn't have to feel the pain ripping through her skull. She knew she was fighting a losing battle . . .

"DeRose knows *you*, not me."

At the sound of Dr. Tippens saying Ian's name, she dragged herself back to the surface. How long had she been under? It didn't matter.

"He somehow found out about this place. He shouldn't have been able to." She shrank away at the sound of Erick so near her cot. "The bastard is determined to get to her. I knew he wouldn't like that I had her, but I didn't know he'd go to such extremes to find her."

Wavy kept her eyes closed and body still. She didn't want Erick to touch her. Revulsion rippled over her skin.

"You're risking everything by keeping her, Erick. She is not a viable candidate. It's not going to work. You need to either kill her or let her go. If we keep this up, it's going to get worse like it did with Bronwyn Rourke."

She knew that name. Why did she know that name? She was who Wavy was supposed to help. No, that was Janice. Who was Bronwyn?

"We haven't gotten to that point yet," Erick responded.

"But we will. The protocol doesn't work with everyone. There has to be a certain aptitude for addiction, plus a number of biological and genetic factors. I was clear about that from the beginning."

She cracked her eyes open. Erick and Dr. Tippens were standing right in front of her. Around them, other patients were being moved, their cots and equipment wheeled away.

"The important thing right now is that we get everyone moved to a secondary location." Erick sounded frustrated. Good.

"The current secondary location has ties to you, so you can bet someone with Ian DeRose's resources is going to find that eventually too," Dr. Tippens said. "We need to move them to somewhere associated with *me*. I have a lab we can use. He doesn't know about me at all, so he'll be much less likely to find us."

Erick crossed his arms over his chest. "Can it hold everyone?"

"Yes. I know you'd like to be in control of everything, but this is a better plan."

"Fine. If it means DeRose won't find us, we'll go with your place."

"But that means I get autonomy in my research. No more bringing in people who aren't viable candidates."

"Fine," Erick said. "The only exception is her." He pointed at

Wavy, and she quickly closed her eyes so they wouldn't know she was listening. "She gets the full protocol."

"That is tantamount to torture. Her body will continue to reject the genetic editing and the drugs. You saw what happened with Bronwyn Rourke."

"I don't care. Full protocol. And you record the whole thing. That'll be a nice gift to send to Ian DeRose. Let him know what it's like to watch someone he loves die painfully."

She struggled to keep her breathing normal, to not give herself away. She had to do something. If they got her out of this lab into that secondary location, Ian would never find her.

There was no way she was going to make it out of this building. She didn't know if she could stand, or if she could somehow get out of this bed.

She only had one option, and she wasn't sure that it would help, but she had to try.

With her eyes barely open, she watched Erick walk away.

"I know you're awake, Wavy," Dr. Tippens said. "I can tell by your heart rate. You are a smart one, I'll give you that, learning to be quiet. We're going to move you. Everybody's getting moved." He reached over and unstrapped her wrist. "We'll have to move you to a rollable cot. Trying to walk right now will make you sick. I know you have to feel sick, Wavy."

She didn't answer. She didn't open her eyes. Maybe he wasn't sure that she was actually awake. She was only going to get one shot at this. Ian was on his way. She had to believe that this was going to work.

Dr. Tippens reached across her and unstrapped her other wrist. This would be the only chance she had. She reached up with every bit of strength she had—oh God, her arms were so heavy—and scratched him as hard as she could at the neck.

She drew blood. That's what she'd been hoping to do. Her arms dropped back down and she prayed it was enough. She had no more strength left.

Dr. Tippens jumped back. "You stupid bitch. Why would you do that? What would it accomplish?"

She didn't respond. It was taking all her effort not to vomit.

"You know what? I would have helped you, would have given you a quick, painless death. I would've told Erick that your heart couldn't take the protocol and you died of a heart attack. But now you get to live through everything he had planned for you. I'm afraid this is going to be a very painful trip to the new lab."

He left, and she laid there, breathing in and out. Scratching him had taken all the energy she had left. Her hands were still unrestrained, but there was no way she could reach down to unfasten her legs.

Moments later, Dr. Tippens was back with two different vials. She watched as he emptied one into her IV. The other, he injected directly into her leg.

She let out a whimper.

He shook his head. "You think that little shot hurts? That's nothing. Just wait a couple minutes, and you'll understand what I mean."

He walked away. He didn't refasten her wrists. That couldn't be a good sign.

At first, she didn't feel anything beyond the normal nausea and throbbing in her head.

Then the burning started.

It started in her leg, then bubbled slowly through the rest of her body, like acid eating her from the inside out. She couldn't stop the whimpers that fell from her throat.

Then it grew. And grew. And grew. The fire spread every-where. She clawed at her skin, trying to stop the burning, but there was nothing she could do to make it go away.

She hoped that the blackness would drag her back under as her whimpers turned into wails, then her wails turned to screams.

Wavy writhed, back arched in agony, as two men came over

and moved her from her bed onto a cot. Dr. Tippens forced a round, wooden block into her mouth then fastened its straps behind her head.

"So you don't bite your tongue off when the pain really starts," he said in her ear.

As they wheeled her away on the cot, her hands jerked open. She tried to close her fist, but her fingers were cramping and jerking uncontrollably like the rest of her.

The piece of the painting, the last connection she had to Ian, fell to the ground.

# CHAPTER
# TWENTY-ONE

SARGE HADN'T BEEN KIDDING when he'd said this lab was hard to get to.

They were scaling a cliff wall to make it up to where the lab was located, cleverly hidden as part of a high-end nursing home off the cliffs of the Tieton River in Washington state.

This place hadn't been on their radar before Sarge had brought it to their attention, and there were a lot of unknown variables in this situation. Their current circumstances were far from what any of them would've called ideal, but time was the most critical factor.

They had a six-man team, including himself. Not the six he would have chosen under ideal circumstances, but both Zac and Finn could pull their own weight.

Finn was currently scaling the cliff wall with Sarge and Ian. He'd agreed to allow them on the team because they'd agreed to take orders from him. He appreciated that both men had Special Forces training, but no mission would be successful without a clear leader.

Isaac and Zac had gone up the wall a few minutes before them. They were responsible for blowing the power at the same time his team blew the door. Both had to be done at exactly the same moment or the backup security measures would lock them out.

That didn't mean they wouldn't get in, but it did mean that the bad guys would have an opportunity to kill everyone inside before they got in there.

That was not an option.

The sixth man had already been inside the nursing home for a couple of hours—Landon doing what he did best: charming people. He was a concerned son looking for a place to put his wealthy, elderly father. If anyone tried to make it out through the nursing home, the legitimate front to the facility, Landon would be there to stop them.

A shit ton of things could go wrong with this mission, so many that they weren't aware of all of them. It was a risk he was willing to take. It was dusk. It would have been better to come in under cover of night, but waiting any longer wasn't an option. Getting anybody out the same way they were coming in was going to be nearly impossible.

That was assuming Wavy was mobile. She'd been in Erick's clutches for eight days now. Ian had no idea what shape she was in. And if Bronwyn was in there, she could be in bad shape too.

*Alive.* They just needed them to be alive.

They silently scaled the rest of the way up the cliff wall and got into position.

"Everyone ready?" He spoke into his comm unit and got affirmatives from everyone involved. "Isaac, Zac, you guys in place?"

"Two minutes," Isaac responded.

"Roger that, we're moving to the outer security door."

Isaac and Zac would shimmy through ventilation shafts to get to where they could cut the power. It would be a tight fit for the big men. Two were going because if one got taken out, hopefully the other could complete their part of the mission. None of them knew exactly what type of security they'd be facing here, but they all knew it would be armed.

"Aries, we're in place. Over," Isaac said.

"Roger that. Blow the power on my mark."

Sarge had already set up their charges, and they stepped back. "Sarge and I will go in high. Finn, you guys go in low. Tranq anything that moves, and we'll sort them out later."

They were using tranquilizers rather than real bullets in case an innocent got caught in the fray. He wasn't going to take a chance on Wavy being injured by friendly fire.

"Detonate on my mark. Three, two, one. *Mark.*"

They all pulled down their night-vision goggles and rushed through the hole where the metal door had been. Finn dropped low to cover Sarge and Ian as they dove inside, then followed on their flanks.

But it didn't take them long to realize there was nobody there. The large room held no one, nor did any of the smaller rooms branching off of it. The place was empty.

"Goddammit. We're too late." He pressed a button to talk to Landon. "Libra, we have nothing down here. Anything up where you are?"

"That's a negative," he replied. "Business as usual here. Got a full tour, didn't see anything that would make me think twice. I don't think anybody here is aware of the lab."

Fury tasted like death in his throat, followed by a huge chaser of fear. They were too late. "Everybody spread out. See if we can find anything useful. Isaac, see if you can get power back on for us."

"Aries, I have two dead bodies left behind out the west door here. Wrapped in a tarp," Zac said. "I can't see their faces, but it's two females."

Cold sweat broke out along his spine as his eyes met Sarge's. They ran to Zac's location where Finn had beat them by a few seconds. He cut through the tarp covering the women's faces.

"It's not her," Finn said. "It's not Wavy."

Ian finally felt like there was enough oxygen to breathe.

Sarge pushed his way past both of them. A few seconds later he said, "It's not Bronwyn either."

"Okay," Ian said.

They all stood in silence for a moment. There were two dead women here, but they weren't *their* women.

But their women were still missing.

"Okay," he said again. "We're going to have to let Callum's team in on this because of the bodies, but let's sweep and see if we can find anything else before we turn it over to them. I'm not going to slow down for bureaucracy."

Not that it was bureaucracy slowing them down. They'd been too late on their own timetable. Erick and Mosaic remained a step ahead of them.

A few minutes later, Isaac had rerouted the power so they were able to look around with the lights on. Landon was already talking to Callum. He'd be getting an earful from him later.

It would've been worth it if they'd gotten Wavy and Bronwyn back.

How long before they'd gotten there had they cleared the building? It couldn't have been too long; those women's bodies hadn't been in rigor mortis. They'd have a more accurate window of when they'd left once the coroner gave them an estimated time of death.

Ultimately, it didn't really matter. Whether they were too late by a day or only a couple hours, they were still too late.

There were no traffic cameras out in this remote area of Washington, but he'd get the tech team on it in case they got lucky.

Even with the lights on, there wasn't much to see in the big room. One gurney along the south wall held both arm and leg restraints.

Had Wavy been restrained in that thing or something like it? He scrubbed his hand down his face. Hopefully, they'd get some answers when the crime lab went through there—both Zodiac's and law enforcement's, but he wasn't sure what they could tell them.

Had Wavy been here? Or was she already dead—a body lying somewhere else wrapped in a tarp?

He almost missed the tiny scrap of paper on the ground. If he hadn't stopped to look at the gurney he would've missed it completely. He knelt to retrieve it.

"She was here. Wavy was definitely here."

"How do you know?" Finn asked.

"She gives me these Post-it-sized paintings all the time, and this is a portion of one of them."

It was so small, less than a quarter of its normal size. It was crumpled, worn.

And it had blood on it.

Despair sliced through Ian once more.

He slipped the tiny piece of canvas into an evidence bag, although he wouldn't be giving it to law enforcement. That was part of Wavy, and he was keeping it with him.

FIVE MORE AGONIZING days passed with nothing. No word. No leads. Erick Huen had gone to ground, and he'd taken Wavy with him.

They'd checked every building Erick or any member of his family had ever had contact with. The lab hidden in that nursing home hadn't been tied to him, it had been tied to his ex-wife, to whom he'd only been married for a year more than a decade ago. Her father had lived at the nursing home for a brief time.

Ian had his team running shifts twenty-four seven, combing intel, putting pressure on or throwing money at contacts who might know anything. But this throwing-spaghetti-at-the-wall-to-see-what-stuck method was not going to get them to Wavy in time. He knew it in his gut.

There were no good options anymore. Hell, there were barely any *bad* options.

There was nothing but the knowledge that every day they didn't get her back, the chances of getting her back at all went down exponentially. If he'd been working for someone else right now under the same circumstances, he would've had the hard talk with them. Tell them they needed to make peace with the fact that their loved one probably wouldn't ever come home.

A silent kidnapper was usually a murderer.

Erick still hadn't demanded anything of Ian or taunted him. His guess was that he was waiting until he had footage of Wavy's death to send him. A reminder that it was retribution for killing Grant.

Never mind that Wavy was innocent and that he'd killed Grant in self-defense. Those trivial facts wouldn't matter in Erick's mind.

He was back in his penthouse, sitting at the large, oak desk in his office, leaning back in his chair. He should be sleeping, but once again, like every night she'd been gone, that was impossible. Every few days his body gave out, and he'd sleep wherever he was.

But until then, all he could do was stay awake and breathe in the air permeated with a mixture of his own terror, fury, and ineptitude.

That tiny painting they'd found at the lab rested in the evidence bag on the edge of the desk in front of him, the same place where Wavy had sat last time she'd been there.

She'd been wrapped in a towel, fresh from the shower, and he'd been on the phone handling some late-night business. She'd proceeded to sit on his desk and spread her legs until they were on either side of his chair.

He'd hung up very quickly after that and proceeded to make a feast out of her.

Ian ran his hands through his hair, barely refraining from pulling it out by the roots. There was nothing he wouldn't give to have her perched on his desk now.

They'd missed them at the lab by only a few hours.

Omega Sector's coroner had determined that one of the bodies was so recently deceased, she'd probably died when they moved her. Mosaic wouldn't have left her there if she hadn't been dead, and she hadn't been dead more than four hours by the time they got there.

So fucking close.

Cause of death for both victims was still unknown. Trauma and blunt-force weapons had been ruled out on scene. But both had shown signs of recent medical procedures—IVs and surgeries. They all knew what that meant. Mosaic was capitalizing on their new method of indoctrination for human trafficking.

He picked up the evidence bag and looked at the canvas again. All the colors on it weren't necessarily paint. Some of it was blood.

She'd bled on that piece of canvas.

The blood was smeared across the two top corners, two lines, like she'd been trying to make some artistic pattern with it. Like she'd taken her nails, dipped them in blood, and used them to paint.

*Wait.* Ian sat up straighter.

Like she'd dipped her nails in blood and tried to paint with it.

What if that wasn't her blood?

What if—oh God, he almost couldn't bear to let himself hope —what if she'd been trying to leave them some sort of clue?

He picked up his phone and speed-dialed Sarge. "Who can we coerce or bribe into getting us a blood sample DNA tested immediately? I think Wavy might have left us a clue."

————

His name was Dr. Sheldon Tippens.

Six hours later, Sarge and Ian were lying in wait in the dawn shadows outside his front door in an affluent suburb of San Diego.

Wavy had pointed them in the right direction by leaving them the blood on the painting. He had no idea if she'd done it on purpose or not, but it was the first solid lead they'd had since the lab.

Sheldon Tippens hadn't been on their radar at all. They'd had no idea he was tied to Mosaic or Erick in any way. They would never have found him without Wavy.

His house was pedestrian at the end of a cul-de-sac with a long driveway. A two-story brick house with fucking flower boxes on the railings. It was a house you lived in when you wanted a good place to raise your kids with the right kind of schools. A bicycle was parked near the side of the house.

He didn't care. He didn't care if the man had a family. He didn't care if he skipped out the door with two kids holding his hands.

He was coming with him, and he was going to tell Ian where Wavy was.

Since Sarge had gotten them an ID from the blood, the nerds had been digging up whatever they could about Tippens and this neighborhood.

No surprise, Tippens was a genetics specialist. He had his own medical and genetics counseling practice. And, evidently, a side job brainwashing human trafficking victims for Mosaic.

Sarge was the only other person who knew they were here. He hadn't contacted Callum to get law enforcement in on this. Even Landon didn't know. The gesture wasn't lost on Sarge.

"What's your plan, Ian?" He didn't call him Ian very often.

"My plan is that Tippens is coming with us, and I'm taking him to an undisclosed location, and he's not leaving until he tells us where Wavy and Bronwyn are. I'm not fucking around anymore."

They both knew what he meant. Torture, dirty and brutal, to get the info they needed.

"I want Bronwyn safe pretty much more than I want my next breath," Sarge said. "But there are some things you don't come back from. If you do this—if *we* do this, then it's going to leave a mark on our souls."

His eyes were still pinned to Tippens's front door. He didn't care. "I will give up my whole fucking soul to get Wavy back. She's in this because of me. Erick figured out, even before I did, how much she means to me. I should have had security on her. I should have never left her alone. I should have known she'd be a target just because she was spending time with me. But I'd been keeping it casual, thought it would never become a factor."

Nothing Ian felt about Wavy Bollinger was casual.

Sarge didn't try to talk him down from this ledge. That's why he was here with him. He was also willing to cross the line. "When Mosaic realizes Tippens has been taken, they might move her again, you know that."

"Then we make him talk quickly. We go straight to the hard stuff from the beginning."

His words were tough but his stomach rolled at the thought. He didn't want to torture anybody. Even someone like Tippens. Someone who was, at the very least, an accomplice in what had happened to Wavy.

But Ian would do it. He would do it without flinching to get her back.

"Okay," Sarge said.

They both relaxed a few minutes later when a vehicle pulled out containing a woman and child. No Tippens. It was better that they were leaving so they wouldn't be around when they grabbed him. Sarge and Ian had worked out multiple scenarios so that no innocents were hurt if it came to that, but if they were nowhere around, that would be ideal.

So they waited in their vehicle, calling the wife's license plate into the nerds so they could follow it.

When Tippens pulled out in his BMW, they made their move. He wasn't all the way out of his driveaway when they rammed their vehicle straight into his. It wasn't subtle, but the neighbors were far enough away from each other that by the time someone called the cops, they would already be gone with him.

They both had masks on and their vehicle was not registered to anyone. Dr. Tippens got out of his car, at first indignant that someone had hit him.

But as soon as he saw them with the masks, he tried to dive back in. Ian grabbed him and pulled him toward their vehicle.

"If you tell me where Wavy Bollinger is right now, you might live to finish this day with all your fingers and toes attached to your body." He wasn't going to waste any time. The more afraid Tippens was, the better this would go for all of them.

"Wavy Bollinger?" His eyes got big. "No. I swear, I didn't want to—"

Ian headbutted him. It was the easiest way to let him know that he meant business without taking a chance on letting him go. "Where is she?"

Blood poured out of his nose and he started blubbering. "I swear I didn't want to do it. It wasn't me."

He dragged him toward their car. They needed to get him off the street.

"Look," he said, "I—"

The impossible happened. A shot rang out from down the street. Tippens collapsed into his arms, a red hole forming on his chest as blood spread across his shirt.

"Shit, he's down." Ian lowered Tippens to the ground.

Sarge was already returning fire. It didn't matter. Tippens was not going to make it.

"Look, you asshole," he told him, "tell me where your lab is. You're going to die. If you don't want your wife and kid to find your body lying here, you will damn well tell me where Wavy is."

He knew his own death was imminent. This was all in his hands now. Nothing Ian could do was going to change things.

"Lab," he breathed out, a gurgling sound in his throat. He was choking on his own blood. "But too late. She's not . . ."

*Too late.* He tamped down panic. "Where, Tippens?"

He almost seemed to relax a little. "Wavy. Told him not viable. But still was able . . ." he trailed off.

"Tell me, please. Even if she's dead, tell me."

"Corner warehouse. City Heights. Industrial district. Chollas—"

That was all he got out before he died.

Ian was vaguely familiar with the warehouse district near

Chollas Creek off the bay in downtown San Diego. He was about to become much more familiar with it.

He could only hope that he'd been telling the truth, because Sheldon Tippens wouldn't be telling anyone anything else ever again.

# CHAPTER
# TWENTY-THREE

A TWO-MAN TEAM for a full offensive wasn't a great plan, but Ian didn't have a choice.

The rest of his team was on their way with an ETA of one hour, but he wasn't waiting. Sarge and Ian had fled the scene of the crime. He'd put a call in to Callum to get his people out there.

Yet another thing he was going to get a lecture about.

Mosaic had killed Tippens rather than let him take him. That meant he had information that they didn't want them to have. And if that information was about Wavy, then he wasn't going to wait, no matter what it might cost him. If Ian got arrested for anything he did today, he would take it.

As long as it was later.

If they moved her again, he might never find her.

Tippens had said it was too late, but he didn't care. He refused to accept that as a possibility until he saw it with his own eyes.

The location Tippens had provided was in the warehouse district down by the docks. Sarge shook his head as they drove around. "There's no way this can be a lab like the nursing home. Too many people coming in and out."

He was right. This was the kind of place to keep dead bodies. *Too late.*

Ian parked way too close to the warehouse for any true stealth, but he didn't care.

Sarge muttered a curse as Ian opened the car door and started running toward the corner warehouse, but he didn't care about that either. He was going in. He wasn't going to wait. He'd wasted thirteen fucking days. He wasn't going to waste one minute more.

If there was so much as a chance that Wavy might still be alive, he would get her.

A flying tackle caught him about twenty yards from the door. Sarge and Ian went sprawling into an alley, hitting the ground hard.

"I don't know what the fuck you think you're doing, but you need to use your brain," he said.

They both jumped back up to their feet, and he grabbed Ian by his shirt and slammed him into the wall.

"What you're about to do is not only going to get you killed, but possibly her too."

Ian swung at him, his fist connecting with Sarge's jaw. He took it without flinching, didn't let go of his shirt. Sarge was older, but he could still take a punch. He swung at him again. This time, he blocked it. "I'm going in. You heard what Tippens said."

"I heard Tippens say it was too late, and if Wavy's dead, then that sucks, and we're going to have to deal with it. Damn it, Ian, I was willing to let you torture that man to find out where she was. If she's in there and she's alive, the guards will have orders to kill if the building is breached. You going in there half-cocked is going to get her killed as well as you. Now use your fucking brain, and let's see if we can get her out alive."

He was right. Ian lowered his fists. It was hard to see through his own cloud of fury. "I'm sorry."

Sarge shook his head. "Don't be sorry. Be smart. We do recon until backup arrives, and then we go in fast and hard. We get her out if there's any possibility to do so."

He nodded. Ian let go of Sarge's shirt, and they headed back toward the warehouse.

"Let's see if we can find some windows or doors and get eyes inside," he said. "We won't engage until help, back-up arrives."

Sarge nodded. "I'll take the south side of the building."

"I'm going up the fire escape. There are some windows up there. We'll communicate via phone."

Sarge was right. Now that he could think through the terror and fury that had consumed him, Ian knew that rushing in was the wrong plan.

If there was any chance Wavy was alive, he had to come at this strategically.

He jumped up, pulled down the ladder for the fire escape, and ascended silently. He didn't touch the door that led out to the fire escape. That would be the most likely place for a booby trap or alarm. Instead, he jimmied open the nearest window and fit himself inside.

Sarge had been right. There were at least eight armed guards. If Ian had gone rushing through the door, he would have done nothing but gotten himself killed.

He was also right that this was not a lab like the previous building they'd infiltrated. No medical procedures could be performed here. There were only guards. But if there were guards, there had to be something worth guarding, especially eight guards.

They were standing and sitting around, chatting with each other, obviously not expecting any trouble.

He reported his findings to Sarge via text. He shot back that there were two guards in a roving patrol around the perimeter of the building.

*Ten armed guards mean something important.*

His response was immediate. *I concur.*

They both continued to observe. No one seemed to be

making radio contact with the patrol guards. That was a good sign.

Landon texted that the rest of the team, including Finn Bollinger, was ten minutes out. Ian let him know that he was inside the building, getting himself into a more strategic position.

Why were the eight of them huddled around that corner of the building? They were young, not necessarily the best guards, and if there'd been a TV or, hell, even a dirty magazine, he would have understood more.

But they were sitting around the large crate in the corner of the room.

He watched them, forcing himself to keep an icy calm. They weren't chatting with each other; they were tossing remarks at the crate. Every once in a while, one of them kicked at the wood or hit it with their fists.

Taunting.

For the first time, hope grew inside him. Someone was inside that crate. He shot a text off to both Sarge and Landon.

*Guards interested in large crate in the northwest corner. Taunting. Someone's in there.*

One of the guards took a stick and poked between the slats, and it was all Ian could do not to pull out his gun right there and kill him.

*Stay frosty, boss,* Sarge shot back.

*Fear does not exist in this dojo.* Landon with another line, this time from *Karate Kid.* He almost smiled.

And then all hell broke loose.

The guards got a call and went on high alert, guns out. They left their taunting to focus on the incoming threat: them.

Five of them turned and headed to whatever posts they were supposed to have been at, but two of them turned their guns inward, toward the crate. Fuck.

Ian typed as rapidly as he could. *Guards on the move. I'm heading toward that crate.*

He shoved his phone into his pocket. He wouldn't have time for any more messages. He pulled out his weapon and bolted for the stairs. He wasn't using tranqs this time, which meant firing would let everyone in the entire building know exactly where he was, but he would rather be the target than Wavy inside that wooden cell.

He stayed in the shadows as much as possible but didn't sacrifice speed for stealth. His eyes were pinned on those two guards, who were unlocking the door.

He pushed faster, hitting the metal stairs with enough noise to wake the dead. He sighted his weapon and shot, hitting the first guard just as he opened the lock. He fell. Was he dead or merely wounded?

As expected, that drew the attention of everybody in the whole fucking building to him. He still ran toward the crate, grunting as he took a bullet in the fleshy part of his side. It didn't affect his ability to run. At this point, nothing short of a bullet through the head was going to affect his ability to run. As bullets flew at his head from the other direction, he fired at the second guard but missed.

And then he heard firing from the other side of the building. Sarge. He was drawing their attention.

Some of the guards turned to go after him, but Ian kept running. He shot the second guard as he opened the door of the cell, and he fell dead to the ground. But now, he was out of ammunition.

Out of the corner of his eye, Ian saw a different guard as he trained his sights on him.

He wasn't going to make it. He had a clear shot. Ian could only hope that he had bought Wavy, if that's who was in that crate, enough time for the others to get here and get her out.

A shot rang out, and he waited for the pain, but he didn't feel anything more than the bullet he'd already taken in his side. A second later, two more shots rang out.

He spun in the opposite direction. Finn and Landon ran

toward him, opening fire without any concern for their own safety. Sarge covered them from somewhere deeper in the warehouse. A few seconds later, all was quiet.

The rest of the Zodiac team covered any guards who were still alive. Ian kept moving toward the crate, praying to a God he'd never put much faith in that it would be Wavy and she would still be alive.

He threw the lock to the ground and pulled open the makeshift door, then came to a halt. Inside, a lone, naked figure lay on the floor near the farthest corner. Inside the crate was dim, but what he could see made him want to vomit.

Then go rip the heads off of every person who'd ever been associated with Mosaic.

It was Wavy, but she was . . . broken.

"Wavy?" He dropped to his knees and crawled toward her slowly. He didn't want to frighten her. What the hell should he do? "Wavy?"

She let out a pitiful moan, and then scooted back, away from him.

Ian's heart broke into a thousand pieces.

He stopped where he was, about five feet from her. "Wavy, it's Ian. We're going to get you out of here, Rainbow."

She still tried to back away, although she could barely move.

"Oh, my God. Oh, my fucking God." Finn's voice came from behind him in the doorway of the crate. "Is she, is she—"

"She's alive," he answered.

"We've got medical on the way," Landon called out.

Finn dropped beside him and crawled closer to her. "Wavy, it's Finn, sweetheart. We're here, honey."

She didn't continue her pitiful attempt to move backward. It was almost like she'd given up.

She was covered in blood and scratches and bruises. There wasn't a clean inch of skin anywhere on her. Finn and Ian crouched lower so they could crawl closer, trying to make themselves as least threatening as possible.

"Wavy, it's Finn, sweetheart." Finn sat up a little bit and pulled off his shirt. "I'm going to cover you, okay? Would that be okay? Are you cold?"

He wanted to say something, anything, but she was responding better to Finn's voice. He was her brother. She'd known him a lot longer and, God, maybe she was never going to want anything to do with him for the rest of her life.

And could Ian really blame her for that?

Finn moved closer and draped his shirt over her torso. Her eyes finally opened. She didn't say anything but her fingers reached out toward them. Finn touched them, and she didn't flinch or withdraw, but she didn't do or say anything else.

Ian sat there next to them feeling more helpless than he ever had in his entire life.

# CHAPTER
# TWENTY-FOUR

"WHY HASN'T WAVY WOKEN UP?" Finn demanded.

Ian stood in the corner of the doctor's office as Finn ranted at the woman who'd been treating Wavy for the past three days.

Finn's wife, Charlie, was also in the room, as well as his brother, Baby. He was here only because Charlie had argued on his behalf. She'd reminded her husband that Ian wasn't the one who had taken Wavy. Wasn't the one who had done this to her.

It was also Zodiac's knowledge of what Mosaic was doing—the gene-editing, neuro-inhibitors, and drug cocktail—that had allowed Wavy to get the immediate medical help she'd needed. It would've taken them much longer to figure out how to treat her otherwise.

But he was still to blame for what had happened to her. He knew it, and Finn did too. Ian didn't blame him for not wanting him anywhere near Wavy. But to make his tiny wife happy, he'd agreed to allow Ian into the room for this meeting with the doctor, so he was going to take advantage of it.

He just wanted to be near Wavy. The thought of being far from her was unbearable.

Once again, his assistants had worked their magic and set him up a makeshift office next door to the hospital there in San

Diego. He wanted to be as close as possible in case she woke up and for some unknown reason wanted to see him.

Dr. Ling, the head of trauma at San Diego's Jackson-Madison Hospital, nodded at all of them at Finn's demand for answers. "Yes, we would've liked Wavy to show some sign of activity by now, but let's look at the positives first. She has brain activity. That's good. She's breathing on her own. That's good too. She had no sign of sexual abuse or trauma—given the fact that she was held against her will, that's even better. She seems to have full movement of all her limbs, so we're glad for all those things."

Dr. Ling had been telling them those facts for three days, and they were all good to hear, but they wanted to address some of the bad things now.

"We're grateful for all of that. But what about the rest?" Finn said. "Why is she still asleep? Why does she have those scratches all over her body, and why is part of her hair missing?"

Dr. Ling bridged her fingers on her desk. "Actually, the scratches point to what we think is part of the reason she hasn't woken up yet."

"What does that mean?" Baby asked.

"Based on the condition of her own fingernails, we think she scratched herself."

They were all silent.

These weren't scratches like *oh, I've got an itchy back*. These scratches had ripped through her skin. The scratches had been what had caused her to be covered in blood when they'd first found her. Even cleaned up now, the scabs covered her entire body.

Thinking about her living through that was agonizing. The knowledge that she'd done it to herself . . .

"Why?" Ian had promised himself he'd be quiet, but he couldn't stop the question now. "Why would she have done that to herself?"

The doctor let out a sigh. "When Wavy was brought in, we knew she'd been experimented upon."

"Because of the bald spots on her head?" Baby asked.

She nodded. "Yes, those were used to monitor brain activity. She also had signs of multiple procedures, which, based on what Mr. DeRose has told us about this group Mosaic and what they're attempting to do, were likely a type of gene editing."

"And that went wrong?" Finn asked. "Made her start scratching herself uncontrollably? Some sort of allergic reaction?"

"Genetic editing is much further along than the government and media would have us all believe. Genome editing tools are becoming more available, which enables geneticists and medical researchers to edit parts of the DNA sequence."

"What does that do?" Charlie asked.

"Normally, good things," Dr. Ling said. "Curing certain types of blindness, diabetes, even some cancers. But what was done to Wavy was the opposite. She wasn't receptive to the gene editing. That, combined with the chemical stimulants and drugs, was basically . . . torture."

"She ripped at her own skin to try to make it stop hurting." Ian rubbed the heel of his hand against his eyes in an effort to push away the image of Wavy in that much pain. It didn't work.

Charlie muffled a sob. Finn and Baby looked like they might be sick.

Dr. Ling sighed. "Maybe in Wavy's overwhelmed mind, she was scratching herself to get to her insides where the pain was. To try to stop it."

"Is she still hurting now?" Finn asked. "Is that why she won't wake up?"

"No, she's not, that's another good thing. Hopefully, it's a matter of her brain figuring that out and allowing her to wake up. All the chemicals have been flushed out of her system, and the edited genes have been reversed. So nothing should be causing her any pain."

Charlie wiped her eyes. "How do we help her?"

"You wait," the doctor replied. "You sit there with her, you talk to her, and you let her brain know that she's in a safe space. And you pray that it's enough."

———

"I was wondering if you might let me sit in with her," Ian asked Finn nearly sixteen hours later.

He'd been very careful not to go inside Wavy's hospital room. Her family had been with her every second, and it wasn't his place to intrude given . . . everything.

So he'd come here at zero four hundred in the hopes of catching her without anybody by her side. He should have known better. Finn was there wide awake, looking as exhausted as Ian felt.

Finn shifted in his chair by the bed. "Look, DeRose, we all appreciate what you've done. Bringing in the specialists so Wavy got the help she needed right away, keeping law enforcement away from her until she's ready to talk. Making sure security is airtight around her."

Yeah, he'd told Callum he'd have to wait. If she woke up and asked to talk to law enforcement, he'd be the first person Ian called. Otherwise, he could cool his fucking jets. He didn't give a shit that his bosses were breathing down his neck. Wavy's well-being was his only priority.

He hadn't known Finn was aware of that or the security. But he was right. There was absolutely no way someone was getting Wavy again. The security in this hospital was airtight. "I wasn't sure you knew."

"I noticed the one intern who happens to be packing a weapon and is always nearby. I noticed the two men at the outside door and the random patrols on the stairs. I noticed the extra security cameras. I'm not sure that the hospital approved those, but I don't care. You're doing what you can to keep her safe. I appreciate it."

Ian should have known somebody with Finn Bollinger's background would recognize security, no matter what form it took. "But you don't want me around her, is that it?"

He couldn't blame him if he never wanted Ian within a hundred miles of his sister again.

Finn leaned forward on his chair and dropped his elbows on his knees. "Did I ever tell you about the time some maniac kidnapped Charlie and nearly beat her to death?"

He froze where he was in the doorway. "No, I wasn't aware of that."

"It was before we were married. She had stumbled onto some intel a terrorist wanted and refused to tell him where it was. Takes a special kind of person to withstand that sort of interrogation."

"What happened?"

He rubbed his eyes. "Charlie is strong. Not in a physical sense—she weighs a hundred pounds soaking wet. She's strong in a way I will never be. My strength is honed, *created* from years of physical and mental training. Charlie's strength is part of her genetic makeup. It's not something that can be taken from her."

Finn looked over at his sister lying in the bed. "Wavy has that same sort of strength. And I can guarantee you that whatever they changed with that gene editing, it didn't strip away her strength. She's never been tested like this, but she's going to come through."

Ian scrubbed his hands over his eyes. "God, I hope so, Finn. I can't tell you how sorry I am about this."

"I blamed myself for what happened to Charlie for a long time. She was in that mess because of me. Charlie was the one who eventually convinced me that the only person responsible for hurting her had been the guy who'd hurt her."

He reached over and touched Wavy's hand. "Same thing is

true in this situation. The only ones responsible for what was done to Wavy are Erick Huen and those assholes at Mosaic. So, I guess what I'm trying to say is yes, you can sit here with my sister. She was so fucking happy before this happened, so maybe she'll listen to you and wake up because God knows she's never listened to me."

He stood up and offered me his chair. "I only have one request."

"Anything, man," he said.

"You promise me that you're going to take down the bastards that did this to her."

"If I have to spend every dollar I have and every minute of the rest of my life, trust me, that will happen."

He slapped him on the shoulder. "I believe you. I'm going to find my wife. Text me if anything changes."

Finn walked out of the room. Ian sat down and placed Wavy's hand in his. It was the first time he'd touched her since before she'd been taken. For seventeen days he hadn't felt the softness of her skin. Even though that soft skin was covered in scabs and scratches, it was the best feeling he'd had in a long time.

He would never take for granted the opportunity to touch her ever again.

"Hey, Rainbow. It's me. You're safe here now. I need you to come back." He kissed her hand. "I need you to paint more pictures, not only for me, but for yourself. Because you still have so many beautiful colors in you, and you need to let them out."

He talked like that to her for hours, letting her know that they were all there and that she was safe like Dr. Ling had told them to do. Eventually, he fell asleep, his fingers intertwined with hers.

Ian hadn't slept in what felt like weeks because it *had* been weeks. His head was resting on the bed next to their intertwined hands when something touched his nose. He batted it away but it came back.

It was Wavy's fingers.

He sat up and saw the most beautiful thing he'd ever seen: her green eyes open and looking at him.

# CHAPTER
# TWENTY-FIVE

EVERY TIME WAVY opened her eyes, she braced herself for the pain. She'd long since stopped screaming. It didn't help, and her voice was broken anyway.

All of her was broken.

When she woke up and Ian was there beside her, Wavy still braced herself for the pain. He'd been beside her before, for fleeting seconds, and the pain had still come.

But this time it . . . *didn't*.

The longer it didn't come, the more scared she got. It would be back. It always came back and was worse than before. She couldn't bear it. She couldn't—

She closed her eyes.

When she opened them again, she wasn't sure how much time had passed. Ian was still beside her.

There was still no pain.

This time, there were other people around. Doctors, nurses. Wavy flinched away when any came near her. She didn't know how she'd gotten back into the medical bed. She'd been on the floor for so long.

Ian crouched beside her. She still kept waiting for him to disappear. Kept waiting for the pain to return.

He touched her hand, but she didn't flinch from him. She stared down at where their hands rested together.

"You're not bound anymore, Rainbow," he whispered, his voice so low she didn't think anyone else could hear it. "You're not alone. You're not trapped. Let your senses tell you what's really happening."

Wavy could feel his thumb brush across her skin. She could feel that. There was no pain anywhere.

"Think about what you can hear, what you can feel. Take it in a little bit at a time, at your own pace. There's no rush. But you're safe."

She did take it in, but time still didn't make sense to her.

She was in a hospital. There were doctors. Finn was there. And Baby, her mom, and Ian. But all of it seemed so far away. Wavy could see them, she could hear them, but it was like she was inside a thick bubble.

She'd seen one out on the lake one time. A giant, plastic bubble. A couple of kids had crawled inside, then run around on the surface of the lake, spinning and flipping—the thick plastic keeping them safe and dry.

That was her now. Everyone outside the bubble was distant and a little fuzzy, but at least nothing in here hurt her anymore.

So she stayed.

She was aware when they moved her from one hospital to another in one of Ian's jets.

She was back in Oak Creek. She knew that because Dr. Anne was here and her friends, and Leeann from the diner. They came in to say hello, but they were all as fuzzy as everyone else.

Wavy was content to lay in her little bubble in her hospital bed where nothing hurt. It took her a while to realize that everyone was waiting for things from her.

So she tried to give them what they wanted.

They seemed so excited when she sat up by herself, when she fed herself, when she walked from the hospital bed over to the chair by the window, even though she couldn't really see out of it.

She could, but it was too hard to focus on anything through the thickness wrapping her mind.

But nothing hurt. Wavy kept the thought of the pain pushed far away. If she let that in, remembered the agony, she would—

Wavy just couldn't think about it at all.

She would keep the thought of it out of the bubble. She'd keep everything out of the bubble.

It took her a lot longer than it probably should have to realize what everyone really wanted from her. They wanted her to *talk*.

But her voice was broken in every possible way. Wavy had screamed until her voice no longer worked, and now she was afraid it would never work again.

She wanted to explain it wasn't that she didn't want to talk to them, it was that she *couldn't*. But that was a lie. She didn't *want* to talk either.

So, everyone continued to treat her like she was a toddler, all but applauding every time she did something very simple, asking her yes or no questions so she could nod or shake her head.

She was disappointing them. Or maybe not disappointing but hurting their feelings. No, that wasn't right either. All she knew was they were worried about her.

In a distant part of her mind, Wavy knew she should put more of an effort into breaking out of her bubble. But she couldn't. She wasn't strong enough. It would take more than she had.

So she stayed like she was. They moved her out of the hospital—she wasn't taking any medicine so didn't need to be there—to her mom's house. That was good. Her old bed was familiar. She didn't have to do anything but listen as her mom talked to her from far away and people came to visit.

Ian came to see her. He was the hardest to see. The only one who caused her to question staying in her bubble. If she stayed in there, she'd never be with him again.

But maybe that was better. What could he possibly see in her now? She could barely get out of bed without assistance. She didn't talk, didn't feel. Didn't have anything left to offer to anyone, maybe ever.

He'd sit next to her, try to talk, but Wavy never spoke back. He would gently touch her hand, but then just as gently let it go, as if he wasn't sure if touching her was okay.

*Please don't let me go!*

The words screamed in her mind, but nothing came out of her mouth. She didn't know how to communicate with him, so she turned away.

Each time. How many times had he been there? So many, it felt like. He was there more than anyone else. He was the one who encouraged her to walk around the house, to walk outside in the sun. Whispered to her to have sweet dreams.

———

Time became the last thing Wavy was truly aware of.

Finn and Charlie brought her a new phone, and she opened the calendar app during one of the few times when there was no one in the room with her.

The red block date told her what today's date was, and she couldn't believe it. The last date she remembered had been more than five weeks ago. That had been the day she'd gone to see Louis Noeya, the "art dealer." But he wasn't an art dealer. He was Erick Huen.

It was the first time she'd let herself think about his name. Wavy waited to see what would happen, if the pain would come back, but it didn't. He couldn't hurt her now.

How had five weeks passed? How much of that had been when she was taken, and how much of it had been since they'd found her? She didn't know.

All she knew was that it was five weeks of her life she was never going to get back.

For a split second, the bubble around her thinned enough that she could see out of it. She was sitting on the corner of the couch in the living room, legs tucked underneath her. No TV, no book, just sitting there.

Her mom was in the kitchen talking to Charlie. The baby—Thomas, *her nephew* Thomas—was sitting in a booster seat, banging away and eating faster than Charlie could give him pieces of banana.

Wavy got up and walked into the kitchen. Her mom and Charlie stopped talking and stared at her. She wanted to say something, but couldn't find her voice. Instead, she picked up the banana and fed Thomas a piece. They started talking again.

Then the bubble snapped back into place. But that was okay.

Every time she looked at her calendar, the bubble thinned, sometimes for only a few seconds, sometimes for much longer. Each time it thinned, she did more. She went outside, even drove herself into town every once in a while. Everyone talked and smiled at her, although nobody seemed to expect a response.

Finn brought an easel and her paints and set it up in their mom's guest room, but she closed the door so she couldn't see it. Wavy had no desire whatsoever to paint. Her colors were gone.

She could see colors around her. She knew her eyes worked correctly. But the colors, the way she used to see them, flowing in patterns and mists and surrounding everything, were gone. And she didn't think they were ever coming back.

Wavy's colors were gone. Her feelings were gone. Her voice was gone.

Who was she without those? If she never expressed herself or felt anything, was she still a person?

Day after day ticked by. Everyone got used to seeing her in town and waving and smiling at her, but nobody tried to talk to her anymore. Ian came to see her regularly, but Wavy knew he had to be getting frustrated. He always asked her questions, ones that required actual *answers,* not like the questions everyone else posed around her to make her feel included. But she never responded. How long before he decided she wasn't worth the effort?

How long until he started posing the non-question questions like everyone else?

Wavy wasn't sure exactly when the anger began to creep in.

All she knew was that the anger disintegrated the bubble more consistently than anything else. The anger didn't make anything better, but at least she could *feel* it.

Every time she looked at the calendar, she was *mad.*

She had lost weeks of her life because of what Erick Huen had done to her. But she had lost much more time because of what *she* was allowing.

She wanted to go to her studio. Not to paint. To rip it all down.

She waved to her mom, who gave Wavy her slightly relieved look, like she was glad she was going out, but she probably ought to be concerned. She gave her as big a smile as she could muster, although it was nothing compared to how Wavy used to grin at damn near everybody.

Her mom had always been kind of fragile, and they'd taken turns caring for her since their dad died more than a decade ago. Being Wavy's caretaker was taking a toll on her. She was hurting her.

For the first time, it felt like the bubble was keeping her trapped rather than safe. But she'd let it surround her for so long, Wavy wasn't sure how to separate it from who she was. They'd melded together.

She drove into town and parked near her studio. She forced herself to walk up the stairs and open the door.

Everything looked the way it had the last time she'd seen it. The unmade cot in the corner. Her sweater thrown over the chair by the tiny table. Her blank canvases and supplies.

All the paintings with their colors so bright and cheerful.

They were garish to her now. So bright they hurt her eyes. Wavy picked up the biggest canvas and threw it on the ground. Stomped on it, picking up the frame until the canvas ripped under her foot.

Then she did the same to another. And another. Destroying canvas after canvas until her weakened body could do no more.

Then she sat down in the middle of it all and cried. Sobbed. She answered the question she'd been afraid to ask herself—did her voice actually still work?

It did. Wavy knew because the sobs poured out of her now, from the very depths of her being.

She wept at what had been taken from her, at what she'd lost, at what she'd given up.

For what she was afraid was gone forever.

Not just her paintings, but her relationship with Ian. She'd shut him out.

*She needed him.*

Just like that, the bubble snapped—gone. All of a sudden, Wavy could see everything clearly, but she was naked and raw without its presence.

Baby and Finn came bursting through the door. Someone must have heard her crying.

She scrambled back from them, unable to explain that she couldn't be touched, not right then while everything was so immediate and painful and raw. They stopped, unsure of what to do. Agony blanketed their handsome faces.

Baby, her younger, gentler brother, crouched on the ground. "Hey, sis, we're just checking on you. Mom said you came to town and, well, we have security cameras set up. And when we saw you in here crying . . ."

Wavy tried to force words out, she really did. She knew her vocal cords worked, but she couldn't manage yet. So she held a hand out toward them and nodded.

Baby stood up and took a few steps closer. He didn't pull her in for a hug, which had to be hard for him—he was such a hugger. But he knew she wasn't ready.

She wanted to explain about how things were changing, how the bubble was gone, how everything, even breathing, felt over-stimulating. About how she knew in the long run, it was probably for the better, but for right now, she couldn't process everything that was happening.

Wavy wanted to explain that she needed to be alone, but that she was afraid to be alone, that she needed a chance to figure out what her new normal was going to be.

She wanted to tell them that she knew she was hurting them, and that was not her intention. And that she was so sorry. That she would try harder, but that she had to figure out how to take those first steps.

Both of them kept murmuring that it would be okay. The same thing they'd been murmuring since she'd woken up in the hospital.

And although they meant it, it was a lie.

Because the truth was, there, where everyone coddled her and looked at her in sympathy and talked in non-question questions around her, Wavy was never going to find herself again. Never going to reclaim herself.

So, for the first time since she'd woken up, Wavy forced words out of her lips.

"I need Ian."

# CHAPTER
# TWENTY-SIX

IAN HAD KNOWN Wavy's whereabouts every single moment since they'd gotten her back. He had round-the-clock security on her. He'd run it past Finn, although he hadn't been asking his permission.

Wavy Bollinger would have a full-time Zodiac Tactical security team watching her for the rest of her life.

She would never again be taken against her will. It didn't matter what happened between her and Ian, this would be a service provided for her for as long as she would allow it. Hell, even if she wouldn't allow it, he would probably still keep a covert surveillance team on her.

At some point, he was going to have to leave her alone—that became more evident every time he visited her and she stayed so distant—but he would ensure her safety until the day he died.

Since he couldn't be at Wavy's side twenty-four seven like he wanted, he'd thrown himself back into running Zodiac Tactical and tracking down any leads having to do with Mosaic. Especially Bronwyn.

Erick Huen had gone to ground. The bastard would show back up eventually, and when he did, Ian would take him down post fucking haste, whichever way he had to.

If that meant hiding his body where no one would ever find it, he'd have a sandwich and a beer afterward.

He was back to working twenty-hour days. It helped drag his mind off Wavy instead of obsessing over her. She needed time.

Ian had to believe that someday she would find herself again. That time would give her that. He didn't allow himself to hope that he would be a part of her future. Right now, it was enough that she had a future at all.

When he got the text from Wavy's detail that she'd gone to her studio, Ian didn't know whether to be happy or concerned.

There was nothing he wanted more than to know she'd taken up painting again. He thought he could be content not being in her life as long as he knew she'd found her way back to that passion. Even if it wasn't her rainbow paintings.

With the next message that both Baby and Finn Bollinger had rushed to the premises, Ian got more concerned. They were both overprotective—understandably—but maybe she wasn't handling the trip to her studio well.

But then again, maybe they needed to just let her be. Let her work her way out of this.

When he received a phone call from Finn a few minutes later, his heart stopped. He answered it after only half a ring.

"Finn."

"Something's happened," he said without any sort of preamble.

Fear roiled in Ian's gut. "What? Is she okay?"

The long-term effects of what had been done to Wavy were something they all worried about. The thought of her being in such pain again was unbearable to any of them.

"Her voice works. Baby and I walked in on her having some sort of a breakdown in her studio."

Ian rubbed his eyes, wishing he were there, wishing he could help. At least Finn was telling him this, but *why* was he telling him this? "Crying might be good. It's at least an outlet. It's at least *something*."

"I agree. Baby and I are both hoping this is a step forward for her. And she looked different too, DeRose. Like she was panicked, overwhelmed."

He rubbed his eyes again, his heart hurting for her. "Again, I'm not sure that that's a bad thing. At least she's coming out of that fucking shell she's had around her. Recovery is painful."

He knew that firsthand. He hated to think of it for Wavy, but the only way to move forward was to take those painful steps.

"I think Wavy wants to get out of Oak Creek," Finn said, voice tight. "I think maybe being around all of us all the time is not what she needs right now."

"Tell me what she needs," Ian said. "You know I'll provide it. Wherever she wants to go, I can set her up with full-time security anywhere in the world. Whoever she wants with her. Family. Friends. Whoever."

Finn was silent for a long minute. Was he considering his offer or offended by it? Why had he called at all?

"I'm going to trust you, DeRose," he finally said. "Trust you like I trust only a handful of people in the world."

"I won't hurt her, Finn." It was a solemn vow. "I will make sure she has whatever she needs."

"Well, evidently what she needs is you."

"What?" That was not what Ian had been expecting. "Why would you say that?"

"I didn't say it. She did. Wavy finally spoke, and her first words were that she needed you."

"I'm on my way."

———

Ian was on his way to Oak Creek not an hour after he finished talking to Finn. Whatever Wavy needed, he would give it to her. Hell, if she'd asked for him because she wanted him to move a couch from one side of the room to the other, he would do it without complaint.

She'd *asked* for him.

He jumped in his car as soon as they landed. His security team let him know that Wavy was still in her studio, so Ian went straight there. Finn and Baby were outside the building talking to each other. Both men shook his hand as he walked up.

"She's different," Baby said, "like something, I don't know, has switched back on inside of her."

Finn nodded. "She's still inside. I had no idea how much she had in that place. I knew she liked to paint here, but I didn't know that she had done such extensive work."

Baby glanced up at the window of her studio. "Although there's less now after what she destroyed. She was mad."

Mad was good. Mad would push her forward. The thought of her destroying her beautiful artwork pained him, but if it was what she needed, then they'd have to let her do it.

"Does she still want me here?" he asked.

God, it would break something in him if she'd changed her mind. But he'd never let her know that. She was allowed to change her mind as many times as she wanted to.

"Honestly, I don't know," Baby said. "But if it helps, I'm not sure she knows what she wants."

Ian nodded and turned to walk up the stairs. He knocked on the door, not expecting her to answer, and she didn't. Finally, he opened the door himself.

She was standing in front of one of her rainbow paintings on a large easel. She had a screwdriver in her hand. This one was about to suffer the same fate as all the ones lying ripped all over the floor.

The sight of it broke his heart. But the sight of her, awake and alive—pissed as hell—put some of the pieces together again.

He got daily reports about her, but nothing was quite the same as seeing her with his own eyes.

"Hi," he said, his voice foreign to his own ears—hoarse, weak, nervous. He wasn't someone who was used to feeling or sounding nervous.

Her arm dropped to her side, and she turned to look at him.

"I'm sorry," he said. "I didn't mean to interrupt you. I'll come back in a little while. Do you want that?"

Like everyone else, Ian had gotten used to talking to her with the yes or no questions, so she'd be able to communicate. He needed to stop doing that.

She shook her head, no. At least she didn't want him to leave. He walked a few steps closer, watching her for any indication that it was troubling her to be alone with him.

But those big green eyes were steady, clear, studying him as he approached.

He gestured to the canvases scattered all across the floor. "Doing a little redecorating in here?"

Her face remained stoic, but she didn't shy away as he came closer.

"Being angry is good. Healthy even. But save me a couple of those, okay? They're some of my very favorite things in the world."

She nodded, then handed him the screwdriver, her fingers brushing his. Ian waited to see if she would say anything, wanting to give her plenty of opportunity to use her voice if she wanted to, but she didn't.

"Finn told me you said you needed something from me. Tell me what it is, Rainbow, and I'll give it to you. Whatever it is, no matter how big or small."

"Go," she said.

He forced himself to show no reaction as the word sliced through him. She was responsive. She had spoken. That was enough for today. If she wanted him to go, he would. "Okay. Maybe I can come back tomorrow?"

She shook her head, and that jagged rip in his heart opened further.

Then she touched her fingers to her chest.

"Me go," she whispered.

Her voice was raspy not only from disuse, but from

screaming for so long when she'd been in captivity, or so the doctor had warned them.

"Where do you want to go, Rainbow? Tell me. I'll get you there, with or without me. Wherever you want to go."

Her gaze dropped, and she stared down at the destroyed paintings around her for so long he thought she was done talking. But finally, she responded.

"Penthouse."

# CHAPTER
# TWENTY-SEVEN

WAVY WROTE notes to her family before she left for Ian's penthouse. She had to explain that in order for her to move forward, she couldn't stay there. And to thank them for taking such good care of her. She owed them that much, and so much more. She knew they'd all understand, and were probably at least a little bit relieved that she was going, that they didn't have to be responsible for her anymore.

The bubble had burst, and Wavy couldn't get back inside it. Everything felt scratchy and raw against her senses—too bright, too loud, too immediate. The bubble had kept her buffered. Part of her wished she could get back to where she didn't feel anything, good or bad.

No. She didn't want that. She couldn't allow herself to want it.

And now sitting in Ian's penthouse, looking down at the Denver area below her, she knew coming here had been the right decision. She couldn't stay in Oak Creek, but she was terrified of being alone.

Ian could give her a balance. He wouldn't baby her, but he would help in whatever way she wanted. He would give her space, but also keep her close.

And . . . Wavy wanted to be *near* him. When he was around, she felt better. She wasn't sure what shape their relationship would take, if any. All she knew was that being there felt right.

He hadn't tried to talk to her the entire flight from Wyoming to Denver. He'd seemed content to be next to her, which in turn had helped her be more comfortable living in the space.

Once they got to the penthouse, he'd left her alone to go out on the balcony to her favorite view. She had stayed out there longer than normal, enjoying the crisp fall air, looking down on the city. Maybe it was because it was night and everything was already muddled and dark so it didn't have to feel unusual. She didn't have to worry that her colors were still gone.

Destroying as many of her paintings as she could hadn't made them come back. All it had done was make her tired.

How did Wavy explain any of what was going on inside her head, how there were big chunks of her memory missing, and what she did remember was fuzzy?

All she could remember clearly was the pain, and she didn't want to focus on that. So she kept it all from her mind.

Finally, the night air's chill got the better of her, and she went inside. She found Ian sitting on his couch, a glass of his favorite scotch in his hand. Wavy didn't know how long he'd been sitting there, but he'd been able to see her from his perch on the sofa.

"Enjoy the night air?"

She nodded, trying to force words, but they wouldn't come.

"It's one of the main reasons I bought this place. I definitely got the appeal." He leaned back in the couch. "If it's okay with you, I'd like to talk about the rules of you living here."

Her eyes narrowed, but the thought of house rules was actually intriguing. It was normal. If they were going to be in this space together, they needed to know how to interact. She liked it.

He gestured to the overstuffed chair across from him and she sat, wrapping her legs under her and pulling a small, thick blanket over her lap.

"Okay. First, this is a safe space. There are only two ways in or out of this apartment. One is the elevator. The second is via the emergency stairway that leads off the kitchen. The elevator is currently set so that only you or I can use it. That means no one will be coming up here without you being aware of it and inviting them. It's always been set so that only a few people had access, but I'm eliminating their access too."

Wavy had to admit, she felt better knowing no one else could use the elevator except the two of them. She nodded again.

"If you want, I can take my access off too. That way only emergency services could override in a fire or something."

She shook her head. He didn't need to remove his own access. If she was afraid of him coming into his own home, then she had no right to be there.

"Okay. I'll leave my access on. You'll still get a notification every time the elevator is on the move. It only stops here and the lobby, and is accessible through a special key, so no one can use it accidentally. The emergency stairs can only be accessed from the inside, except for emergency services."

She nodded.

He leaned forward and rested his forearms on his knees. "There are security cameras on the balcony and in the foyer where the elevator exits into the apartment. I have someone watching those security cameras twenty-four seven. So if you decide to dance around naked, you might want to avoid those two areas. There are no other cameras anywhere else in the penthouse."

Wavy could feel the beginning of a twitch at her lips, but it disappeared before it could form into an actual smile.

"I guess those weren't so much rules as they were security specs, but I wanted to make sure that you understood. I want you to feel as safe as possible in this place."

She nodded again. He took another sip of his scotch, then leaned back.

"Okay. So let's talk about actual rules. First, you are welcome here as long as you want, with or without me being here. If you decide to reside in this penthouse for the rest of your life, that's okay."

She wasn't about to kick him out of his own home, but she nodded.

"As you know, I have four bedrooms here. My bedroom, the guest bedroom, my office, and the fourth room. All of those spaces are completely available to you. I will still need my office, but that can be moved to a different room if for some reason that space is more comfortable to you."

She shook my head, brows furrowed. This was getting ridiculous.

He held out a hand. "Before you argue, let's talk about the second rule, equally as important as the first."

He stopped and leaned forward, placing his drink on the coffee table. "When it comes to recovery, what you need is what you need. Sometimes it's not going to make sense and sometimes it's not going to be convenient. But it is what it is."

It didn't seem right that he would be the only one inconvenienced by what she needed. Wavy scowled. He smiled a little at that, then continued.

"There's a reason I know that, Rainbow. Because I had a recovery of my own, and believe it or not, it had to do with Mosaic. I never told you about it before because it's ugly, and I don't like to talk about it. But if you want to hear it sometime, I'll tell you."

Her scowl fell, and she leaned forward in her chair, studying him, fingers running over the blanket in her lap.

That changed things.

If he actually knew about recovery, had suffered something similar, then maybe for the first time she had someone who wasn't merely trying to fix her. He was somebody who *understood*.

This time Wavy forced out the words. "Okay. Thank you."

It sounded like a croak, but Ian broke into such a big smile you would've thought she had offered him the most precious of gifts.

"Good. All right, rule number three. Recovery is not linear. I guess that's not really a rule either, but it's still true. Recovery will not always be forward in progression. It'll be one step forward, eleven steps back. But that's how recovery is. The important thing to remember is that you *are* actually recovering."

He leaned back, propping his arms along the back of the couch. "I want to help in any way I can. I have extensive resources at my disposal, and you should not be afraid to take advantage of them. If it's okay with you, I'd like to bring in Dr. Rayne Westerfield. She does a lot of work at a place called the Resting Warrior Ranch in Wyoming, and she specializes in dealing with extreme PTSD. She is the very best in the business. She helped me when I didn't think that was going to be possible."

The fact that Ian had needed a psychiatrist to talk to about whatever he'd been through told her it had been a pretty big deal.

"Okay," she whispered, and got another smile. It was almost worth talking, worth forcing her voice to work, to see him smile. For the first time, Wavy realized how exhausted he looked. "Tired." The word came out a little choked.

"You're tired?" he said. "Had enough talking for one night? I totally understand."

She pointed at him. "You tired."

He stared at her for long seconds, then wiped a hand down his face and got up. He walked slowly over to her—obviously waiting to see if she was going to freak out—and crouched down at her feet.

She wasn't going to freak out. Ian would never hurt her. She touched the hair over his ear like she'd wanted to do that very first time she'd seen him. She could remember that. Her memories from her captivity were muddled, but that was crystal clear.

"Oh, Rainbow. You are never going to be anything but

amazing to me. That you could see that I'm tired? Your heart is incredible. So big and strong."

Wavy wasn't sure about any of that, but she knew that he needed to rest. She touched his temple again before her arm fell back to her side.

"I am tired," he admitted. "I don't think I've slept for more than a couple of hours at a time since you were taken. Even once you were back, I haven't been able to rest. Maybe now that you're here, I'll be able to."

She nodded. Maybe they both would be able to.

"The last rule," he said, still perched there at her feet, "is that I'm bringing in your painting supplies and easels."

Wavy tensed. "I can't."

She wanted to say so much more than that. She wanted to tell him that her colors were gone, never coming back. She was never going to paint like she had before.

"You can," he said. "It might not be the same, but it's an important part of you that you can't give up without a fight. If you want to gain two hundred pounds, that's fine. Hell, if you want to drink yourself into oblivion every day, I'll help you do that too. But I'm not going to allow you to give up painting. I'm asking that once a day you go in there and put at least one stroke on a canvas. If that's all, that's fine. Will you do that for me?"

Wavy nodded. She would do it for him.

"It doesn't have to be the same as before. But you can still paint your emotions, whatever they are. The anger, the fear, the bleakness, the despair, you take it, and you put it on a canvas. If you do that, at least try every day, I'll show you what I did as part of my recovery. Deal?" He reached out his hand to shake.

She took it, tilting her head, intrigued by the thought.

He gave her another smile. "Believe me. It's not nearly as creative an outlet as yours, and I'm pretty sure I'd get teased if my team knew about it, but it helped me get through."

She shook his hand. Painting would be worth knowing what he'd done. Some sort of sword fighting? Tae kwon do?

He pointed at the blanket in her lap. "That was one of my recovery pieces."

She stared down at it, then back at him, befuddled. He smiled.

"Knitting. Mostly blankets, but some potholders here and there, especially during therapy sessions. Having something that kept my hands busy allowed my mind to work through a lot of my trauma. Maybe painting will do the same for you."

Wavy pulled the blanket closer. Ian, with his brilliant mind and trained warrior instincts, had knitted this. And it had helped him. That, somehow, gave her more hope than anything else he'd said tonight. She brought the blanket up and rubbed it against her cheek.

His smile broke out again. "Welcome home for however long you want it to be yours."

# CHAPTER
# TWENTY-EIGHT

FOR THREE DAYS, Wavy had a showdown with her paintbrush.

She wanted to do the one thing Ian had asked of her, since it was such a reasonable request. The first day, she stood there in front of the easel for more than an hour, trying to figure out what color to use. Finally, she opened the nearest paint container, marked the canvas with something that could barely be called a stroke, and left.

The second day wasn't much better. Except that she'd decided to forget about picking a color and went with black. Not having to worry about colors made it much easier. She painted a few strokes—nothing specific. She wasn't trying to create anything. The paintbrush wasn't awkward in her hand like she feared it would be. It felt natural—an extension of her.

As long as Wavy stuck with black. As soon as she tried to reach for one of the colors neatly stacked all around her, she panicked. It was all she could do not to vomit and throw the canvas across the room.

She couldn't use colors. Color had no place in her life or her painting. She was tired of fighting that.

*What you need is what you need. Sometimes it's not going to make sense.*

Ian's words came back to her. What Wavy needed was to not paint colors. It didn't have to be logical. She simply had to accept that it was her new reality.

So this morning, when she'd woken up before dawn in the guest bedroom, her fingers itching to paint, she'd gone back to the easel but stayed far away from the colors. Black was fine. White wasn't a problem either. That gave her an endless array of grays to work with.

Wavy set the tray out in front of her and let the brush do what it wanted to do—what her subconscious wanted her to do. Over the next couple of hours, she filled up a small canvas. The end result wasn't particularly pretty to look at—it mostly resembled a thunderstorm. But she had *painted*.

"All forward progress was progress," she said, echoing what Dr. Rayne had said to her more than once over the past two days.

She was younger than Wavy'd expected but was definitely an old soul. Her eyes screamed that she'd seen things. She would understand whatever Wavy might tell her. They'd sat down in the living room, since she'd flown out from whatever that ranch was she worked at in Wyoming.

Dr. Rayne had seemed content to do much of the talking. Wavy'd tried to answer questions when asked, but when she'd asked her if she preferred not to talk, she'd nodded. She wasn't ready.

She'd given her a gentle smile. "When you're ready, you'll talk again."

But Wavy did want to discuss one of the things that was bothering her the most. "I don't remember."

"All or parts?"

"All," she whispered. Well, all except for the pain. She should be able to remember *something* about her captivity, but it was all a blank. No details, all blurry.

"The memories will come when they come," she said. "Just like the talking, when you're ready."

"What if they don't come?" she whispered, her voice shaky.

"Then they don't come. You've done your part, Wavy. You survived. You've come out of this whole, or at least in big enough pieces that you're going to be able to put them back together again."

Somehow, that was the most encouraging thing she could have said to her, that yes, she was in pieces, but that they would fit together again to make a whole. She was holding on to that.

Every minute Wavy spent there in the penthouse, she felt a little safer, a little less fractured.

Sometimes Ian was there, sometimes he wasn't. He ate most of her meals with her, even when she ate them at weird times. Usually, he fell asleep on the couch, watching a movie with her, and she placed a blanket as gently as she could over him. He was still so tired, still concerned about her.

Now it was late. Ian had already gone to lie down in his bedroom, although he'd left the door open for her in case she needed him. Her fingers were itching for the paintbrush again. As she walked toward the room she'd already started calling her studio in her mind, a flash came to her: medical beds lined up in a row. Machines beeping. Her wrist strapped to the bed.

Wavy's breath faltered, but instead of forcing the thought away, she made herself breathe through it. To look around herself in that memory.

Was this where she'd been? The only hospital bed she remembered was after she'd woken up safe. But this wasn't that. This was much bigger, like a dormitory. But her wrists and ankles had been restrained.

And then the vision was gone.

Wavy stopped and looked around, getting her breathing under control. She was still in the penthouse. She was safe. She could hear Ian snoring lightly from his bed. She was okay.

She walked the rest of the way into the studio and picked up her paints. All derivatives of black and white, but she didn't care. She painted a full canvas the way she would have before using colors: rainbow, but monochromatic.

She didn't think, she just felt. Let her fear from the flashback bleed onto the canvas. Her strokes were jagged, but she didn't care. She let her mind do what it wanted to do.

She got lost in the painting, adding detail after detail. Details she hadn't been aware of while using only blacks, whites, and grays.

But as Wavy finished and stepped back, she realized it was beautiful in its own stark way. Ian had been right. She needed to allow herself to paint the bleakness, the fear, the anger.

She looked over at the clock and realized it was nearly three o'clock in the morning. She was exhausted. She cleaned up her brushes and left the room. She wanted to take a shower, but the shower in her room wasn't nearly as nice as the one in Ian's room. She would go in there and take a shower. He wouldn't mind.

He wouldn't join her either. And Wavy wasn't sure exactly how she felt about that. She wanted him to, she really did. But she didn't know if she could trust herself not to freak out. What if something he did triggered something in her? Then they would both feel horrible. And he wouldn't risk that unless she asked him to join her.

The shower felt good. The memories of all the times they had spent there felt even better, surrounding her and pouring over her like the water. It felt like one more piece of her was slipping back into place.

When she got out, she put on one of Ian's T-shirts that she'd stolen before her captivity. Wavy knew she should leave, go back to her room, but instead of doing that, she walked over to the bed. He was still lying on his side, but those brown eyes were looking at her.

"Doing okay?" he asked.

She nodded, then forced herself to use words. "Yes."

Then she forced herself to ask for what she really wanted, even more than the shower she'd come in for. "C-can I sleep with you?"

He didn't say anything. He just moved over on the bed and held up the covers. Wavy slid in next to him and put her back to him so that he surrounded her. His arm wrapped around her waist.

"This okay?"

She pressed her hands over his. "More than okay."

Another piece of her glued back into place.

# CHAPTER
# TWENTY-NINE

"WE NEED to talk to Wavy. She's been back a month, and she hasn't had a single law enforcement debrief."

Callum had been calling him every day for the past week. Ian had finally taken his call today because he couldn't put off his calls forever. Definitely not because he had any intention of letting him near Wavy.

"She's not ready yet," Ian told him.

"I know she's talking."

He ground his teeth together. "How do you know that?" Nobody in his organization should be talking about Wavy at all.

"Simmer down there, Aries," Callum shot back. "I know because I've talked to Wavy's family, not because any of your people are feeding me secrets."

Wavy *was* talking, and every word out of her lips felt like a minor miracle. She was painting too, and if she never left this penthouse, as long as she talked and painted, he would consider his life a success.

"She doesn't remember anything, Callum. You coming in and putting a lot of pressure on her is not going to help her mental health, and to be honest, that's the only thing I give a fuck about right now."

"She's not the only one involved in this situation. You can't keep acting like she is. We know she was being held with other people. We need details."

"No."

There was no way Ian was letting him talk to Wavy. If she decided she wanted to talk to law enforcement down the road, that was fine, but he was not going to ask her to do it.

"Goddammit, Ian, I am running interference for you left and right. Do you think that there are no repercussions when dead bodies rack up around you? First Varela, then the two at the lab, then Dr. Tippens. I'm happy that your girlfriend made it out alive, but somebody has to be held accountable for the dead people."

"Are you trying to say that Wavy is responsible?" He would burn the world to the fucking ground before he'd let someone suggest she had anything to do with any of this.

"No," he responded, "of course not. What I'm saying is that she may have information that would allow us to figure out who they were, how they died, and who *is* responsible. We know it's Mosaic, but we don't know more than that. I've got to give my bosses something. Especially now that—" He cut himself off.

"What?"

"Nothing."

Ian let out a sigh. "Don't start holding out on me now, Webb."

"How come that sentiment only goes one way? You have no qualms about leaving me out of the loop when it suits your fancy."

He scrubbed a hand down his face. "It's not you. When it came to Wavy, I wasn't willing to wait for things to go through a committee. There was too much at stake, and time was always of the essence."

There was a moment of silence before Callum spoke again. "I'm not in the inner loop here anymore. I'm pretty sure I'm one dead body away from getting fired."

Ian winced. "Fuck. I didn't know—"

"I'm a big boy, DeRose. I can take care of myself. What I was going to say is that we've had some other intel come in about this brainwashing concoction Mosaic is developing. Turns out the end goal isn't human trafficking at all, at least not in the traditional sexual sense."

He sat up straighter in his desk chair. "What is the end goal?"

"Human *weapons*."

His curse was vile, even by former Navy SEAL standards. "How do you know?"

"We got intel on an assassination plot on a senator. We were able to stop it, but the perp committed suicide in the process. This perp had the same genetic mutations as the two bodies found in that lab. Same type of gene editing attempted on Wavy."

He rubbed the back of his neck at the knot of tension forming there. "Sadly, that makes so much more sense than Mosaic going to all this trouble to develop glorified sex slaves."

"This is next level now. We need to question Wavy."

Ian couldn't stand the thought of anything reversing Wavy's tentative progress. "I'll talk to her therapist and see what she thinks about presenting Wavy with the option of talking to you. That's all I'm willing to promise."

"You're going to have to do better than that. She's a material witness to multiple murders and may know something more about potential crimes. There will be subpoenas if she's not willing to talk to us voluntarily."

"Don't do that, Callum."

"It's out of my hands. My bosses aren't asking my opinion anymore. I'm working other angles as best I can."

"What other angles?"

"If it amounts to anything, I'll let you know. Right now, the best thing you can do is let us talk to Wavy. If she comes in voluntarily, that gives you more options. We could come to you instead of her having to come into a law enforcement facility. You could be with her the whole time."

Neither option was going to happen, not until Wavy was damned well ready for it. He didn't know if Callum had tipped his hand to him on purpose, but he'd provided Ian with important info he was definitely going to act on.

He would keep Wavy safe from anything, good guys included. Nothing was going to cause her pain again as long as he had any say in it.

"Thanks for your call, Callum."

"We'll be in touch soon. Do the right thing."

He would do the right thing. It was time to see if Wavy was interested in going on a little field trip.

---

Once Wavy started painting, she couldn't seem to stop for three solid days. It was all she wanted to do. Ian had to see the finished products because he was the one who'd made sure she had all the supplies she needed.

For the first day, it was all black and white. But by the second day, her grays were tinted silver and blue. She'd added the hues without being aware of it because she'd needed them to capture her feelings on the canvas. Then it became easier to add other hues.

They still weren't colorful by any means, and definitely nothing like what she'd painted before her abduction, at least in their final appearance. But in other ways, they were the same. They were still expressions of her emotional state—of what her mind and heart and soul were feeling.

For three days straight, Wavy painted every spare moment until her fingers cramped up, then crawled into bed at night with Ian. She thought they both slept better together, even though they hadn't done so much as kiss. They slept, limbs wrapped around each other like they were clinging to one another for survival, which was probably accurate in her case. Maybe his too.

She'd spent every morning talking to Dr. Rayne for at least an hour via video chat since she'd gone back to Wyoming. Wavy was frustrated that she hadn't had any progress with her memories. None whatsoever.

Dr. Rayne kept saying the same thing: that they would come when they came. But with every passing hour, that became less and less acceptable to Wavy. She needed to remember. She didn't know why she needed to remember, but she knew that she did. Wavy wasn't going to heal until she did.

But it wasn't just about her. There was something she *needed* to remember. Or maybe . . . *someone*. But that didn't make sense. Dr. Rayne had told her she'd been alone when they'd found her. And she was a little too scared to push for more details.

Wavy'd told her she felt like she got the closest to remembering when she was painting. She kept having those flashes. But were they real? Dr. Rayne encouraged her to keep painting and let her subconscious sort it out. She wasn't going to get any argument from her, but still, the frustration built.

So when Ian came out of his office and smiled at her, it was a welcome distraction. "Want to go on a field trip?"

Wavy had not been expecting that. She hadn't left the penthouse since she'd arrived almost a week ago. "Together or by myself?"

He walked over to the kitchen where she was making dinner and leaned against the counter. "Together."

That already sounded better. "Where would we go?"

His smile widened. "If I told you, that would ruin the fun. And besides, it's not necessarily a set destination."

She paused over the salad she was tossing. Their nights had been easy—she crawled into bed with him after she was done painting for the evening, and they wrapped around each other.

But their days weren't so easily defined. They'd been circling around each other, neither of them knowing how to make the first move or what the first move should be.

But she thought they both wanted to.

"How long will we be gone?" Wavy asked.

He raised an eyebrow. "Why? Do you have an appointment somewhere?"

She liked it when he teased her. It made her feel normal. "Maybe. Maybe I have all sorts of social engagements you don't know about."

Ian gave her a little laugh. "Okay, Miss Social Butterfly. I'll make sure you're at any social engagement you let me know about. As long as I can come too."

She nodded. "You can."

"Good." He stepped closer. "So, the field trip is on?"

"Can I paint?"

"Absolutely. As a matter of fact, I think you're going to find you want to paint even more."

Wavy looked down at her feet before looking back up at him. It was okay to ask this question she knew, but it was still hard. "Can I still sleep with you on the field trip?" That wasn't worth giving up. No matter where he took her, if she couldn't sleep in his arms, it wouldn't be worth it.

He walked over and tilted her head up with his thumb. "I wouldn't have it any other way."

A smile formed on her lips before she realized it was happening. It wasn't forced. It wasn't thought through. It was natural. His eyes widened and he inhaled. "There it is."

He bent down and kissed her. The softest, most feathery of kisses, like he wanted to catch her smile with his lips.

He leaned back, about to say something, but she wasn't done. She put her hands on his shoulders and pulled him closer, kissing him again, this one much more than soft.

He seemed happy to oblige her, his hands falling to her waist, keeping her tucked against him.

So they stood there in the kitchen and kissed and kissed and kissed, for she didn't know how long, like a couple of teenagers. Or like two people getting to know each other again.

They kissed until their lips were chapped and their stomachs were growling.

And it was everything she wanted and needed.

AN IAN DEROSE field trip was not to be missed.

Wavy didn't know what she'd thought they would do. Maybe stay at a nice hotel suite for a business meeting he needed to attend. Maybe fly to Asia—one of the Zodiac offices was in Singapore.

A yacht in the French Riviera was *not* what she'd been expecting. Moreover, seeing Ian so relaxed was even more unexpected. It was a big boat, bigger than anything she'd ever been on. Ian told her it wasn't his. He'd borrowed it from a friend.

"What kind of friend lends you a yacht this size?"

He grinned. "The kind who is a famous actor. We guarded him when a stalker tried to kill him."

He told her the name and her eyes grew big. "Wow."

"When I remembered the name of his yacht was *Rainbow Bright*, I took him up on his offer to borrow it anytime."

Ian's grin was bigger than she'd ever seen it. It had been that way the entire four days they'd been on the *Rainbow Bright*.

He was out on the deck, like he had been since they'd come onboard. He loved to be outside, no matter what the weather. She'd found him up there day and night, sunny weather and cloudy. Even when the waves were larger than she was comfortable with from a couple of storms they'd had.

At first, she'd thought it was because he really liked being out on the water. But as Wavy watched him now, itching to paint him once again, she realized it was because he was *outside*. No walls, no ceilings, nothing boxing him in.

Like he could *breathe*.

She stiffened. She had no idea how she'd missed it before. "You're claustrophobic."

Ian looked up at her from his laptop on the deck table where he was doing some work. "I am."

"Have you been that way your whole life?"

"No." He closed his computer. "That was the thing I mentioned that Dr. Rayne helped me with. I've had to learn how to adjust to my phobia."

"I remember in the cave you were . . . not nervous exactly, but tense."

"Yes." He nodded. "I'm uncomfortable in most enclosed spaces, and that's probably never going to go away. The elevator up to the penthouse is something I live through each time I use it. Cars aren't great for me either, but at least there are a lot of windows."

"Windows," she whispered, understanding more with each moment. "That's why you have so many of them in the penthouse."

He leaned back in his chair, pivoting so he was facing her. "It had the most windows I could find. And it's why I like spending so much time out on the patio."

"Will you tell me what happened?"

He came over to sit next to her where he'd been lounging and looking up at the stars. "I will, but I don't want to do anything that causes you undue stress. Right now, you have to focus on you. I don't want you to worry about me."

"Maybe it's time for me to start worrying about someone else *besides* me. Maybe that's what I need. Maybe I've been so focused on myself that I can't heal. And I know you. I know that if this is something you're still struggling with years later, that it must've been pretty bad."

He ran a hand through his hair. "I need you to know that this is not the Pain Olympics. What I went through, what you went through, it's . . ."

"It's not something that we compare. I get it."

He looped his arms around his knees, looking out at the glittering lights of France in the distance. "I guess I should lead with the worst. My brother, Grant, was the person who originally created Mosaic. He wasn't into human trafficking then, but he had a laundry list of other criminal activity—weapons sales, espionage, drugs."

"Oh." That's why he'd been sad about his brother. Not merely because of his death.

"My dad was into a lot of illegal activity, too, when I was growing up, so the apple didn't fall far from the tree. I joined the navy as soon as I could to get away from it all, and my family disowned me. Dad, at some point before he died, had a change of heart, went straight."

"That's good, right?"

He shrugged. "Yeah. Although I still wasn't interested in having anything to do with him. But I'm glad he at least tried to undo some of the damage he'd done over the course of a lifetIme."

Damage to Ian too, although she knew he wouldn't say it. "Did you get to see him before he died?"

"No, although maybe I should have. Instead of leaving his fortune to Grant as both Grant and I expected, Dad left it to me. Grant never quite got over that."

Ian laid down beside her so he was also looking up at the stars. "I was approached by a law enforcement agency back when I was still in the navy about taking my brother and his network down. I had the perfect alibi for joining their group. All I had to do was convince Grant that I wanted to get back into the family business. That I had seen how lucrative it could be based on what Dad had left me."

"You helped make a bunch of arrests, right?" That much Wavy knew.

"Yeah, but not before Grant found out I was working to take him down. He lost it. Me doing that, plus Dad leaving me the money . . . I'd underestimated how much he hated me." He fell silent.

"We don't have to talk about this if you don't want to." Not talking was definitely something she understood.

He took in a breath, and his words came out in a rush. "When Grant discovered I was working undercover against him, he locked me in a wooden casket—an old one like something out of the Wild West—and buried me alive."

Her entire body froze. This was so much worse than she'd thought. "How did you survive?"

Wavy reached over to take his hand, but froze midmovement, afraid that was the wrong thing to do. For the first time, she understood his hesitancy when he touched her, finally under-stood wanting to touch someone so badly to offer your support but knowing that your comfort might make things worse. This was about what *he* needed.

Her hand fell back to her side. "Did someone rescue you?"

"No, I wasn't rescued. I died."

She swallowed, bile burning in the back of her throat.

"Once I ran out of air, Grant dug me back up and had me resuscitated. After I was conscious and functional, he put me back in the box and buried me again."

"Oh God. How many times?" Damn it. Why had she asked that?

"Honestly, I'm not sure. My mind has kind of protected me from remembering it in too much detail. I remember certain things, my nails coming off because I scratched at the wood so hard. Trying to headbutt myself to unconsciousness one time, hoping I would die while I wasn't awake. But they all blend together. I think probably half a dozen."

He had *died* half a dozen times. Wavy had no words. How did someone come back from that?

"What I remember most was the overall feeling of helplessness. That's something Dr. Rayne and I worked on a lot—my claustrophobia is tied to it. All my training, all my strength . . . none of it was enough. No matter how hard I pushed on that wood, I couldn't do anything to save myself."

She put a hand over her mouth to hold back her sob.

"At some point, I realized there was a camera inside the coffin with me. That was how they knew when to dig me back up. The sick bastards wanted to watch."

"Your brother did this to you?" Given Wavy's relationship with her brothers, how protective they were of her, it was impossible to wrap her head around.

"Yes. Grant and his best friend, his second in command." Ian looked over at me. "Erick Huen."

Full circle. "You killed your brother. That's why Erick Huen hates you."

"Yes. I knew that I wasn't going to survive another time in that coffin, and when they resuscitated me, I came out fighting with whatever strength I had left. I knocked Erick unconscious and strangled Grant with my own hands. Erick came to, and he would have taken me out, but by then, my team had realized things had gone wrong and had breached the area."

She couldn't stop herself this time. She reached out and grabbed his hand, closing her eyes in thanks when he didn't shun her touch.

"Erick got away by jumping over a cliff. We thought he was dead. Obviously, he wasn't."

"You couldn't have known that."

They both stared up at the stars.

"So, I've spent the past two and a half years learning how to keep my panic under control," Ian finally said. "And believe me, it hasn't been easy, and it's taken a long time."

"You've taken something horrible and created strength from it." She knew she should be horrified at what had happened to him, but that was all that she could really see: he'd recreated himself into something better, something stronger because of what had happened to him.

He scooted a little closer to her. "Was telling you the wrong thing to do? I know it's a pretty gruesome tale."

"No. I'm so sorry for what happened, but . . ." Wavy hoped he would understand what she was trying to say—that it wouldn't seem like she was making light of it in any way. "You found strength in something terrible. I want to do that, but I'm afraid I'm never going to."

Ian wrapped an arm around her shoulders and pulled her so she was lying half on top of him. "You're already in the process of it. I can tell every time you put a new color into your paintings. You don't have to be a warrior in order to be strong. Quiet strength is the most enduring."

It was the most perfect thing he could've said, because someone with his strength recognizing it in her meant everything.

She wanted to make love to him right there out on this deck. She wanted to absorb more of his strength through her pores. She eased her leg over his hips until she was lying on top of him.

"Can you make sure that this deck is cleared and no one will come out here?" she whispered.

She wanted to make love with him there, in the open, in a place where he had no restrictions or fears pressing on the back of his mind. Where they could focus on being with each other.

He grabbed the walkie-talkie that was always nearby. "Tristan, can you see that we have complete privacy on the rear starboard deck? Including cameras."

"It would be my pleasure, boss."

She raised an eyebrow. "Is that Tristan Zimmerman?"

Ian nodded. "I needed at least one of my inner team on board, and we wanted someone you knew on the ship. He's been keeping a low profile."

In case she freaked out, he meant. But honestly, it was a fair concern. "I'm glad he's here. And I'm glad he's giving us some privacy."

Ian reached up and brushed the hair off of her face before cupping her cheek. "We don't have to do anything if you don't want to. And you can change your mind at any point for any reason. We can just kiss. Or lie out and watch the stars."

"Both. All." Wavy knew she was back to not using full sentences. She didn't want to talk, but not for her normal reasons. She wanted to be with him. Breathe him in. Feel his strength in every possible way.

She sat up, straddling him, and pulled her shirt over her head. She ought to be nervous, but the feel of him hard beneath her, the heat in his eyes as he watched her, chased away any fears before they could form.

This was Ian. This was her. There was no space for demons between them.

Wavy unbuttoned his shirt, trailing her nails across his chest as she eased the material to the side.

This time was different, and they both knew it. They'd made love almost every way a couple could. In the six weeks before she'd been taken, it had been the urgent passion of a new relationship: the discovery, the teasing and the delight, and all the pleasure. It had been wonderful, and she'd loved every second of it.

But this time was different. This time, they both knew what it was like to have almost lost each other. This time was with reverence and with the knowledge that no tomorrow was ever guaranteed.

This time, when she looked at his strong fingers as they slid from her hips up her back to her shoulders, she could imagine them bloody and torn where he'd scratched to get out of that casket. And she saw their strength now.

This time, they weren't taking anything for granted.

She eased herself off of him so she could remove the rest of her clothes, trusting him when he said that there was no one watching. It was just him and her and the open seas and the stars above them.

He unbuckled and unzipped his pants. They came back together, her lips crashing onto his, the feel of his naked skin against hers intoxicating.

"I want to be on top," she whispered.

He slid his arms under his head, a slow grin spreading across his handsome features. "Yes, please."

Normally, on top wasn't her favorite. She liked to have him over her, surrounding her with his strength, or behind her, his hand fisted in her hair.

But today, she wanted to be the one in control. He knew that and was more than happy to let her.

Wavy straddled his hips again, this time with nothing between them. Air hissed out of both of them as she lowered herself onto his length. His fingers gripped her hips, the force almost bruising, but she didn't care. She knew what it meant. He felt the same way she did. That they'd both been afraid that *this* would be lost forever, but it hadn't been.

She fell forward and braced her hands on Ian's chest as she took him all the way inside. And then she began to move. His brown eyes watched her, burning.

"I wanted you out here," she said. "I wanted you out in the open, the way you belong. I wanted to ride you while we couldn't feel anything against us except each other and the night air." Her voice sounded different to her ears.

The doctor had told her that she would always be a little hoarse given the damage she'd done to her vocal cords. But now that she had found her words, she couldn't seem to stop talking.

The fact that he jerked a little bit with everything she said made her want to talk all the more.

"You're the most beautiful thing I've ever seen," he said, thrusting up into her. "You've always been beautiful to me from the first time I saw you, but right now in this moment . . ."

Now he was the one who'd lost his words.

"Make me yours, Rainbow." His fingers gentled on her hips, stroking up and down as she leaned forward and ground herself against him in a pattern that had both of them breathing hard within seconds. She teased them both, loving the feeling of control. Easing backward to slow things down when either of them got too close. His laugh was as hoarse as hers. "You're very good at this."

She rose up on her knees so that he was almost all the way out of her, then slammed back down. He groaned, and she did it again. Like she'd been learning with her painting, she let the rhythm take her, let her body do what it wanted. Faster, then slower, than finally at a pace that left her burning with anticipation. She couldn't tell where she ended and Ian began.

"Help me," She whispered.

He knew exactly what she needed without having to ask. His fingers gripped her hips once again, and he set a pace for them that drove them both up and up.

"Yes." Her voice was hoarse, but not weak. "Yes, Ian."

Wavy's fingers scratched along his chest as the orgasm ripped through her. He pulled her down hard against him and ground up, calling out her name. She collapsed against his chest, and his arms came around her, both of them breathing hard.

Many things had been taken from Wavy during her captivity, things she might never get back.

But this wasn't one of them.

# CHAPTER
# THIRTY-ONE

IAN STARED up at the starry night as Wavy lay sleeping in his arms. He didn't think he'd ever been as thankful and reverent as he had been the past hour.

Not for the sex. He was thankful for that, too, and damned well reverent, but the closeness, the turns that she was taking, the healing she was doing. She couldn't see it in herself, but he could.

He'd been willing to give everything he owned to get her back, and then everything he owned once again to help her heal, but it ended up that Wavy could heal herself.

He was beyond honored that she was letting him stand beside her as she did it.

Bringing her out there had been the right thing to do. It had nothing to do with getting her to sleep with him—he'd been more than content with all the kissing they'd been doing the past few days.

But international waters meant nobody at Omega Sector, or any other law enforcement group they might try to involve, had jurisdiction to bring Wavy in for questioning.

He'd made Dr. Rayne aware of the situation, and she'd encouraged him to tell Wavy that Callum wanted to talk to her.

Dr. Rayne had also concurred that Wavy healing and remembering on her own time would be the best way to ensure she didn't have any further emotional fallout. That trumped everything as far as Ian was concerned, at least for now.

If he went back and remembered all the details about the worst hours of his life, what would it bring to light? He remembered the fear the first time he'd died—the knowledge that that was really *it*. He was going to die in that box at his brother's hand. The second time he only remembered how agonizing it had been to actually run out of air. The rest of it was a blessed blur, protection from his own mind.

All of Wavy's worst days were a blur, and if it stayed that way forever, maybe it was for the best. She didn't have to remember the agony she'd lived through that had caused her to rip at her own skin.

But fuck, Mosaic developing human weapons? That was scary as hell. Ian already had his team reexamining any and all data they'd acquired over the past few weeks with that angle in mind. There might be patterns they'd missed the first time because they hadn't known what to search for.

He was wide awake now but wanted to get Wavy inside before she got chilled, and because eventually the boat staff would need to get back on that area of the deck. He slipped on his pants, then wrapped her in his T-shirt before lifting her in his arms. She still hadn't gained back all the weight she'd lost in her captivity, but she was healthier than she had been.

She stayed asleep as he walked them both down to the master stateroom. It was only when he laid her on the bed that she murmured and reached for him, pouting in her sleep when he scooted away.

That brought a smile to his lips. Even though they hadn't been making love, they'd been sleeping together every night, and she had no idea how much that meant to him. How having her near had helped him get more rest than he'd had in weeks.

But right now, there was work to be done. It was time to get some of their rogue Zodiac agents on this Mosaic situation. Most of them were difficult to get ahold of, but they needed them. If Mosaic was creating killers, they needed to utilize the members of their team who thought most like them. The members of the team who struggled with the gray themselves.

He'd spent a couple hours sitting at the desk near the bed putting those plans into motion when Tristan interrupted on the walkie-talkie.

"Boss, come in."

Ian turned the volume down so it wouldn't wake Wavy. "Go ahead."

"We've got an incoming helicopter landing in ten. It's Sarge."

"Okay." Why was Sarge coming in on a helicopter? Anything he had to say to him he could do via phone or message.

"Sarge said you weren't going to like this, but it was the only way."

"I'm heading up to the landing pad." He pulled on the rest of his clothes and moved silently out the door. Hopefully, Wavy would sleep through all of this. He had a bad feeling about whatever it was Sarge had to say.

When he saw who was with him as they got off the chopper, Ian let out a curse. Callum Webb. He got on the walkie-talkie with Tristan.

"Under no circumstances is Callum Webb to take Wavy off of this ship, you got that?"

"What the fuck is Webb doing here?" Tristan responded.

"I'm about to find out, but I can tell you this. We're in international waters, and he has zero jurisdiction. He's not taking her."

"Roger that, boss. No worries. Sarge wouldn't want that."

He didn't know what the hell Sarge wanted. Or what he was thinking, bringing Callum here.

Ian nodded at both men, and they walked toward the conference room in silence—the rotors making too much noise to talk anyway. It wasn't until they were inside and the door was closed behind them that he turned to the two men.

He pointed at Sarge. "I'm going to assume that there is a reason why I don't need to fire you." His pointed finger turned to Callum. "And throw you overboard."

"He knows something about Bronwyn," Sarge said. "But he would only talk to you face-to-face."

Ian ran a hand through his hair. "Fine. You're here. Talk."

Callum sat down at the table. "We have Bronwyn Rourke in custody."

His eyes flew to Sarge.

"What?" he roared, standing.

He put a hand out to stop Sarge from jumping over the conference room table and beating the shit out of Callum, law enforcement officer or not.

"What are you doing, Webb?" he asked quietly.

"We have video footage of her breaking and entering and robbing a well-known crime family in New York a few weeks ago. She took out three guards and fought hand to hand with an unsub that showed up out of nowhere." Callum leaned back in his chair. "Now that I think about it, the unsub had your coloring and build, Sarge. Know anybody like that?"

Ian knew there had been more to Sarge's time in New York.

"You know there are other circumstances involved with that robbery," Sarge spit out. "Not to mention she wasn't stealing from the most upstanding people."

Callum shrugged. "I'm not saying she didn't do the world a favor. All I'm just saying is that she robbed someone, we have it on video, and she's in our custody."

He sat back in his seat. Callum wanted to play, they could play. "Charge her then, so I can send in my lawyers. You came a long way for what could've been said in a three-line email."

"What if we're not looking to charge her? What if I'm looking for a trade?"

"What the fuck are you talking about, Webb? You're wasting my time."

"I'll release Bronwyn into Sarge's custody for a chance to talk to Wavy."

Sarge didn't say anything, but his eyes shot to his. Ian knew how much he was willing to give to get Bronwyn off the streets and somewhere safe. He would pay damn near any price. But he wasn't the one who would have to pay this one. It would be Wavy.

"Goddammit," he said.

Callum slammed a hand down on the table. "Hell, DeRose, I'm not asking for a chance to interrogate her in a ten-by-ten room. I'm not going to fucking waterboard her. I just want to see if there's anything she remembers and ask for her help. That's not unreasonable."

Ian knew it wasn't unreasonable, but everything inside him said to protect her at all costs. He remembered what she'd looked like naked in that crate when they'd found her.

The three of them sat staring at each other for a long minute, and then there was a tap on the door. "May I come in?"

Wavy. *Shit.*

She stepped inside. "I tracked down Tristan, and he told me you were in here." She turned to Callum. "I've seen you before. You were at the hospital."

Callum nodded. "I was."

She turned to him. "The two of you were fighting."

"Yes," Ian said. "This is Callum Webb. He's an agent for Omega Sector, the law enforcement team I worked with to bring down Mosaic the first time."

"And you guys are working together to try to bring them down again?"

"Sort of," Callum answered, before he could tell him to shut the hell up.

Wavy was too damn smart for her own good. "You want to talk to me, don't you?"

Callum shrugged. "You are our only viable lead left, but . . . we haven't wanted to impede your recovery."

She crossed her arms over her chest and looked at Ian. "I'm going to take that to mean that Agent Webb has been asking to talk to me, and you've refused to let him, and this field trip was to keep me out of his reach. Is that right?"

He reached an arm out toward her. "Wavy."

She raised an eyebrow. "Did you or did you not bring me onto this yacht to get away from that man?" She pointed at Callum.

Ian wasn't going to lie to her. "Yes, I did, and I'm not going to apologize for it. Your mental and physical health are the most important things to me. You may or may not be able to help with his case, but I wasn't going to let you suffer in order to find that out."

"I'm getting stronger, you know that. Remembering stuff."

He stood up and walked over to her, tucking a strand of her hair behind her ear. "I know that. But you don't have to do this. We will find other ways."

"No." She shook her head. "Other ways might take too long."

She peeked around him at Callum. "I've been seeing stuff. I'm not sure if it's dreams or memories. I'm not sure what's real and what is just in my mind. But if I can help you, I will try to figure that out."

He had to hand it to Callum. He didn't look smug. He only looked grateful. "Thank you. I'm not sure what you know about the whole situation."

She looked embarrassed, and he wanted to stop this before it got started. "Not very much, I'm ashamed to admit. I've buried my head in the sand."

Callum's smile was gentle. "I don't blame you for staying away from it as much as you could."

She nodded. "Tell me what you know."

"Mosaic has developed new technology, a blend of chemicals

and genetic editing to control people. We thought it was for human trafficking. But it's more than that." He rubbed his forehead. "It looks like Mosaic is using their protocol not to turn people into more pliable sex slaves, but to develop a team of assassins and spies."

"Protocol. I remember that word. They used that on me. I remember being hooked up to medical equipment."

Ian's hand fisted. Wavy's voice was barely more than a whisper, and they hadn't gotten to the hard part. She turned to look at him.

"What if I'm an assassin? What if they did something to me to—"

"You're not," he told her. "Your body rejected the treatment they tried to give you. It's one of the things we found out about when the Linear guys cracked the computer drive. It can't be used on everyone."

"How do you know I rejected it?"

"The pain, Rainbow. That's why you don't remember much. Your brain has blocked out the pain." Now it was Ian's voice that was hoarse. "When we found you, we thought you'd been tortured. You had scratches and bruises all over your body."

She sat down in the chair beside him, staring straight ahead at something no one else could see. "I did it to myself. To try to stop the fire burning me inside. It was boiling me alive."

Ian turned to Callum with a glare. This was why he'd kept him from her. Because all they were doing was causing her pain without getting any usable intel. "Yes. We didn't find that out until you were in the hospital and the doctors saw what shape your fingernails were in. The scratches, you'd done to yourself. But the people who'd held you had driven you to it. They could've stopped the pain at any time."

Finally, she dragged herself back into the room. She looked at Callum, taking a steadying breath. "Does this help you? I would think you need other info."

"You don't have to do this, Wavy," he said.

She shook her head. "I do. I do have to do this if I ever want to move on with my life."

He offered her his hand. Thank God she took it.

"Ask me what you want to know," she said to Callum.

"We know you were held in at least three places. The first was a lab where Ian found the small painting that had Dr. Tippens's blood on it. Tippens told Ian about the warehouse where you were found. But there was a second lab. That's the one we don't have any info on, the one we need to find."

"Dr. Tippens," she whispered.

"Do you remember him at all?" Ian leaned closer.

She blinked at him. "He was working for Erick Huen, the man I thought was Louis Noeya. I was dizzy and sick . . . in a hospital bed. He and Erick were talking. They knew you were coming so they wanted to move—oh God."

"What, Rainbow? It's okay. You're safe now." Her grip on his hand was like iron, and he covered their hands with his other one. "They knew we were coming so they wanted to move you? Is that what you were going to say?"

"*Us*," she croaked out. "They wanted to move *us*. There were dozens of people in beds like mine. One of them was a girl, a teenager named Janice."

"WE NEED TO TRY AGAIN. And this time don't stop me if I get a nosebleed."

They'd set up the guest bedroom at the penthouse as an office for Dr. Rayne and Wavy to use for their sessions. She'd made Ian bring her home immediately, because how could she stay out in the middle of the Mediterranean on a yacht when she'd left people behind in hell? People she'd *forgotten*. People she might be able to help.

*Janice.*

Dr. Rayne had worked with her for hours in the five days since they'd been back in Denver, trying every method of therapy and counseling she was comfortable with, and a few she wasn't, to help Wavy remember more. Sometimes, it felt like she was making progress, actually remembering stuff, especially when it came to the teenage girl.

Helping find her had become Wavy's number one priority.

Talking about Janice seemed to ground her the most, maybe because she was what Wavy felt most guilty about. How could she have forgotten about her for weeks? Who knew what had happened to her in the time since she'd been gone? She'd been coddled and catered to by everyone . . . and she'd been trapped in hell.

Her hands clenched into fists.

"Getting frustrated to the point of a setback isn't going to help," Dr. Rayne said. "I know you want to do what you can for the people who are trapped, but we're not going to lose you in the process."

"I don't understand why sometimes it's so hard to remember and sometimes it's so easy." Wavy took the tissue she offered, knowing it meant there was blood about to drip from her nose again.

This had been one of the hard sessions. They'd been trying hypnosis, not either of their favorites. Every time they tried it, Wavy ended up with terrible headaches and nosebleeds. But then again, she ended up with terrible headaches half the time they were talking anyway.

They were trying to pinpoint any information she might have in her subconscious about the unknown second location. Ian had found her in a warehouse, but she'd been pretty much left there to die. They also knew about the first lab. But where had Mosaic kept her in between?

She'd remembered part of a conversation between Dr. Tippens and Erick Huen, them arguing about where to move them. She'd remembered scratching Dr. Tippens in the hopes his blood on the canvas would provide Ian with a clue.

It was all a lot foggier after that, since that's when they'd started the protocol on her. Once that happened, merely staying alive had been hard enough. No memories were clear from that point on.

If Wavy's mind was to be trusted, she'd been on a plane twice. She'd been consistent in that memory, no matter which method Dr. Rayne had used to get the information. So they were trusting it as the truth.

She also remembered fans and being hot. She remembered

windows that had been cracked open, which Ian agreed told them quite a bit about the location. Hot in September with fans and windows open meant that they'd been somewhere isolated, but tropical. The flights suggested an island. It would make sense, given the human experimentation. The Zodiac Tactical team and Callum Webb—finally working together—were investigating ties Dr. Tippens had had with any possible location that fit those parameters.

She'd tried to describe the people she saw while she was held, but that was all fuzzy to her too, except for Janice. Her face, Wavy could see more clearly in her mind—freckles, big, terrified eyes. But anybody else, it was nosebleeds and headaches.

"It's understandable," Dr. Rayne said. "You want to help Janice most of all. So your brain has focused on her."

She would have stayed and worked with Dr. Rayne every hour of every day, but she wouldn't allow it. She said Wavy had to let her brain rest. As if letting her brain rest was going to help those trapped people. Ian concurred with her and was waiting at the door as they finished every session.

She was exhausted, maybe pushing too hard. But what choice did she have, really? Even when she painted, it was hard on her body. Just like with the talking, sometimes it was fine—no pain, no stress. But sometimes her painting brought on the nosebleeds and the headaches too.

"Let's go again." Wavy could do one more hypnosis session.

"Nope, we're done for today."

"Rayne, come on. It's only midafternoon."

She shook her head. "You've had enough. Two separate nosebleeds. We'll try again tomorrow."

She started to argue, but she held out a hand to stop her. "The more you force this, the longer it's going to take. Unfortunately, you don't get to control what causes you pain. All you can do is manage it wisely. So, no painting either if it's going to cause your brain to hemorrhage out your nose."

Wavy let out a groan. "Thanks for that visual."

The doctor took off her glasses and reached across the table to grab her hand. "I've seen your nose bleeding and you flinching in pain more often than not in the past week. We're walking a fine line. Your brain can only take so much before it shuts down. And if you're in a coma, you're no good to anybody. Not to mention, Ian will kick my ass."

As if Ian would ever raise a finger to hurt the five-foot-nothing doctor.

"Fine, then I'll go bother him in his office." She stood up, aware she sounded like a petulant four-year-old.

Dr. Rayne smiled. "Good, he needs a break too. It's hard on the big, alpha males when all they can do is stand by and watch the women they love suffer."

"*What?*"

"He'd rather take on the pain him—"

Wavy plopped back down in the chair. "No, I mean the *love* part. Ian and I don't love each other."

"If you say so." Rayne stared at her, head tilted, like she was not terribly bright.

She didn't feel terribly bright. "Why do *you* say so?"

"Ian DeRose would move heaven and earth to give you what you need."

"He feels guilty about—"

She held out a hand to stop her. "Let me ask you a question. Do you love him?"

"Yes." The word was out of her mouth before she could stop it. Yes, Wavy did love Ian. She was in love with the man and his strength, his courage, his utter tenacity when it came to doing what he thought was right.

"And if someone said your feelings were transference—hero worship, that you love him because he was the one who rescued you, what would you say?"

"I would say that's not true. That's not even part of what my feelings for him are. If someone else had rescued me from Mosaic, I would still love Ian just as much."

Dr. Rayne smiled. "Good. Then don't allow his feelings to be trivialized with talk of guilt either. He does feel guilty. He will always feel guilty about what happened to you. But his feelings for you are both separate and more than that."

"We haven't talked about love."

She reached for her hand. "You've had a lot of other things that needed to be talked about. To quote a brilliant psychiatrist, 'The words will come when they come.' "

Wavy smiled at her. "I hope to meet this brilliant psychiatrist someday."

She laughed and shooed her out with her hands. "Get out of here."

She took the elevator down to Ian's office, waving to his assistants as she walked by. They'd been given strict instructions to let her in, regardless of what he was doing. Wavy knew she was probably the only one in the world who had that privilege, and she didn't take it lightly.

After her conversation with Rayne, she wanted to see him. Wanted to wrap her arms around him. Maybe they weren't ready to use any love words, but they both needed the connection they had to each other.

She didn't expect to hear the conversation she heard as she approached the cracked door to his office.

"Please, Ian, let me talk to her. That's all I'm asking."

Damn it, it was the same tone Callum Webb had used on the yacht last week. Wavy stopped.

"François, I know that I was the one who contacted your office in the first pl—"

"Yes, you were," François said, interrupting Ian without any qualms. There weren't a lot of people who did that. "And I'm so glad you did. Please, let me talk to her. If she says no, she says no, but please."

Enough. Ian was obviously trying to protect her once again. If law enforcement needed more help, then she needed to suck it up and make that happen. Wavy pushed the door open. "Let you talk to me about what?"

Both men stood as she entered. "Rainbow . . ."

She turned to François. "Are you another cop?"

The man scoffed. "Do I look like I'm a cop?"

No. He very definitely didn't. He was in his fifties, hair styled neatly and dressed in a suit that probably cost more than she made in a month at the diner. "No, but otherwise, why do you want to talk to me?"

He gave her a charming grin. "I wanted to talk to you about getting more of your paintings and including them in an exhibit showcasing new artists I'm putting on next week."

That was not what Wavy had been expecting. "How do you know I'm an artist at all?"

"Darling Ian"—he gestured in Ian's direction—"sent a couple of your paintings to my office several weeks ago now. It took a while for them to make it to my desk. Then I have spent the past three weeks trying to get in touch with him, but he hasn't returned my calls. So, finally, I came out here myself."

She looked over at Ian, who gave her an apologetic shrug.

"I'm not sure why Ian has had such an about-face from when he sent your work," François continued. "Perhaps you've already accepted other representation?"

"No, I think Darling Ian is a little skeptical since the last person who wanted to look at my artwork tried to kill me."

François crossed his arms over his chest. "Sounds like any given Tuesday in the art world, although usually it's one agent wanting to kill another. I can assure you that that is not my plan. I would like to instead make us both very rich."

"You're already rich, François," Ian muttered under his breath.

"Fine, then I would like to make her rich and me richer."

"You're François Nester," she said. "Holy hell."

Anyone who'd ever had anything to do with art had heard of him. He had blasted careers from obscurity to fame overnight.

He smiled and extended his hand. When she took it, he raised her hand to his lips. "I am. And you, Darling Ian's darling, are about to become a household name in the art world."

"I CAN'T BELIEVE you had François Nester in your office. You know he's a legend, right? That he's famous for procuring new artists for the stars?"

Wavy was lying in bed naked with Ian, trying to wrap her head around the fact that François Nester wanted to display *her* work at *his* show.

Not only that, he'd been adamant her work would be a success and people would want to buy her paintings. He'd taken it as a personal affront to his reputation when she'd questioned that.

"I meet a lot of interesting people in my line of work, although François is admittedly one of the most memorable."

"Why do you say that, Darling Ian?"

He chuckled. "Honestly, I had forgotten I'd sent your work to his office. I wasn't actually trying to get it in front of him, just one of his associates. If it didn't go anywhere, then no harm. It was . . ." he trailed off.

"What?"

His arms tightened around her. "I sent the paintings a couple of days before you were taken. If I had mentioned it to you, you wouldn't have gone to that meeting with Erick. You wouldn't have been taken."

"But we're going to end up rescuing a lot of people because I was taken, so let's focus on that."

He reached over and kissed her as if they hadn't spent the past two hours driving each other crazy in this bed. "Rayne says you're pushing too hard."

Wavy rolled her eyes. "I'll rest once we get those people home safe and out of Mosaic's clutches."

She was missing something. She knew it, but she couldn't put her finger on it. It had come to her after she'd left Ian's office today. She'd been overwhelmed by everything—the conversation with Rayne, the conversation with François . . .

She didn't want to get so caught up with all the great things happening in her life that she lost the urge to help Janice. To help the others.

Wavy wasn't sure why some memories came so easily and why some didn't, but it was the key to what was happening.

Ian tucked her closer to him. "Hey, superhero girl. How about you go for twenty-four whole hours without a nosebleed, and then we can start pushing hard again?"

A nosebleed was nothing compared to what some of those people might be going through. But for right now, she would rest. "How about we sit here and think about what's going to happen when François meets Finn? I would give a lot of money to see that play out."

Ian laughed, the sound always beautiful. "Oh, me too. Although François will bring a ton of assistants with him to Oak Creek. So even if Finn had the entire Linear Tactical crew, I'm not sure they'd be a match for François and his gang."

She couldn't help the giggle that escaped her. François was so petite and flamboyant and Finn was so big and brawny. "I'd love to see them in a room together."

"God, that sound. It fills every dream I have. The best ones, at least."

"What sound?" she asked.

"Your laugh. I love it, Wavy. I love *you*, Rainbow."

She sat up so she could see his face more clearly. "Did you talk to Dr. Rayne?"

"About your nosebleed, yes. She said you needed to rest."

"About anything else?"

His eyes narrowed. "No. Why? Did something else happen? Are you okay? Damn it, I don't care what law enforcement needs. If you're hurting yourself to rememb—"

Wavy leaned over and kissed him. Rayne hadn't told him what they'd talked about. And Ian was more concerned about her health than that she hadn't declared her love in return.

*The words will come when they come.*

It was time for them to come from her. She leaned her forehead against his. "I don't know what I remember of being kidnapped is true and what isn't. But I very distinctly remember thinking that this couldn't be the end for me because I hadn't let you know how important you were, how I've loved every second I've spent with you. I love you, Ian DeRose."

He kissed her until they were both breathless, then eased back.

"I'm not going to let anything happen to you, Rainbow. And if that means keeping you safe from yourself, then I'm going to do it. Tomorrow, you get a day off from Dr. Rayne."

"Fine. One day off," she said. "But you have to promise that if anybody else wants to talk to me, you'll let them. No more running interference. Completely open with each other, right?"

"Agreed. Although, in my defense, I wouldn't have kept François from you. I didn't know if it was the right time given, like you said, the last art representative who contacted you tried to kill you."

"Fair enough."

He tucked her against him, and a few minutes later, his breathing evened out. He was tired, and she was glad he was getting rest.

Wavy was still too keyed up to sleep. She couldn't wait to see what pieces François chose for the art show. She was keyed up just thinking about it. After an hour of lying there, she decided to get out of bed so she wouldn't wake Ian.

She wanted to paint. More than that, she wanted to use *colors*.

This time, she wouldn't take them for granted. She knew that they could be taken from her at any time. That made them all the more precious.

She walked into the room they'd made into her studio and laid a barrage of colors out in front of her as well as a large canvas. She started with blues, then added purples a little bit later.

But her subconscious seemed to have other plans. It wasn't long before her color choice and brush strokes came from a place deep inside. She wasn't choosing any of it anymore. The painting was guiding her, rather than her creating it.

Wavy felt the pain start, the same headaches that sometimes happened, but she ignored it and kept painting. The colors were coming faster than had ever happened before.

She filled an entire canvas in record time, then pulled out a second one without stopping. She *couldn't* stop. Her head throbbed, and she almost couldn't see the colors in front of her.

Everything became muddled, but she kept painting, kept putting the paint on the canvas as the wildness demanded.

She couldn't stop.

She didn't know how to stop.

She kept going—stroke after stroke, color after color.

Even when her arms screamed from overuse and her mind spun with agony, she couldn't stop the frenzy.

A hand gripped her wrist. "Wavy, enough."

She pulled away from Ian to try to continue with the painting. It wasn't done. She had to keep going.

He lowered her arm to her side, and she let out a sob, fighting him. She had to keep going.

"Wavy. Look at me."

She spun toward him. "What?" She snarled.

"Put the brush down," he said.

"No, I need to—"

"Now, Wavy. Put it down."

She did, allowing it to drop to the ground. And with it, whatever had controlled her eased, draining from her. As did every bit of energy she had.

Ian caught her as she collapsed and lifted her in his arms, carrying her into the bathroom. She caught a glimpse of herself in the mirror.

There was blood dripping all down her face. It had soaked the front of her shirt. His shirt, the one she slept in.

"What? I don't understand. I've only been painting for a few minutes."

"You've been in there for hours, Wavy. I just woke up and came in. You have four completed canvases that weren't in there when I went to sleep."

"That's impossible. I couldn't do that in one session. I don't remember any of them."

He set her down on the counter. "You were in some sort of trance. I've never seen you like that."

He was worried. She could see it in his brown eyes, "I'm sorry," she whispered, "I didn't mean to—"

"I know." He wet a washcloth and stroked it down her chin and under her nose. "You weren't doing it on purpose, but I think this is your brain saying that you've been pushing too hard. A final warning. You have to rest."

"Okay, I will. I'm sorry. I'm sorry." She hated the look of fear on his strong face.

"Rainbow. It's okay." He cupped her cheek and kissed her. "We'll rest together."

# CHAPTER
# THIRTY-FOUR

NEARLY EVERY HAND here at François's makeshift art show held a glass of champagne. The glass in his held sparkling water. Ian was not taking a chance on even a sip of alcohol dulling his senses tonight.

It was Wavy's debut in the art world, and he wanted everything to go perfectly. But mostly he wanted her to be safe.

Roughly every third person roaming around was a member of Ian's security team or knew Wavy through Linear Tactical. They were needed.

François had worked his magic. He'd created the kind of buzz about this show, and Wavy's work in particular, a debut artist would normally only dream of having. Unfortunately, that buzz had included splashing Wavy's identity all over the press.

François had cried actual tears when he'd told him that the only way she was going to be at the show in person was to hold it there in Denver, in the Zodiac Tactical building, rather than in Los Angeles as originally planned. But the man was no dummy. He knew what he had in Wavy's art. He would have had the show in Timbuktu if it had meant being the exclusive dealer who exposed her to the world.

There had been places in LA that they could have secured,

but he didn't want it to be just secure. Ian wanted Wavy to feel comfortable so she could enjoy the evening. What better place than the building she'd been living in for weeks?

They took half of the lobby-level offices and turned them into a space François was happy with.

Making François Nester happy wasn't the easiest thing in the world. But all the work and money had been worth it to see Wavy beaming now. She stood beside François, who was introducing her to some bigwig or another.

You didn't have to know anything about art to know that her work was a success. Everybody in here was talking about it. Buzz, indeed.

Ian watched her from a discreet distance, wanting to give her all the opportunity to chat with what would certainly be future owners of her work. This was her night.

His job was to never let her out of his sight, which wasn't a problem. He'd barely let her out of his sight for a second since she'd scared the hell out of him last week with that painting trance.

He'd lost ten years off his life when he'd walked into that studio and found blood running down her face and soaking her T-shirt. It had taken five minutes of trying to talk to her before she'd realized he was in the room with her. And then he'd thought she was going to deck him when he tried to take the paintbrush from her.

She hadn't been asleep, but she hadn't really been awake either. Definitely hadn't been aware of what was happening.

Once Ian had gotten her away from the easel, cleaned her up, and put her in bed, she'd slept for fourteen hours straight. But fitful sleep, her hands attempting to paint even while she was unconscious. When her fingers worked at all. She'd held the paint brushes for so long, her fingers had cramped, and he'd had to massage them.

He'd called Rayne immediately, afraid Wavy had had some sort of mental snap. Rayne had admitted what he'd already known. They'd been pushing too hard. Wavy was on some sort of mission to remember everything she could about what had happened, which was great, but it couldn't be at the price of her own health.

They'd agreed to encourage her to focus only on things that didn't cause her pain, things that didn't cause a headache or a nosebleed. Whatever those were, her brain obviously wasn't ready to process them.

They'd even gotten François in on helping them. Ian had explained some of the situation and, having lived through a violent situation himself, convinced Wavy to help him select her works for the show—both of them going through the paintings in her loft she hadn't destroyed.

And while Wavy had obviously seen their ploy for what it was, she'd still agreed. The night of trance painting had scared her too.

Four full canvases in a few hours. That should have been impossible, especially with the level of detail in them. They were incredible. When François had seen them, he'd immediately wanted them in the show, and she'd agreed.

But the first thing Ian had done was make sure François knew he was purchasing them. He could charge him whatever he wanted, but those paintings weren't going home with anyone else. They were the first time since her abduction she'd embraced the use of color, and Ian wanted that memory in his possession— in *their* possession, because he planned to be wherever Wavy was for the next fifty years or so—forever.

He glanced at them now, featured prominently on the south wall, still as entranced as he'd been since the first time he'd seen them. They were, by far, the greatest things Wavy had ever created. If this was a sign of where her art was going, she'd not only be a known name in the art world, she'd be a known name in the world, period.

Ian could only hope future works didn't come at the terrible price she'd paid for these.

Landon came over to talk with him, a striking image in his suit. "Those are pretty damn impressive."

"Awe-inspiring. There's something almost familiar about them." That was the other reason he wanted them, not that it made any sense. The paintings were just vivid colors over other vivid colors, no rhyme or reason to them.

"Maybe it's the Wavy in them that feels familiar to you."

He nodded. "I always feel that way about anything she's painted, like I'm connected to it in some way, but this is different. It's like it's drawing on a piece of me I'm not sure I'm still in touch with."

He took a sip of his non-champagne champagne. "I'd like to say something profound here, but I'm not sure what that means."

Ian chuckled. "Me either."

They both turned toward Wavy. "She seems comfortable, enjoying herself. I'm glad to see it. And I'd say she looks gorgeous too if it wouldn't get my ass kicked."

"I won't kick your ass for stating the truth. And she does look relaxed. She deserves it more than anybody. Any security problems?"

"Nope, quiet on every possible channel. We've got doubled-up guards everywhere and half the waiters are our people. I've got men on the roof and men on the roofs next to our roofs. Nobody is getting in here."

Ian believed it but still kept on high alert. The event was invitation only, and every person attending had been thoroughly vetted and matched with their photo ID as they arrived. Holding the show in their building meant they knew all the vendors and were more familiar with the details than even François.

All of his men would take a bullet for Wavy, and all of her Linear Tactical family would do the same. Nobody was getting to her. Not tonight.

Her smile was back. Her colors were back.

Tonight, she got to enjoy that.

# CHAPTER
# THIRTY-FIVE

"IT WAS AMAZING. It was amazing, right?" Wavy's voice was high and excited as she slipped out of the black dress she'd been wearing.

She obviously didn't understand what seeing her standing there in only stockings, garters, bra, panties, and heels did to him, but Ian forced himself not to throw her on the bed like he wanted. The drooling, on the other hand, he couldn't stop.

"It was amazing," he said. "You were amazing."

She spun around, that huge grin still on her face. "The show *sold out*. I thought maybe you or François were pulling some strings, but he swore on his mother's grave that it was all legit." She pointed at him. "Is that true?"

Ian held up a hand. "Scout's honor. I had nothing to do with any sales, except for the four that I bought before the show started."

He couldn't believe the price François had charged him, but he swore, again on his mother's grave, that it was the price he'd been able to get for all of her paintings. At this rate, Wavy very definitely would never have to work as a waitress again.

He walked over to her and hooked an arm around her waist.

"When you're super famous, promise me you'll still take me out on yachts and have your way with me."

She wrapped her arms around his neck, her grin turning into something very feminine and beautiful. "I will have my way with you on every yacht and every other possible surface for as long as you'll have me."

"That's going to be a very long time. Quite a lot of surfaces." he slid his arms down and hooked them under her hips, lifting her so they were face-to-face.

"Oh, I hope so," she said, bringing her lips against his.

He carried her toward the bed. "Can I talk you into wearing this all the time around the house?"

She chuckled against his mouth. "*Around the house*. I like that."

She was so happy, so relaxed and comfortable. It was all he could do not to let out a curse when his phone chimed. It was Landon, given the ring tone. He wouldn't be calling unless it was something important.

Ian lowered Wavy down to the bed, sliding his hand down her thigh. "Hold that thought and that position," he said with a wink before grabbing his phone from the nightstand.

He called him, not wanting to take time to text. "What's going on?"

"We need you down here."

He stiffened. "What happened?"

"We got another video from Erick Huen. He mentions Wavy by name, Ian."

"Fuck. I'm on my way."

Wavy was staring at him now, sitting up. She knew something was wrong. "What is it?"

"Don't worry about it. I'll handle it and then be back up when I can."

Her eyes narrowed. "Is it something Zodiac Tactical–related or is it something related to Mosaic?"

Damn it. He wanted to shelter her from this, didn't want her to have to carry it, especially tonight. "We received a video from Erick Huen."

"Then I'm coming with you." She was already moving off the bed.

"You don't have to do that."

"No more secrets, remember? We work this out together."

Ian nodded. She was right. Loving her meant loving her enough to let her do the hard things when she needed to, even when he wanted to shelter her from them. "Okay, let's go."

They were dressed and down in the office less than ten minutes later. Landon was there as well as Isaac. Sarge was still MIA with Bronwyn. He hadn't seen him since Callum had traded her to Sarge for talking to Wavy.

Landon nodded at them as they came in the door. "I've got Callum on video call. He's already seen the footage once. I've also got the tech team standing by. They're running everything they can on it."

"Good." Ian led Wavy to a seat at the conference table next to him, then turned back to the screen. "Thanks for being here so late, everyone."

"Are you sure Wavy should be in here for this?" Callum asked.

"Wavy can speak for herself." He grabbed her hand. "And if she wants to be here, then yes, she gets to be here. This involves her as much as any of us. More."

Landon sat back down at the table across from them, next to Isaac. He smiled gently at Wavy. "I don't disagree, but I want to warn you that it's pretty brutal. It's Erick Huen being his asshole worst on it."

"Totally up to you, Rainbow." If she wanted to leave, that was understandable. Nobody would judge, and definitely no one would think any less of her.

"I'll be okay," she whispered, but her hand trembled in his.

He nodded at Landon to start the footage. As soon as Erick's face came on the screen, Wavy went ramrod straight.

This was probably the first time she'd seen him since her captivity.

Ian held a hand up and Landon stopped the footage right away. He leaned over so that only Wavy could hear him. "Hey, not too late to change your mind. You can go upstairs, and we can take this a piece at a time later."

She shook her head. "I'm all right."

She didn't look all right, but he nodded at Landon to continue.

Erick was leaning back in an office chair, arms crossed over his thin chest. He looked smug.

"I'm sad that I wasn't invited to Wavy's art show," he said. Ian wanted to rip his throat out of his body. "I'm glad she's doing so well. The last time I saw her, she didn't seem quite as lively. I'll admit I've missed having her around. Maybe you'll let me borrow her sometime, Ian? I'm sure we could work out some sort of a deal."

He would torture him slowly before he killed him.

"Come on," Erick continued. "*Mano y mano.*"

"Ian," Wavy whispered. He held out a hand for Landon to stop the footage again. "I remember something. I remember something. I need to draw. Please."

Isaac rushed out of his chair and grabbed her some paper and a pencil.

"Do you want us to wait?" He asked her.

She shook her head, pencil already racing across the paper. "No, go ahead."

He watched her for a few more seconds. This didn't seem like the painting the other night, which had hurt her. Now her expression was almost peaceful. Her hand flew over the paper, but there was no nosebleed.

He nodded at Landon to continue.

"Your woman has such a beautiful scream, Ian. Sometimes I watch the video footage just so I can hear it."

Ian's hands clenched into fists. That fucking bastard was going to die.

"Of course, you had a nice scream. I have that footage too. Maybe we should run a comparison."

Everyone was looking at him, but he didn't give a shit what Erick said about him. It was Wavy he didn't want upset. But it was like she wasn't listening to what Erick was saying now.

Good. Let the fucker monologue. Ian was glad she wasn't paying him any mind.

"You want to kill me right now, don't you, Ian? Like you killed Grant. It must be frustrating how I've been hiding from you. Don't worry, I'm not going to be hiding for much longer. I'll see you soon, Ian. You too, Wavy."

He waved his fingers, bye-bye, taunting them like the petulant child he was.

She was still drawing as he asked Landon, "Is that it?"

"Yep."

He would watch it again, but not right now. Not in front of Wavy in case she did decide to pay Erick any attention.

"What was the purpose of this?" Ian asked no one in particular.

"He's trying to provoke you is our best guess," Callum responded.

Landon leaned back in his chair. "Erick has never been terribly stable, boss. He doesn't like that Wavy had an art show and that you guys are getting back to a normal life. He's trying to shake things up."

That sounded right. "Let's use his own arrogance against him. What can we find out from the video itself?"

"Jenna and the rest of the tech team are checking for ambient noise," Isaac said. "There was a little bit, but we don't have anything definitive yet. We'll see if it matches any island."

"That's daylight behind his window," Callum pointed out. "But I'm not sure that helps us at all."

"It tells us he made the video before the actual art show

unless he sent it from fucking Australia. Why would he wait until nearly midnight to send it?"

"I think he's still messing with you like Landon said." Isaac leaned forward in his chair. "He waited until you were settled in for the night, then sent it."

"Or maybe he had something planned for earlier and it didn't go the way—"

Ian stopped midsentence as Wavy touched his arm. "Ian, this place, this is the place. I don't know why I remembered it now. Something in Erick's voice. I've been here. I'm absolutely positive."

There was no way anybody could doubt the sincerity in her voice, and there was no sign of any trauma or nosebleeds or pain. Maybe like Rayne had been saying all along, her mind would tell her when it was ready.

And evidently hearing Erick Huen's voice again was what it had needed to be ready.

The fact that he might be instrumental in his own downfall made this all the more poetic.

He looked at the drawing, then held it up so everyone else could see.

The drawing was exceptionally detailed, and much of the architecture of the building she'd drawn was quite unique.

"That looks like a church," Landon said.

Everyone else agreed.

"A church building converted into a lab, that could work," Cullum said. "Scan that over, and I'll get our systems on it as well."

Wavy stared at the picture.

"This is it?" He asked her again. "You think you were held in this building?"

"I think so. I remember a cold floor and this stone . . . it could definitely be this stone."

That was enough for him, given that and the other things

she'd remembered with Dr. Rayne's sessions. Sunny, the sound of a bird, perhaps seagulls.

"We need to concentrate on the islands off the California coast," he said. "You were taken to San Diego in that warehouse, left there to die." His throat constricted as he said the words, but they were true. "If you were on an island off the coast of San Diego, that would make sense."

She stared at the picture again. "I'm sorry I'm not more help, but this image, I can't explain it. I had to draw it. It's definitely something I know."

He grabbed her hand. "Your mind was ready to remember. That's enough for us." He was glad it hadn't caused her any pain to come up with it.

Landon had already scanned it and sent it to the tech team. They watched the video again. This time, Wavy flinched as Erick spoke.

"I think I'll go upstairs," she finally said as they looked at it once more. "I don't want to see or hear him anymore."

"Okay, I'll come with you."

She shook her head. "No, you need to stay down here. I'll be fine. You know how secure this building is."

Ian stood up anyway. "There's absolutely no way in hell I'm allowing you to go upstairs by yourself. You're not going anywhere by yourself."

She smiled, relief evident.

He cupped her cheeks as they stopped by the door. "Hey, this total honesty thing goes both ways. If you're feeling nervous, even if it seems like you shouldn't be, you tell me. That's how it works. We don't keep things from each other."

"You're right." She leaned her forehead against his. "I'm sorry."

"Come on, let's get you up to bed. Try not to let this thing ruin your big night." As soon as he said it, he knew that was true. "That's probably what Erick was trying to do. Steal your night. Don't let him, Rainbow."

She straightened in front of him. "I'm not going to let him take anything else of mine."

"That's my girl." He kissed her. He didn't care if anyone else was around. Then he wrapped an arm around her and led her toward the elevator.

"Holy shit!" Landon yelled and they both stopped. "Tech team has a match, like a goddamn literal match for what Wavy drew. You're right. It's a private island off the coast of San Diego."

She looked at him, eyes wide. He cupped her cheeks and kissed her again. "Looks like you just turned Erick's plan against him."

# CHAPTER THIRTY-SIX

THEY DIDN'T WAIT. As soon as they confirmed the location of the building Wavy had drawn, they put plans into motion. They were making their move tonight.

Normally, Ian would have waited. He would have gathered intel to amass every possible tactical advantage he could get. But now, he had to balance those potential advantages with the element of surprise.

And that Ian really, *really* wanted to take that fucker down.

Erick Huen thought he was untouchable. They were about to show him otherwise.

He'd been prepared to fight Callum, thinking he'd want to send in his own law enforcement team. But he'd surprised Ian by only insisting he come with his team unofficially. That was good because he was not waiting for official channels to move on this. They also got Finn Bollinger onto their six-man team, mostly because he knew Finn wanted to kill Erick as much as he did. If for some reason Erick slipped past Ian, Finn would be there to stop him.

The only person he'd been unsure about for their team had been himself. He hadn't wanted to leave Wavy, not even to finish this.

If she'd asked him to stay, he would have. There was nothing he wouldn't give her if she asked, but she hadn't. She'd been remarkably calm, sitting with her feet tucked under her on the couch in a robe as he'd explained the plan.

"It's a private island, which works well for us." Ian pulled on the formfitting black shirt that would go under his tactical gear. "Fewer civilians, less chance for casualties."

"Kings Fork Island," she murmured.

He glanced over to see if the name of the island caused her stress, but she seemed okay. "Yes, there's a church that matches what you drew. We couldn't have asked for something more affirmative."

She nodded. "That's it. I know it is. You have to rescue Janice."

Landon had agreed to stay behind with Wavy. He knew he hadn't done it lightly. He might be one of the most charming members of the Zodiac team, but he was deadly in the field. Besides himself and maybe Sarge, there was no one else Ian would trust with Wavy's safety. If Mosaic got word they were coming and tried to turn the tables, he would get Wavy to safety.

Ian didn't leave until he was up in the penthouse, armed and ready. Then he kissed Wavy softly on the lips. "I love you."

For the first time her facade cracked. "Ian? I-I . . . love you too."

"I'll be home soon, and this will be over."

That must've reassured her enough. She walked into the bedroom without another word.

He rubbed the back of his neck. This must be harder on her than she was letting on, and she'd been keeping it together for him. They both needed this to be *finished*.

He turned to Landon. "Try to keep her away from her paints, or make sure it's not a nosebleed session if she does want them."

Landon held his hand out for him to shake. "I'll guard her with my life."

He pulled him in for a brief hug. He knew he would.

Ian and the team were on their way less than an hour later, taking the Zodiac jet to the closest large island since landing on Kings Fork under stealth would be impossible. Then they'd switch to two rigid hull inflatable boats, the same RHIBs he'd used in the SEALs.

On the jet, Isaac laid out a large map of the island on the table in front of them so everyone could see it. "Our drop-off point will be this beach less than a kilometer from the church. Satellite imaging shows us movement in and out of that building as of a few hours ago. We also have heat signatures inside."

"How many?" Callum asked.

"At least two dozen. That could be good or bad. Good if they're the other victims. Bad if they're all Mosaic guards."

Everyone was armed with both tranquilizers and real guns. Tranquilizers were the first and best option, but they were all willing to change over to bullets if it meant stopping whatever was happening there. Even Callum.

"Aren't you risking your job by being here?" Ian asked him as the others studied the map.

He shrugged. "I'm hoping this all goes smoothly, we bring in Erick Huen and possibly other members of Mosaic, and we eliminate a human trafficking/assassin ring. Hopefully, that'll be enough to get back into my bosses' good graces. If not, I'm assuming that you're going to create a position for me in Zodiac when I get fired."

"I'm sure we have a position open for a janitor or something."

He let out a laugh. "Let's just take Mosaic down, and then we'll see where the chips lie."

They landed at San Amado Island, Finn muttering about how it had been much nicer when he'd been there a few months ago for a wedding, then they headed out on the rafts. Even if someone was looking, the six of them in black, the raft in black, motoring across the black water of the Pacific, were nearly invisible.

They were silent, everyone knowing their job and what was expected of them. Finn and Ian would breach the northwest door. Isaac and Callum would each come in from a far window. Nate and Garrett, two of his most trusted agents, would come through what used to be a wine cellar. The plan was to tranquilize anyone they saw and sort them out later.

Once they got off the raft, they approached the church at rapid speed. They only had a couple hours of darkness left, and they wanted to use that cover to their advantage. Before he went in, Ian made one last contact with Landon back at the house.

"Everything okay with you and Wavy?" he asked on a separate comms channel.

"Affirmative. She hasn't come back out of the bedroom. I checked on her briefly. She wasn't painting, just sitting on the bed. I'm sure this hasn't been as easy on her as she wanted us to believe."

"It'll all be over soon," Ian assured him. It was a promise to him, to himself, and to her.

They split up and went their separate directions. There was no sign of any guards, which could mean a number of different things. That they weren't expecting to be found, or Mosaic was so confident in their location they didn't feel like they needed perimeter lookouts.

Or they knew they were coming and had fallen back into a more secure position.

The church had stone footings and then grew into wood, making it a unique structure, even in the darkness. Ian waited for everyone to get into position and report in.

It was time.

"On my mark, we go," he said in a low voice. "Everyone head toward the heat signatures, and watch your asses."

A chorus of "Roger that" echoed in his head.

They maintained silence as they entered the building. Finn and Ian split up into the two different hallways as soon as they entered. They'd be coming from different directions, hoping to catch any tangos off guard.

He moved down the narrow passage. It was quiet, which didn't make him feel better. This wasn't a great location—it would be way too easy for him to get trapped there if guards started coming in from behind him.

He spotted his first bad guy facing the other direction and pulled out his tranquilizer gun. He fired two shots, frowning when they hit the man and made a sort of clank, and he didn't fall.

"Be aware tangos are wearing some sort of body armor," he said into his comm unit as he dropped to one knee, waiting for the guy to turn around. He'd have to take him out in his leg or shoulder. Not as easy a hit, but it would still get the job done.

He didn't move.

He didn't spin. He didn't fire. He didn't yell, nothing. There was something very wrong here.

"Aries, we've got some sort of problem," Isaac's voice came in his ear. "The tango I took out is not . . . human."

Ian ran toward the guard he'd fired on, realizing the same was true about him too. What the hell? It wasn't a robot or even a machine. It was something made to look vaguely like a person from a distance and wrapped in some sort of cloak.

It only took him a few seconds to realize what the material was. It magnified heat. The only reason to use it like this would be to give the impression of body temperature.

"Everybody out," he yelled into the comm unit. "Get out right now. It's a trap."

"Are you sure?" Garrett asked. "Everything looks clear on this end."

"Just do it." Ian ran back for the door, hoping everyone was doing the same.

"Maybe there's still something down here," Nate said. "I can see someone up ahead."

"No!" he yelled. "Get out *now!*"

He was barely three feet out the door before the building blew up behind him in a raging inferno, propelling him through the air and hard onto the ground. He tried to move, tried to breathe, but he couldn't do either. Darkness overtook him.

———

Ian woke to somebody pulling on him and started fighting them.

"Ian, it's me, buddy. It's Isaac. Cut it out."

"Isaac?" He stopped taking blind swings as his brain fog cleared and his eyes focused. "What happened?"

"The building exploded. It was a setup, man."

He remembered now. "Oh fuck, is everybody okay?" Ian turned so he could see the flames in the darkness.

"Finn's over there. He's unconscious. I think he has a concussion. Callum is alive, definitely a broken leg, maybe more. I haven't heard from Nate or Garrett yet. Shit, they would've checked in if they could have. You've got some burns on your back, man."

He could feel them. "I'll be fine. Are you okay?"

"Yeah, I'm fine. I want to do a perimeter sweep and see if maybe Nate and Garrett are unconscious somewhere. God, I hope so."

"They knew we were coming." Ian repeated back the words Isaac had said a few seconds ago. It was the only thing that made sense.

"It looks like it. They had dummies inside to make it look like heat signatures."

"They knew we'd be looking here."

Isaac squeezed his shoulder. "If you hadn't called it when you did, we'd all be dead, man."

He shook his head. He still might have been too late to save everybody.

Isaac shook his head. "I guess Erick Huen was trying to eliminate you once and for all."

"Or at least get me out of the way so he could . . ." Terror crashed over him like a tidal wave as a new thought hit him. "Shit, I've got to get Landon on the line."

Ian got to his feet with Isaac's help and stumbled farther away from the burning building. His comm unit was down, so he grabbed his phone. He tried Wavy's number first, but when no one answered, he tried Landon. The call connected, but there was no sound on the other end.

"Landon, are you there? Landon?" Still nothing. He didn't want to hang up. Had his phone been damaged in the explosion and he couldn't hear? "Landon, you need to expect trouble. They knew we were coming."

Ian held his hand up to his other ear to hear better. "Landon, do you read?" Something muffled came through the phone, and then he pulled it away from his head and looked. He was turning on video.

The first thing Ian saw when the picture came through was blood. "Shit, what happened? Are you hit? Where's Wavy?"

"I'm sorry, boss. I'm sorry." Landon's voice was weaker than he'd ever heard it.

"Shit, Landon. What happened? Were you attacked?"

"Wavy," Landon whispered. "I'm sorry, boss. Wavy." He didn't say anything else.

Ian kept the line open and yelled over to Isaac. "Isaac, you got a phone? Landon's down. They've been hit back at the penthouse." But Isaac had gone to hunt for Garrett and Nate.

"I've got one." It was Callum. He couldn't walk, but was dragging himself toward him. Ian ran over to him.

"They hit us in Denver too," he told him. "I don't know what's going on, but I think Landon's down."

He couldn't think about his best friend possibly being dead, and he definitely couldn't think about what might've happened to Wavy.

"That place is the Fortress of Solitude," Callum said. "How could anyone get in there?"

"I don't know. We must've missed something." Ian used Callum's phone to call the rest of the team back at the building in Denver. "You need to lock down the entire fucking building now," he told them. "And get medical help up to the penthouse. Somebody find Wavy and tell me where she is."

He brought his face toward his phone. "Landon, hang in there. Don't you dare fucking die on me. Help is on its way. Just keep breathing." Something like the gurgling of air responded, which wasn't good, but at least it meant he was still alive.

Within minutes, Ian had Andrew and Tristan on the phone. Both of them would need to get out there to mop up this situation. He needed to get back to Denver. When he saw Isaac walking back toward them, grim look on his face, he knew the worst had happened.

"Both of them?" he asked.

"Yeah, they're nowhere around the perimeter. They must not have made it out in time."

Goddammit. "Landon was hit too, and we don't have eyes on Wavy. I've got Tristan and Andrew coming out here. I'm heading back. We've got medical help coming for Finn and Callum and the others just in case."

Isaac nodded. "It's all right, boss. You can't be everywhere at once. Get to where you're needed most."

That was it, wasn't it? Ian was needed *everywhere* most, but right now, Wavy had to come first. If Landon was down, she had been taken. He couldn't let himself dwell on that. He had to focus on what he could do and believe it would be enough.

He forced himself to do that as he got on the raft, then on the plane that took him back to Denver. Ian was on the phone the entire time, working every angle he could, getting the tech team to look for any signs of anyone coming into the building, anyone scaling the building. Hell, anyone parachuting to the fucking roof of the building.

Someone had found a hole in their security and made it into the penthouse. They needed to find out how and who. He should have never left Wavy alone. Erick had played them like they were his damned instruments, and they'd let him.

He also coordinated with Tristan and Andrew about the disaster on Kings Fork Island, Nate and Garrett were probably dead, Callum and Finn wounded. The brothers would get out there and be his eyes and ears.

A final helicopter took Ian the short distance from the airport to the penthouse. Two of the building's security team met him on the roof landing zone, updating him as they went. He wanted to see the footage from the penthouse.

"What's Landon's condition?" he asked.

"He's been taken to the emergency room. He was shot in the chest."

His jaw hardened. "I want to see all the penthouse footage from the elevator foyer and the emergency stairs and the balcony."

The two men looked at each other and then at him. "Mr. DeRose, we've already scoured this footage multiple times. Nobody came into that penthouse. We've already had the tech team double-check the footage to make sure it hadn't been manipulated. It wasn't. Nobody has gone in since you left."

"Gone *in*?" Ian repeated. "What does that mean?"

"It means that somebody went out," Brinker said. He was a good man. Older, not necessarily the brightest, but he was a solid member of the team.

"Someone we recognize?" he asked him.

"Yes, sir. Miss Bollinger."

"Wavy went out. I get it. Somebody took her."

"No, sir," Brinker said. "She walked out of her own accord, got on the elevator, and left through the front door. Nobody thought to stop her because, you know, she's . . . her."

Dread filled his stomach once again. "Nobody went in, and Wavy left on her own?"

Both men nodded.

Ian wiped his hand down his face. "I need somebody to get

Dr. Rayne here. Tell her if she has any recordings of her sessions with Wavy, we need them right away."

"Yes, sir," Brinker said. "Do we still need to keep looking for whoever shot Landon?"

He nodded, praying what he thought had happened was wrong. "Do a search of each floor in this building, and I want every single security camera run through the tech team to be sure it hasn't been manipulated."

But Ian already knew who had shot Landon.

*Wavy.*

# CHAPTER
# THIRTY-SEVEN

IAN WATCHED the footage of Wavy leaving the building for the hundredth time, leaning forward in his chair to relieve the ache from the burns on his back. Nothing was any different than it had been any of the other times he'd watched it.

She was calm, looked straight ahead, relaxed and unhurried. She wasn't antsy, wasn't looking over her shoulder, wasn't nervous.

She was calm.

Just like she'd been before he'd left to go to Kings Fork Island.

Rayne was sitting next to him, also watching the footage.

Ian rubbed the back of his neck. "I don't understand what's going on here, Rayne. Look at her. Nobody's coercing her. She's not in a hurry. She's unnaturally calm."

Rayne had arrived a couple hours ago and had been briefed on what had happened. He'd also been caught up on the details of the current shitstorm that was his life. Garrett and Nate had both been confirmed dead. They hadn't made it out of the church before the explosion. Landon was out of surgery, the bullet having missed all major organs and arteries, thank God. He was still sedated, but they thought he would pull through without a problem.

"We must have been wrong," he told Rayne. "Mosaic's protocol must have worked on Wavy after all. She was some sort of sleeper agent. Whatever genetic changes they made in her worked and what we thought we knew was wrong."

Rayne leaned back in her chair. "I don't think that's the case. Honestly, I don't think that Erick Huen would have waited this long to trigger her if he could've used her as a tool to hurt you from the beginning. I think they wanted to make her an assassin, but they couldn't."

Ian shook his head. "She shot Landon. She was the only person in that room. It had to have been her."

"I don't disagree that they did something to her, but if she was an assassin, you'd be dead now. We don't have all the facts."

No, they didn't have all the facts. But they had enough to know that Wavy wasn't herself.

There was a short knock at the door before it opened. "Hey, boss."

Ian closed his eyes for a second, relief surging through him. With Landon out of commission, there was nobody else he'd rather have in this office. "Sarge. I'm damned glad to see you."

"I heard what happened," he said. "I'm here to help."

"And Bronwyn?" he asked.

"I have her hidden away. More like locked away. It's . . . complicated. I'm going to have to get back to her as soon as I can, but I wanted to help."

Ian nodded. "Thank you."

"Get me up to speed."

He wasn't sure he knew where to start. "Wavy fed us fake intel and then shot Landon and left the building of her own accord."

Saying the words out loud made it even harder to wrap his head around them.

"I know it looks bad now, boss, but you have to focus on the most important things."

"I'm not sure I know what those are anymore."

"Finding her and getting her back are the most important things. You deal with all the rest afterward, but first things first."

Sarge was speaking from experience. And he was right. Rayne was nodding too.

Ian took a breath, blowing it out slowly. "We have to assume that Mosaic picked her back up." He had to force the words out, barely able to stand the thought of her being back in their clutches after what she'd gone through the last time.

"I concur," Sarge said, "but this is personal for Erick, so you know you'll be hearing from him again soon."

His jaw clenched, and he bit back a curse. He didn't want to wait while Erick held all the cards and then watch as the hand played out.

Ian's phone rang, and for a second, he wondered if it was Erick, but it was the hospital. That could be worse. He connected the call.

"Ian DeRose," he barked.

"Mr. DeRose, this is Dr. Faxon at the hospital. Landon Black is awake and insisting on talking to you. I told him whatever it was needed to wait, but he refuses. He is causing problems for the hospital staff and endangering his health in the process, so I was wondering if you could please come here immediately."

"I'm on my way," he said, standing.

Sarge stood up too. "I'm coming with you. You need two sets of ears and eyes on everything right now. Nothing is what it seems."

That was the damn truth.

"I'm going to stay here," Rayne said. "I need to reexamine the footage of my sessions with Wavy over the past week. There were two distinct types of sessions. I have a potential theory. I'll let you know if that still holds true after I watch the footage."

Sarge and Ian were silent on the drive to the hospital. He

wanted to ask how Bronwyn was doing, but he didn't have the emotional bandwidth for that. Sarge seemed to understand.

When they got there, Landon looked like hell. He'd obviously refused any pain medication and was suffering for it. When he saw them, he tried to sit up.

Ian put a hand on his shoulder. "We're here. Just relax as much as you can."

"Wavy," he croaked out. "Wavy."

"She shot you. We figured it out."

"I don't think she meant to."

"Like, it was an accident?"

He shook his head, then grimaced in pain. "No. She only picked up the gun when I tried to stop her from leaving. She had to get out of the penthouse. I don't know how to explain it. She was compelled to leave."

"But she wasn't trying to kill you?" he asked.

"No, not until I stood in front of the elevator door."

He looked over at Sarge. That was something at least. She hadn't tried to murder him in cold blood. "So she only shot you when she tried to leave and you wouldn't let her?"

"Yes," Landon whispered, "and, boss, she had a headshot. She had a gun pointed straight at my head, but she fought it. Her nose was bleeding, she was sweating, but she lowered the gun to my chest and then took the shot when I wouldn't move."

Ian tried to wrap his mind around what he was saying. "So, she was fighting it? Whatever it was she was . . . *compelled* to do, she was fighting it?"

"Yes," Landon whispered, getting weaker. "I think if I had gotten out of her way, she wouldn't have shot me at all. But as it was, she took the chest shot rather than the kill shot."

His breathing was getting more labored. Nurses gathered at the door, shooting them worried looks. Ian leaned down and kissed his friend on the forehead. "You've done enough, Landon. Now you rest, okay? We're going to get her back, and we're going to get to the bottom of this. You've helped so much."

His eyes closed. Sarge and Ian left.

"You look like you've discovered something," Sarge said as we walked back down the hall.

"I have. We've been encouraging Wavy to focus on the wrong things."

"What do you mean?"

"I'm pretty sure Dr. Rayne has gotten to the same conclusion. Wavy's had two types of memories over the past couple weeks. Ones that caused nosebleeds, headaches, vomiting, and ones that were easy."

"Let me guess," Sarge said. "The church on the island that blew up, those were part of the easy memories?"

"Yep. The easy stuff is what Mosaic planted. So we need to look at the things that cause her pain. Those are the things her brain is trying to remember. Her *real* memories."

———

He'd been right.

Dr. Rayne had come to the same conclusion they had. Now they were all poring over any conversation or action over the past two weeks that had caused Wavy pain.

"Janice," Rayne said. "Every time Wavy talked about Janice, she was upset, but no nosebleeds or flinching. I think Janice was somebody they planted in her mind to make her want to get back somewhere. I think that may be the only reason she was trying to leave the building. We can ask Landon when he wakes up, but I wouldn't be surprised if Janice's name was mentioned."

They'd all spent the past six hours searching through the footage of Dr. Rayne's sessions with Wavy. Filtering them with the information they now had, it was easy to see the pattern.

They'd done something to her that made bringing forward any real memories from her subconscious very painful. But the memories they'd planted came forward without any problems at all.

"The fact that she fought to access the real memories is a testament to her mental strength," Rayne continued. "Most people wouldn't have had the strength to fight the pain. Mosaic probably wasn't counting on that."

"I'm not surprised. Wavy has always been strong." She wouldn't have survived the first time if she hadn't been.

They needed to figure out how to find her.

Sarge leaned in toward the monitor. "The video from Erick was used as the trigger. Watch Wavy as soon as he says '*mano y mano.*' That was the phrase. I'm sure of it."

Wavy had been ramrod-straight as she'd watched the first couple of minutes of Erick's video, obviously disturbed by seeing and hearing him. Then, sure enough, as soon as he said *mano y mano*, everything about her changed. The tension and worry faded from her features.

And she began drawing the church Erick had used as a trap.

"She stayed that same eerie calm the entire night. I thought she was hiding her fear for my sake."

Sarge turned to Ian. "I looked through the research found on the drive again about the gene-editing protocol not working on everyone. I'm pretty sure that's what happened with both Bronwyn and Wavy."

Rayne nodded. "Mosaic knew it wasn't going to work the way they wanted—getting her to kill you—so they did what they could with her, which was to lead you somewhere they wanted you to be. She wouldn't hurt you, but that didn't mean that she couldn't be used to lie to you. You had no reason not to trust her, and they knew it."

Ian rubbed the back of his neck. "But this doesn't help us find her."

Rayne sat back in her seat. "I've been looking at the footage of our sessions, concentrating on the things that were hard for her to talk about. Nothing about islands or churches or anything like that. I'm convinced any helpful info we'll find is in the conversations that were hardest for her. The headaches, the nosebleeds. The worse it was, the harder her mind was working to get the truth out."

That was a good place to start. "The worst nosebleed and pain I saw her have wasn't in conversation. It was . . ." Ian trailed off.

"What?" Rayne asked.

"Her paintings. The ones she did the other night, before we made her stop anything that was hurting her. I remember it was so bad, blood was pouring from both nostrils. I'd never seen anything like that."

He got up and went into his office next door to the conference room. Rayne and Sarge followed. He still had the paintings from the show because he wasn't sure exactly where he wanted to put them yet.

Sarge whistled through his teeth. "Those things are absolutely breathtaking, but in the same way, hard to look at."

"I know. They've called to me the whole time."

Ian set them all out side by side.

"There's a pattern in them." Rayne pointed to the ones that were primarily made of blues and greens. "See right there."

"It's also in the red one, the one with the gray too," Sarge said, running his finger along the same pattern, this one farther up in the corner.

Oh God. Oh, holy hell. It felt like he'd taken a hit to the solar plexus.

Ian took each of the paintings and flipped them so they were upside down from how they'd been facing.

"I know where this is. It's a compound in the Sierra Nevada."

"Are you sure?" Dr. Rayne asked.

"Very sure. The shapes of these two buildings together are unique—the dome and then the A-frame. I know it. It's where I killed my brother."

Both Sarge and Rayne let out curses.

"It would make sense that Erick would take her there. This has always been about me killing Grant. He wants revenge."

Rayne nodded. "I agree. Everything that Erick has done orbits around that event. I'm sure he would like the chance to bring his fight with you back around to where it began."

Ian walked over to a map hanging in his office. "The compound is hard to get to. Grant loved it because he was a paranoid bastard. Lots of exits and panic rooms, including some underground tunnels."

"Good thing is, you're familiar with it," Sarge said.

"Yep, and we're going to use that against Erick. Sarge, I need you to lead a team, a big one. As many as we can get."

He side-eyed him. "Are you sure that's the way you want to go? If we go in there guns blazing, Erick will disappear with Wavy or maybe kill her outright."

"He won't kill her until he knows what's going on. I need you guys to distract him and the majority of his men long enough for me to sneak in a back route and get Wavy out."

That was the good thing about having spent so much time there. Ian didn't want to go back to where he had died, but at least he was already familiar with the compound itself. Once again, they didn't have a lot of time to figure out their best tactical approach. Time was of the essence.

Sarge nodded. He could see why he wanted to go this route. "It's still risky. Erick's not going to send every single man he has after us. If you get caught, it won't be pretty."

Ian nodded. "I'll wear a tracker just in case, but I'm not going to get caught. The only thing I'm going to do is get Wavy back."

# CHAPTER
# THIRTY-EIGHT

IAN HADN'T DONE a lot of parachuting since his time in the Navy SEALs, but he still had the skills, despite the pain from the burns on his back. Parachuting into the mountains under the cover of night in the rain was not his forte, but if it meant getting Wavy back, he was willing to do it.

The timing of this operation was delicate. Their biggest advantage was that Erick didn't know Wavy's subconscious had sent them clues about this location. They needed to keep that advantage for as long as possible. That meant him getting into place well before Sarge and his team started making their moves to draw Erick out.

His landing wasn't as smooth as it could have been, but Ian had to admit he was reaching the ends of his reserves. He hadn't slept in more than fifty-two hours, and the stress and fear of Wavy being held, not to mention the deaths and injuries of his team members, were certainly taking their toll. But he made the landing without breaking anything, so he would call it a win.

Despite the storm around him, Ian pushed hard the five miles to the compound. Every minute that he could gain was another he could use to get Wavy out. He had no idea what condition she was going to be in. But he would take any condition, as long as she was alive and she was here.

He moved silently through the wilderness. He couldn't deny the effect this place had on him as he caught sight of the compound in the moonlight. Ian had died here multiple times. Everything in his psyche demanded he not go back, that this was a place to stay away from. But he kept moving forward.

He had weapons this time, and a team that would move heaven and earth to come get him if he needed them to. Ian also had a tranquilizer—not for use on any of Erick's men, because any Mosaic guard he saw was going down for good.

The tranquilizer was for Wavy. If she was in some sort of catastrophic state, he had to be prepared to render her unconscious to carry her out. That wouldn't be easy, but Ian had the equipment and was prepared to do it. He'd strap her onto his back like a damn Sherpa if he had to.

Ian cut around the south end of the compound. He found the tunnel he wanted, glad Grant had been such a paranoid bastard. It allowed him to come up through a grate inside the main wall of the compound. Now, all he had to do was not get killed and find Wavy.

There was a lot that could go wrong here. He couldn't communicate with his team because any signal coming in or out would be caught by Mosaic's defense system. He had forty-five minutes remaining to find Wavy and get her out before Sarge and his team made their move. Once they did, there would be chaos, but they would also lose the element of surprise. Erick might not move Wavy immediately, but he would certainly sic a shit ton more guards on her.

Ian made his way on silent feet into the living quarters. It was almost too much to hope that Erick would be treating Wavy like a guest, but they were the closest and the easiest to eliminate as a possibility. He took out two guards on his way, dragging their bodies into the dark so they wouldn't be found until after he was gone.

That gave him free access to the living quarters' control room. There were cameras in all of the bedrooms here. That was how Grant had discovered Ian had been an undercover operative. He'd thought he had dismantled the camera in his room, but they'd placed another one he hadn't found.

He ran through the cameras in each room. There was no sign of Wavy. But he did spot Erick. He was playing cards with a few of his men in the main living room. The fact that he wasn't asleep wasn't good, but it didn't look like he was on high alert.

That also provided him intel about where they might be keeping Wavy. They didn't have her hidden away, because they weren't expecting an attack, at least not yet. Ian knew by looking at Erick's smug face that it would suit his fancy to put her where they'd kept him when they found out he had betrayed them.

In the cages.

———

Wavy should be happy she wasn't in the agonizing pain she'd been in the last time Erick Huen had kidnapped her. She had some bruises and probably a broken wrist from when she had tried to fight back once whatever trance he'd had her in wore off. Nothing compared to trying to rip her own skin off like last time.

But all she could think as she laid there in that metal cage was that she'd killed Landon.

The past few hours—God, she wasn't sure how many—were a blur. The last things Wavy remembered clearly were her art show, then almost making love to Ian.

Then Erick's video.

Somewhere in the middle of that, everything had changed, and she'd been watching a movie starring herself.

Drawing a church she'd never been to.

Letting Ian leave her and not being concerned in the slightest.

Being compelled to come to this place, to rescue *Janice*.

She'd killed Landon to get here to rescue someone Erick had

taken great delight in telling Wavy had never existed. Mosaic's protocol hadn't worked correctly on her, and they hadn't been able to make her into Ian's assassin as Erick had planned.

So, they'd stopped trying to make her a killer and made her someone's *savior* instead.

A small sob escaped her throat. The fact that she'd killed one of Ian's closest friends to get here and save "Janice" had been a mere bonus.

Wavy had no idea where she was. She couldn't expect anyone to come rescue her. Even if they knew where she was, why would they bother after finding Landon dead in the penthouse when it had only been the two of them there?

So what if she had shot him in the chest rather than the head? She'd still shot him. He was still dead. Maybe she deserved to die in this cage. She couldn't be trusted anymore.

Whatever compulsion Wavy'd been under had ended once she'd arrived, but what if it came back? What if she tried to kill Ian?

That's why, when her name came from the darkness surrounding her cage in Ian's soft voice, she scampered away.

"Wavy, it's Ian. It's okay, Rainbow."

"No," she said, holding out her good arm in front of her. "Stay away from me."

"I'm not going to hurt you," he said. "I'm here to get you out."

"No, Ian, no. You have to stay away from me. I killed Landon. They might be using me to kill you."

He stepped forward, placing his hands on the bar, bringing his face close enough that Wavy could see him. "No, listen. Landon is alive. Remember, you took the chest shot rather than the head."

"So?"

"That saved his life. I spoke to him a few hours ago."

"We don't know—"

"Think about it. Really think about it. Were you trying to kill Landon? Is that what you were trying to do?"

She rubbed her eyes with her good hand. "N-no. I was trying to save Janice. All I knew was that I had to get into the elevator, and he wouldn't get out of the way."

"Exactly," Ian said. "You weren't trying to hurt Landon. You're not going to try to hurt me now. And when I get you out of here, we'll make sure you can never be triggered like that again."

Wavy didn't know whether to believe him or not. Her brain was still muddled. She started to cry. She felt so stupid.

"Hey Rainbow, come on," he said. "Be strong for me a couple more hours. Let's get out of here. I promise you Landon will be very happy to see you."

"You'd say that even if it weren't true. You'd do whatever you had to do to get me out of here."

He leaned his head against the bars, a smile pulling at his lips. "You know me well. But I promise Landon is alive. Right now, we've got to go. How badly are you hurt?" He gestured at her wrist.

"I'm pretty sure it's broken. I tried to fight some of Erick's men."

"I hope you gave as good as you got."

"Well, I'm the one who ended up in the cage. So, not exactly. But a couple of them probably have broken noses and boy parts that won't work right for a while."

He chuckled a little at that. "I love you, Rainbow. Let's get out of here."

He grabbed the key for the padlock that the guards had left just outside her reach and unlocked the cage. She was stiff after being inside it for so long and everything ached, but she pushed it all down and followed Ian into the night.

He kept hold of her good hand as they moved through the rainy night, only letting go when he had to eliminate a guard. At first, he dragged the bodies out of sight. But once they got farther away, he left them as they fell.

He took Wavy down into a tunnel and then out the other side, which brought them into the wilderness. They hadn't gotten very far before it became obvious that the Mosaic guards were aware there was a problem. Lights went on all around the compound behind them. There were shouts.

"Shit," Ian said, "I was hoping for more time. It'll still be another fifteen minutes before Sarge makes his move."

"What move?" she asked.

"We'll know it when it happens. Right now, we've got to move faster. It won't take them long to figure out which route we took, given the trail of bodies we left."

They ran through the woods. Wavy kept her broken wrist close to her chest, trying to brace it as much as possible, ignoring the throb. It wasn't long before there were shouts behind them.

"Isn't this how we first started?" She asked him between breaths. "Running through the wilderness with Mosaic guards chasing us?"

He squeezed her good hand. "Almost exactly, except for the rain. They would have had me that first day in Reddington City if it hadn't been for you. So let's call this returning the favor."

They continued to run in silence. An explosion in the distance caused her head to pivot in that direction, but Ian didn't slow down.

"That was Sarge," he said. "It will get the attention of some of Erick's men, but not the ones on our tail."

Even with Sarge's distraction, they weren't going to outrun the men behind them. She wouldn't be able to keep up this pace much longer.

Ian pulled her around a boulder that gave them a little bit of shelter. "Rainbow, I need you to listen to me. I want you to keep following the river straight south. It's getting light now and that route will take you toward Sarge and then into the next town in a few miles."

"Okay," she said. "We can make it."

"I'm not going with you."

"What? I can't go by myself. You have to come with me. We have to stay together."

He cupped her cheeks. "I can handle these guards, but it will be much easier for me to do it on my own. I'll catch up with you."

That made sense, but Wavy didn't like the thought of him going back into the fray just to save her.

He leaned his head against hers. "Let me do this for us, Rainbow. I can make it. You can make it too. You know how to navigate wilderness. Just keep going, make it to Sarge or make it to the town. Either one will keep you safe." He pressed one of his guns into her hand. "Take this. I have another one."

"You'll catch up with me, right?"

"Absolutely. But you have to go now. Run."

His lips brushed hers, and then he turned and ran back toward danger as she made her way toward safety.

THERE WERE TOO many of them.

Ian had realized about half a mile ago and known they weren't going to make it, not at the rate Wavy was slowing down. The rain wasn't helping. What he'd told her was true. He had a much better shot at taking out those guards without having to keep her safe also.

But what he hadn't told her was that there was no possible way he'd be able to take them all out. Still, as Ian circled back toward them, he would eliminate as many as he could, give Wavy as much of a fighting chance to escape as possible.

He did everything short of starting a game of Marco Polo to let the Mosaic soldiers know where he was. This plan only worked if they came after him. Ian took the silencer off his weapon and fired it, taking down a guard while letting the rest of them know where he was.

*Come and get me, you bastards.*

He headed toward the compound. There were at least four behind him, and two more were cutting around to the west side to head him off. That was probably almost everyone, and he could only hope that Wavy would be able to handle any that had followed her down to the river.

They were closing in. He was going to get taken. His only hope was that they wouldn't kill him outright, that their instructions were to take him back to Erick. Ian was counting on his theatrics to buy Sarge time to follow his tracker and get him out.

Ian slowed a little more. Timing was imperative. He wanted them to call back anyone who might be chasing Wavy because they needed help apprehending him. It wouldn't be long until they pressed in for the capture.

Sure enough, ten minutes later, one of the men who'd circled around to cut Ian off made his move in the form of a flying tackle. They both hit the ground hard and seconds afterward there were four other men on top of him.

He wasn't dead outright, which told him all he needed to know about Erick wanting him alive. This plan was going to work.

Ian had to believe that.

Unhappy with the long chase, the Mosaic soldiers made their displeasure known with boots and fists. Ian struggled to hang on to consciousness as what now looked like seven men each got their blows in before dragging him back to the compound.

One eye was already swelling shut, and he had at least one cracked rib by the time they dropped him at Erick's feet. The entire compound was in a great deal more chaos thanks to Sarge's tactics. Everyone was vacating—computer systems and weapons were being shoved into vehicles and driven or flown off.

Erick crouched down so they were almost eye to eye. "I was wondering how my pretty little captive got out. With all the dead bodies, I thought maybe we'd been wrong and she could be molded into an assassin after all. Alas, nothing quite that exciting. Just you doing what you do best: killing."

"You'll never get your hands on her again." His words were mushy from the blows he'd taken to the jaw.

Erick smiled. "Why would I need to get my hands on her when I have *you*?"

That at least reassured him that he wasn't sending anyone else after Wavy. She was safe. That was all Ian needed to know. "You're done. Law enforcement will be breaching any minute now."

That wasn't true, but Ian could only hope he didn't know that.

His eyes narrowed. "How did you know we'd be here?"

"Wavy's mind is stronger than you think." he spit out a mouthful of blood. "She left us clues."

He stood back up. "Honestly, I'm glad you're here. This will allow me to quit playing these silly games and kill you here where it should've happened years ago. Because you murdered Grant."

Ian forced himself to his feet, despite the world spinning around him. "Can I remind you that Grant killed me first multiple times? He put me in that casket, and you guys watched me die."

"Because you betrayed him. You deserved it."

He wasn't going to convince Erick that wasn't true, so he didn't bother trying. He needed to stall as long as possible. "If there had been another way besides killing Grant, I would have done it. I know he was your best friend, but he was my brother. I didn't want to kill him. Not until he started killing me."

"He was more than my best friend," Erick spat. "I *loved* Grant. He was my everything. We were in love with each other."

Ian's breath hissed out in surprise. His brother had been psychotic and sadistic, but the one thing he hadn't been was gay.

"He didn't feel the same about you, Erick." Was this line of reasoning the best way to go? Too late now. "He was straight. He had women around him all the time. You know that. He was notorious for it."

Erick shook his head rapidly—almost comically. "Deep inside, he did care about me. He would've figured that out if you hadn't killed him."

He wasn't surprised that Erick had created yet another illusion for himself. There would be no convincing him that Grant would never have loved him. Erick had been smart enough to disguise his adoration as friendship, which was probably why Grant had kept him around. Grant loved to be the center of attention, loved to have others fawn over him.

Ian stared up at Erick with his good eye. "Grant was never going to love you, especially not in that way. Hell, I don't think Grant was capable of loving anyone but himself."

For a second he thought maybe Erick was seeing reason, but then he motioned to the guard next to him. Ian doubled over as he took a gun butt to the gut.

"You don't get to say what Grant was. You walked away from him and only came back to betray him. Grant would've loved me eventually."

"If that's what you want to tell yourself. Sounds a little bit like you had a work crush and he didn't feel the same."

That got him another blow to the gut. And now Erick was pissed.

"You ruined everything, and now you're going to die the way you died all the previous times." Spittle flew out of his mouth. "Convenient that we already have the casket and the hole dug, although honestly, I hadn't thought I'd be able to use it on you. This gift had been for Wavy, but I'm sure we can make you fit." He stepped a little closer. "I dare say your friends aren't going to make it up the mountain in time to find you."

Ian's eyes fell to the hole in the ground a few yards away from them. Sweat dripped down his back at the thought of being thrown into a casket again. It was everything his nightmares were made of.

"Not so smug now, are you?"

He couldn't help it. This time when Erick's men dragged him, Ian fought. His mind wouldn't allow him to be thrown back into that death hole without fighting. He knew he was giving Erick the show he wanted, but it didn't stop him.

Once again, there were too many of them to fight off. Erick

stopped them right before they got to the hole he was all too familiar with.

"I'll be watching as you die again like I watched all the other times. It's what Grant would have wanted." He crouched down in front of him. "No one is coming to help you this time, Ian. This time, when you die in that casket, you're actually going to die. At least you can look forward to that."

Ian looked down into that hole and a calmness fell over him. He was right. There was no way his team would make it to him in time, even if they followed the tracker.

But goddammit, if he was about to die, he'd make sure something came of it.

He stopped struggling, stood up a little straighter. He knew what he needed to do.

"I forgive you, Erick."

Erick's eyes narrowed. "That's not going to stop what's about to happen."

"I'm not trying to stop what's about to happen." Ian just needed his men around him to relax their grip the slightest bit.

His words had confused him, that much was obvious. Erick stepped closer on the other side of the hole. "What is your end game then?"

"Call it religion. If I'm going to die, I don't want to go with hatred in my heart."

His eyes narrowed and he took another step closer. "*What*?"

"I forgive you. It's okay."

This time when he took another step forward, Ian lunged across the hole that would become his grave, ripping the tracker off his own wrist as he did so. Erick rocked back, but he grabbed his foot. That was all he needed to plant the small, clear sticker on the heel of his shoe. It wasn't perfect, but it would be enough.

It would be enough to get Sarge and his team to Erick's location, wherever he went.

He laughed as he scooted back away from Ian, and his men grabbed him once more. "I knew this was a ploy. I knew you hadn't forgiven me." He actually looked relieved, like he wouldn't have known what to do if that had been the case.

It didn't matter. He had no forgiveness for him, and if Ian burned for it, so be it.

"Time to die, Ian. For real this time." He smiled at him as he said the words.

Ian met his eyes. "I'll see you in hell, Erick."

This time, as they dragged him back toward the hole, he didn't fight. When they threw him in, Ian refused to give Erick the satisfaction of watching him panic. He didn't know that he'd be able to keep this calm once the air started to run out. But right now, face-to-face, he was determined to give him absolutely fucking *nothing*.

Erick was right that the casket wasn't meant for someone Ian's size. It barely fit the span of his shoulders. His legs had to bend at the knees to squeeze in. A smaller box at least meant less air—a quicker death.

There was nothing he could do as the guards lowered the casket's wooden lid, cutting off the sound of Erick's laughter. There was nothing he could do at the sound of the dirt covering him once again. It wasn't very deep, probably no more than a foot, but it was enough.

Enough weight so Ian couldn't push the casket's lid open. Enough mass so that there wouldn't be air soon.

He did everything he could to fight off the panic. Used every method Rayne and he had come up with to get him through his claustrophobia.

Although the ones they'd worked on most—his re-envisioning himself as not being helpless while trapped in this box, being able to use his strength and SEAL training to get out successfully—had been based on the assumption that Ian would never actually be trapped again. It was something he'd created in his mind to help *past* Ian.

It wasn't going to help *current* Ian in any way.

Because *fuck* it was impossible to keep the panic at bay. His nostrils flared, and all he could hear was the rasp of his own breaths as they came faster and faster.

It was only the thought of Wavy, the fact that she would never know the horrors of being inside this damned hell, that comforted him.

Ian would die a hundred times—even this way—to spare her this.

It didn't take long before the air thinned. The tiny beam of light Erick had left so he could watch his sick footage was worse than complete darkness. He found his hands pushing at the lid, but he knew the weight of the dirt was more than any human could move.

He closed his eyes and tried to picture Wavy's face over his. She'd be safe. This was worth it. In the end, the panic would overwhelm him, but Ian would hold on to her as long as he could.

He heard sounds outside the box, the sounds of dirt moving, but that was just his mind playing tricks on him. It had done that when Grant and Erick had buried Ian the first time, his mind wanting to believe that someone was coming to rescue him.

It hadn't happened then. It wasn't happening now.

So Ian closed his eyes once more and concentrated on Wavy's green ones, her smile, the light through the window bringing out the auburn tints in her hair when she'd looked back at him from her easel one day, wearing nothing but his T-shirt as he watched her from the doorway.

He focused on the rainbow paint on her wrist. *His* rainbow. She'd brought all the color into his life and changed him in ways Ian had never known he'd wanted. Definitely hadn't known he needed.

Her phantom voice filled his ears.

That would be enough . . . being able to hear her voice in his ears and see her rainbow as he died. Better than all the other times.

Ian's body started to shake as the lack of air—real or imagined—wrapped its claws around him.

". . . don't you die on me, Ian. I'm coming."

More sounds, more scratches.

"Hang on. Hang on, Ian. I'm almost there. Please, Ian. *Please.*"

*Was that real? Wavy?*

"Talk to me. Can you? I know it's hard. Talk to me, my love. I'm coming."

"Rainbow?" His voice was hoarse, too weak for her to hear him. Ian almost couldn't bear to hope. He forced himself to try again, louder. "Wavy?"

"Ian?" A relieved sob. "Ian. I'm coming. Hold on."

He could hear the dirt moving more clearly now. She was really here.

*Wavy.* He forced his mind to focus. She was here. Possibly in danger. She was injured but trying to get him out.

"I've almost got the dirt off. Hang on."

Hanging on was hard as Ian realized the air really was almost gone in this tiny box. He was lightheaded.

"Talk to me, Ian."

He tried. He couldn't. His breaths growing louder, the box growing smaller.

More shifting of dirt. Ian coughed and knew what that meant. This was going to be close.

"Survive for me, love. Breathe for me. Remember what you worked on with Dr. Rayne. Find that strength."

Strength Training. Rely on the things engrained in him. Maybe all those sessions *could* help current Ian.

Because he'd be damned if he'd lie there and die when he was so close to survival. So close to *Wavy.*

First thing Ian did was inch himself up so his head covered the light and the camera. Erick was undoubtedly watching, and if he found out Wavy was there helping him, he might return to eliminate the problem.

He forced himself onto his side until he could wiggle up his elbow. With one sharp jab, the camera was of no more use to Erick.

He'd probably be throwing a hissy fit, but at least he wouldn't know the truth. Ian should've done that way fucking earlier.

Without the tiny beam of light from the camera, the box fell into complete darkness. He'd been wrong. Some light had definitely been better than no light at all.

"Ian." Wavy's voice was clearer now, but much more frantic. "I can't get the casket open. My fingers won't . . ." Her words were cut off by her sob.

But he knew. She couldn't get a grasp on the coffin lid because of her broken wrist.

"Move for me, Rainbow." Ian used the last of his air to get the words out.

She scrambled away, and he wedged his hands up over his chest. Using every bit of strength—and oxygen—Ian had, he pushed.

He pushed to save himself.

He pushed because Wavy had risked everything to come back to save him.

He pushed because *he was* not *going to die in this fucking box*.

The rest of the dirt moved, and the lid finally creaked open, blessed air and light rushing in.

Wavy jumped down and helped with her good arm, getting her shoulder underneath and hefting the lid the rest of the way off.

Ian sat up, breathing deep, his eyes meeting hers. She was covered in mud, obviously in pain, but still smiling.

The rain had stopped, and over her shoulder at the end of the tree line—

A rainbow.

Ian reached out and touched Wavy's cheek. He didn't need a rainbow in the sky. He had one with him all the time.

# CHAPTER
# FORTY

ONE YEAR *later*

Wavy thought the physical agony she'd survived at Erick Huen's hands the first time he'd taken her would be the worst thing she'd ever survived. Or at least would haunt her nightmares the longest.

She'd been wrong.

The physical pain was easier to handle than what Erick had stripped her of the second time.

The ability to trust herself.

Within three hours of Wavy digging Ian out of that grave, Erick had been caught and arrested, thanks to the tracker Ian had placed on him.

Erick never made it to trial. He'd been killed by his own lawyer—a Mosaic plant—at their first meeting not twenty-four hours after his arrest. The lawyer had then killed himself.

Erick could never get to her again. His voice could never trigger her in a way she couldn't control. The multiple genetic specialists she'd seen had explained that what Erick and Dr. Tippens had managed to do to her had been a one-time thing.

And risky at that. They were surprised Wavy hadn't suffered permanent physiological damage from what Erick had attempted to do. All of them had mentioned the protocol must have been *extremely uncomfortable*.

Yeah. Bad enough that she still woke up in the middle of the night screaming about it.

But that wasn't the worst. The worst had been that she couldn't walk by the elevator in the Denver penthouse without knowing she'd almost killed Landon.

The worst had been the knowledge that two of Ian's men had been killed because of the false information she'd unwittingly provided. That Callum and Finn had been injured in that same explosion.

Everyone was quick to say they didn't blame her.

But Wavy blamed herself.

Especially because a tiny piece of her still itched to rescue Janice, even though Wavy knew she wasn't real. The thought of her had been a tool placed in her mind to manipulate her.

But there were *other* Janices. *Real* Janices. Ian and his team had been working diligently to take down the rest of Mosaic. She hadn't seen much of Sarge, Landon, or Isaac over the past few months. They'd been undercover, although she didn't know the specifics.

Wavy hadn't seen as much of Ian either.

It wasn't that she didn't love him. God, she loved him more each day. But she'd needed space. A chance to find herself. To figure out who she really was after all the dust had settled.

To figure out how to trust herself again. How to stand on her own. How to be Wavy *and* be Ian's Rainbow.

She hadn't thought that journey would bring her to her current location—on the sidewalk in front of a small Craftsman-style house in Highlands, New Jersey, about an hour outside New York City.

*Ian's* house. Or one of them.

Wavy'd been all over the world with Ian in the past year,

enjoying the privileges of his wealth via almost every mode of transportation available. They'd spent time on yachts, jets, trains —and had made love in all of them.

But despite the multiple times he'd asked her to make their relationship more permanent—moving in, marriage, pinky promises, whatever she was most comfortable with—she'd said no.

Wavy kept running from him.

She'd show up for a few days, then leave again. Always saying it was because of her art. Which was true. Her career as an artist had skyrocketed over the past few months. So much so that Ian had moved his office to New York since she was there so much of the time.

And because she'd never recovered from what she'd done in the Denver penthouse. Despite Landon's forgiveness, that space would never be safe for her again. So Ian, being Ian, had worked the problem. He'd gotten a different penthouse, one with no blood-soaked memories for her. It also happened to have a view of Central Park with plenty of windows for him.

But even in a new place, Wavy'd still kept running from him. And they both knew her art wasn't the problem. *She* was the problem.

A few nights ago, it had all come to a head.

*What are you waiting for, Rainbow?*

A question in the middle of the night as she'd tried to slip out of his bed, thinking she was leaving him in his sleep. The way she had too many times.

*I'm afraid I'll lose myself again.*

*If you lose yourself, I will find you. No matter what it takes. No matter what it costs. The same way you did for me. At some point you're going to have to believe that, or we can't go any further. Mosaic may have stolen parts of your past, but you're the one handing over your future.*

Wavy'd left, not wanting to face the truth of his words. She'd gone to the separate midtown apartment she kept—one she could more than afford due to her art's success—and tried to paint.

Nothing would come. Not that night. Not any day or night since.

This wasn't like after her kidnapping when she wasn't sure if she'd ever paint again. This was the deepest part of her, the part where her art flowed from, digging in its heels. Refusing to be used as an escape mechanism any longer.

Forcing Wavy to face what she was doing to herself. To Ian.

To *them*.

She'd once asked him to let them stand together to face whatever needed to be faced. Not protect her from the hard things.

But then she'd been the one who'd run from their united front.

Wavy was done running. She wanted her painting back. But more than that, she wanted *Ian* back. She wanted to take the next step forward with him.

She wanted to trust that he would find her if she lost herself.

He hadn't been at his office or the penthouse yesterday when she'd stopped by. For the first time ever, no one at Zodiac would tell her where he was.

So, she'd taken matters into her own hands today. But this Jersey house that needed another coat of paint wasn't where she'd expected to find him.

By now the security detail he had following her would've notified him she was out of pocket, but they'd still assume she was somewhere in the art gallery in Manhattan, not knowing she'd slipped out the back door immediately upon entering the building. They'd be searching.

Panic wouldn't start until they couldn't find her. Probably soon. Wavy didn't want anyone freaking out so she crossed the street and knocked on the door, unsure of exactly what she would find.

He was talking—voice deep, gruff, never failing, even now, to do something to her body that she wasn't sure anyone else in the world could do—as he opened the door. "Whatever you're selling, I don't have time for it toda—"

His words cut off as he caught sight of her. He was holding a computer tablet in one hand, a phone tucked between his shoulder and chin.

He switched mental gears in less than a breath.

"Landon, the situation is under control. Have Zodiac stand down." He pressed a button on his tablet, then threw it at the small table next to the door, eyes still glued on her.

"Finn," he said into the phone, "I've got Wavy here with me. She's fine. I'll have her call you soon."

Wavy winced as he hung up with her brother. She should've known he'd call Finn right away if she was missing for even a minute.

"And one last text to Zac Mackay before he sends out the entire Linear Tactical team." Ian typed rapidly with one hand before tossing the phone on the side table with the tablet, his brown eyes never once leaving hers. She didn't have to read the message to know it contained no errors, even though he hadn't looked at it.

He stepped out onto the small porch and into her personal space like he belonged there. Like he had every right to have his big, hard body pressed up against her even though their last words to each other a few days ago had been terse.

He yanked her to him and kissed her, his kiss a force of nature, like the man himself. Protector and predator rolled into one.

Gentleness didn't come naturally to him. Not in life and not in his kisses. One arm banded around her hips like iron. Possessive fingers of the other hand threaded through her hair so he could hold her in place and kiss her the way he wanted.

Wavy knew with one word he would release her. He'd proved that more times than any one person should have to prove it to another.

But she didn't want him to. She wanted to keep feeling

those greedy lips on hers, tongue joining in to soothe after gentle nips of his teeth. She loved how he took possession of her mouth.

Loved that he never treated her like she was breakable.

Why in the world had she been running away from this rather than straight to it?

They were both breathing heavily by the time he lifted his lips from hers. Wavy was a little surprised he didn't drag her inside and take her against the door.

That had happened before. And they could both use it.

He leaned his forehead against hers, his arms still around her. "Only you could cause such a brouhaha in eleven minutes and fifty-two seconds, Rainbow."

Wavy raised an eyebrow at him. "I didn't think you'd call out the entire national guard in that short a time."

He ran his thumb down her cheek. "I'm glad you're here. Let me take you out to eat. There're some seafood places nearby to die for."

She leaned into his hand. He always fed her—still trying to make up for the meals she hadn't gotten during her captivity. Normally, she would let him, because hell, she loved to eat as much as he loved to feed her.

But not today. Not while they were here at this *secret* house.

"You're not going to let me in?"

He pulled her closer, lips falling to her neck. "Let's go back to Manhattan. We can be there in less than an hour. I'll have you naked and bent over that chair in front of the window thirty seconds after that."

"No."

His lips moved up to her jaw. "You're right. I won't be able to wait until all our clothes are off. You'll be lucky if we make it out of the elevator—you are the only person I'd willingly stay in an elevator for."

She swallowed hard, her insides clenching at his words. She wanted that as much as he did. Had loved how they'd spent time in the elevator over the past year giving his brain new—and very dirty—things to associate with that space.

But not until she knew what was going on here.

"What is this place, Ian? You might as well tell me because you know I'm not leaving until I have answers."

He didn't move out of the doorway. "How did you find me here?"

"I bugged one of your men's phones." She ignored his amused chuckle as she looked past him. "Do you have a family in there, Ian? That's the only thing I can think of that you would go to such great lengths to keep hidden from me."

"What? No. Trust me. When I have a wife and kids stashed in a house somewhere, you'll know. Because you'll be the one wife-ing and kid-ing with me."

Before today, Wavy wouldn't have doubted that. But she kept staring at the doorway, not sure what to say.

His brows furrowed when she didn't speak. "You really thought I had a wife and two point five kids I'd somehow hidden away from you? In fucking *New Jersey*?"

She scrubbed a hand over her face. "No. No, of course not. I . . . this wasn't what I was expecting. I thought you had a dojo or something. An indoor shooting range. Not a cute little Craftsman where you evidently like to hang out."

His lips pursed as he scratched at a day and a half's worth of stubble. "I needed a place a little outside the city, and I wanted something normal, so I bought it."

She stared up at him. She was so used to Ian being open that this cryptic answer was jarring to her system. There was some-thing in that house he didn't want her to see.

"You know you're going to have to let me in, right?" Wavy kept her tone steady, gentle. Like he'd done with her so many times.

"I don't want you to go inside, Rainbow. What's in there . . ."

Her eyes latched on to his. "I have no secrets from you. You've had a front row seat to my nightmare. If this is the place where you go to be yourself, that's fine. Whatever you have inside, I'm not afraid."

That was a bold-faced lie.

But whatever he had behind that door she could—she *would* —handle.

"I . . ." His voice faded.

She touched his arm. "Hey, if necessary, I'll call *Hoarders*, and you can be on their TV show."

He smiled, but when she tried to step around him, his hand covered hers. "Rainbow . . ."

Hearing the uncertainty in his voice was hard. Ian was many things. Uncertain wasn't one of them.

Wavy stroked the hand covering hers with her thumb. "Whatever it is, we face it together. I'm not running anymore."

Ian stepped aside, then behind her. She could feel him at her back as she stepped into the small foyer.

No tarantula collection. No huge piles of junk. No little wifey in an apron baking muffins.

Just a hallway. Perhaps the most memorable thing about it was that one of her paintings hung along the south wall over a wooden console table. One from her very first show. She knew he'd bought the ones that had led him to find her and them to rescue each other, but she hadn't known he'd purchased this one too.

She'd forced François to give any family or friends who wanted to purchase some of her work a steep discount. But knowing Ian, he'd probably paid full price for his piece, wanting to support her.

The relative normalcy of the hallway gave her more courage. She walked into the small living room on the left.

Still no vampire bats or human skulls. Just a small couch and two armchairs with an antique oak coffee table in front of the three pieces. They were all tasteful, expensive. Maybe slightly out of place given the cost of the house, but not much. Another one of her paintings hung on the wall over the fireplace.

She turned and rolled her eyes at him. He was still two steps behind her, studying her. Waiting for her to figure it out. Whatever *it* was. Smart enough not to incriminate himself by offering any info.

That didn't reassure her.

Wavy brushed by him and crossed the hall into the kitchen. Nothing unusual there. She grabbed an apple from the bowl of fruit, smelled it, and then bit into it gingerly. It was real. Not some sort of staging.

She munched on the apple as she walked farther down the hall into the half bath. No drug paraphernalia, just a nice hand towel set.

The family room held more evidence of Ian. A comfortable couch and lounger faced the huge television. On the far wall was . . .

Another of her paintings. One from her show a month ago. Ian hadn't been able to make it to that one.

So how was that particular painting on his *family* room wall? She set the apple on the table.

This time she didn't look at him as she stormed up the stairs and into the bedrooms.

Her paintings. Every single room had at least a few, some many more. And when she got to the last room, the one he was obviously using as an office, she was surrounded by them all over the walls. Two dozen probably, all sizes, artfully arranged so they somehow didn't clash with one another. If she could be objective, she'd be impressed with the emotion the paintings as a group conveyed. It was everything she'd always wanted her art to be.

But Wavy couldn't be objective. Her world was crumbling to dust.

*He'd bought all her paintings.*

"What have you done?" she whispered, still staring at the art —*her art*—surrounding her. She couldn't look at him.

The level of betrayal was unfathomable. He'd known that. It

was why he hadn't wanted her in here. Why he had this secret house in the first place.

"Rainbow . . ."

"No!" The word roared out of her as she spun to look at him. He reached toward her, but she jumped back. His arm fell to his side. "You bought all my paintings."

"Yes, but—"

"No." She stopped him with one word.

She was such a fool. She thought she'd made a successful career for herself. She thought that something wonderful had come out of the hell she'd lived through. That it had provided her, in some serendipitous fashion, the means to be independent. To live the life she'd wanted instead of waiting tables back in Oak Creek forever.

Every time her brush had hit the canvas, she'd felt like a phoenix. She'd burned to ash in the most horrific way possible, but what had risen had been better, stronger. More majestic and powerful.

Maybe most people would tell her it didn't matter that Ian had been the one to buy her paintings, but it did.

Once again what she'd thought was real had been an illusion. She couldn't trust anything anymore.

# CHAPTER
# FORTY-ONE

IAN WOULD GIVE every dollar he had to never see that expression on Wavy's face ever again.

It was nowhere near the blank, broken expression she'd had when they'd finally gotten her out of that hellhole in San Diego. But it was similar enough to throw him into his own panic.

Wavy and Ian both had triggers. Tight, enclosed spaces might be one of his, but seeing her suffer in any way was much worse.

He'd endure closed-in spaces for the rest of eternity if it meant she never suffered another minute in her life.

"These paintings are pieces of you." He said the words rapidly. He was careful not to crowd her in any way, but he kept himself between her and the door, as if blocking it with his body would keep her from remembering it was there.

Ian didn't have long to make her understand.

He *needed* her to understand.

"They were your heart and soul. Your fears and passions. I wanted them surrounding me. *Just* me."

God, he sounded like a fucking stalker. No wonder she was looking at him with something barely short of horror in her eyes.

That's why he'd kept this place a secret. Because he'd known she wouldn't understand. How could she? How could *anyone*?

Since that day she'd saved him, she'd been running from him —from *them*. Ian would reach the point where he thought they were finally moving forward in their relationship, and then he'd wake up, and she'd be gone.

He never panicked. He had the security team watching her. Plus, he knew she'd be back—a couple of weeks, a few days, an hour . . . however much time she needed.

And Ian was willing to give her that. He'd promised himself he would give it to her. Because she'd lived through what would've broken most people beyond repair.

Because she deserved the chance to do whatever she wanted for as long as she wanted to.

Because he was in love with her beyond reason and would do anything to meet her needs. Even pretend he was asleep so she could slip out the door without a battle.

But being without her . . . he didn't think she had any concept of what emptiness her absence caused each time. Wavy wasn't an unkind person. If she knew the agony she left behind when she ran—the gaping hole in his chest—she wouldn't do it. She'd pay the price herself and stay rather than get out and get whatever it was she needed.

So Ian had never said how much it hurt him. He'd never made a big deal of it when she came back. Just made sure she knew she was welcome. That he loved her.

The paintings had become his way of keeping her with him when she ran. They were a distant second to the woman herself, but at least they were *something*.

But he'd known it was wrong. Why else would he have bought a house in the middle of fucking New Jersey and never had a single other person there?

Because this bordered on insanity. And crossed the stalker line way before that.

And now she knew. She knew, and she was afraid of him.

Ian took a deliberate step away from the door, giving her a

clear path if she wanted to leave. But he started talking again in hopes she'd listen.

"I never wanted to make you feel trapped. After everything you've been through, the strength you've found . . . I wanted you to be free. But these"—he took a step toward the paintings, giving her a clear path to the door—"these helped me feel close to you, even when you weren't around."

"*You bought all my paintings.*" Her voice was choked.

"Yes. Well, most of them." There were still seventeen she'd sold over the past year he hadn't been successful in acquiring.

"Do you know how that makes me feel?"

Ian closed his eyes but didn't turn. "I can only imagine that it makes me seem very similar to Erick Huen." Bile rose in his throat.

She took a shocked step back. "*What*? Jesus, Ian, why would you ever say that? That's not what I meant at all."

Now he turned to face her. "I bought all your paintings because I want to be surrounded by your emotions all the time. That's sick like he was. I don't blame you for feeling betrayed."

She threw up her hands. "No, dumbass. You couldn't be like Erick if you tried. I feel betrayed because I thought I had a successful career. That I was independent. Turns out I don't have that at all, just a wealthy benefactor who lets me have art shows to make me feel important, but then buys all the paintings himself."

"*What*? No—"

Her eyes narrowed. "Oh, and fucks me every once in a while when I want it. He's a full-service benefactor."

His eyes narrowed. "Watch it, Rainbow."

"I'm not afraid of you, Ian." She backed the statement up by walking over and poking him in the chest. "So don't take that tone with me. But I am pissed as hell. I hate to be coddled. Why would you let me pretend to have a career like that?"

He grabbed that pokey little finger before it drilled a hole through his flesh. "I've never pretended anything with you."

She didn't yank her hand back, but her anger slid away, leaving her looking smaller, more vulnerable. "You bought all my paintings without telling me. You had to have gone to a lot of trouble to make sure I didn't notice. The records of sale from the gallery were all in different names."

Ian finally understood. And for a moment had a sliver of hope. "No. Rainbow, *no*. Your shows were real. Your sales were real. I never once used any influence to get people to buy your works. The opposite, actually."

"But all these . . ." She gestured around with the hand he wasn't holding against his chest. At least she was still letting him touch her.

"I tracked down the owners afterward and bought them. Well, not me personally. My people, under different names and using different approaches. I am a businessman, after all. If word got around that there was a growing demand for your paintings, it would cost me a lot more."

She shook her head, eyes crinkling in confusion, but at least that vulnerable air around her had disappeared. "Why didn't you buy them from the gallery directly?"

"And have someone accuse me of being a wealthy benefactor who keeps my painter-in-residence happy by fucking her occasionally?" He raised an eyebrow.

"I would've given you the paintings, you know that, right? Any of them. *All* of them." She slid her hand out from under his and walked around him. "I can't understand why you would want this many. They're all so similar."

He turned so he was right behind her and put both hands on her shoulders. "Similar because they're all pieces of you, but each piece is unique."

Ian turned her to face the collection on one part of the wall that were mostly reds. "Your anger and strength."

He eased her toward the deep purples. "Your passion."

The yellows and orange. "Your happiness."

The grays—the hardest to look at. "Your fear that you'd never find your colors again."

He turned her to face him. "They're all pieces of you, and I want them all. I welcome them all. I never want to stop you from running when you need to run, but these allowed me to feel like you were with me, even when you weren't."

She reached up and wrapped her arms around his neck, and the last of the fear that had eaten at him since he'd seen her at the front door melted away.

"You're going to have to stop buying my paintings, Ian. They're redundant."

"Not to me. Like I said, they're unique—"

She put a finger over his lips. "Redundant because I'm not running anymore. All those pieces of me you have hanging on the wall aren't going to be necessary because you're going to have the real canvas"—she pointed at herself—"with you. I love you, Aries. Do forever with me. And let me paint you naked like I've wanted to from the first minute I saw you."

Ian closed his eyes and leaned his forehead against hers as all the pieces of his world finally clicked into place. Because she was his world. "Yes. Always. I love you. I'm not sure forever is long enough."

He wrapped his arms around her slim hips and lifted her until they were face-to-face and kissed her. No artist, not even one as talented as her, could capture the emotions surrounding them now. The love, the passion, the trust.

But he'd give her forever to try.

And they could start by her painting him naked. As long as she was naked when she did it.

•••

The Zodiac Tactical series continues with **CODE NAME: VIRGO.**

# ALSO BY JANIE CROUCH

All books: https://www.janiecrouch.com/books

LINEAR TACTICAL: OAK CREEK

Hero Unbound

Hero's Flight

Hero's Prize

ZODIAC TACTICAL

Code Name: ARIES

Code Name: VIRGO

Code Name: LIBRA

Code Name: PISCES

Code Name: OUTLAW

Code Name: GEMINI

GILDED EMPIRE (as MJ Crouch; series complete)

Broken Crown

Damaged Kingdom

Fierce Monarch

Vicious Throne

RESTING WARRIOR RANCH (with Josie Jade; series complete)

Montana Sanctuary

Montana Danger

Montana Desire

Montana Mystery

Montana Storm

Montana Freedom

Montana Silence

Montana Rain


LINEAR TACTICAL SERIES (series complete)

Cyclone

Eagle

Shamrock

Angel

Ghost

Shadow

Echo

Phoenix

Baby

Storm

Redwood

Scout

Blaze

Hero Forever


INSTINCT SERIES (series complete)

Primal Instinct

Critical Instinct

Survival Instinct

THE RISK SERIES (series complete)

Calculated Risk

Security Risk

Constant Risk

Risk Everything

OMEGA SECTOR SERIES (series complete)

Stealth

Covert

Conceal

Secret

OMEGA SECTOR: CRITICAL RESPONSE (series complete)

Special Forces Savior

Fully Committed

Armored Attraction

Man of Action

Overwhelming Force

Battle Tested

OMEGA SECTOR: UNDER SIEGE (series complete)

Daddy Defender

Protector's Instinct

Cease Fire

Major Crimes

Armed Response

In the Lawman's Protection

# ABOUT THE AUTHOR

"Passion that leaps right off the page." - Romantic Times Book Reviews

USA Today and Publishers Weekly bestselling author Janie Crouch writes what she loves to read: passionate romantic suspense featuring protective heroes.  Her books have won multiple awards, including the Romance Writers of America's coveted Vivian® Award, the National Readers Choice Award, and the Booksellers' Best.

After a lifetime on the East Coast, and  a six-year stint in Germany due to her husband's job as support for the U.S. Military, Janie has settled into her dream home in Front Range of the Colorado Rockies.

When she's not listening to the voices in her head—and even when she is—she enjoys engaging in all sorts of crazy adventures (200-mile relay races; Ironman Triathlons, treks to Mt. Everest Base Camp...), traveling, and hanging out with her four kids.

Her favorite quote: "Life is a daring adventure or nothing." ~ Helen Keller.

facebook.com/janiecrouch

amazon.com/author/janiecrouch

instagram.com/janiecrouch

bookbub.com/authors/janie-crouch